Under the
INFLUENCE

A Point Pleasant Beach / Cordelia Corbett Mystery · Book 1

Cover and interior design by Jacqueline Cook

ISBN: 978-1-61179-432-8 (Paperback)
ISBN: 978-1-61179-433-5 (e-book)

10 9 8 7 6 5 4 3 2 1

BISAC Subject Headings:
FIC022100 FICTION / Mystery & Detective / Amateur Sleuth
FIC022070 FICTION / Mystery & Detective / Cozy / General
FIC022040 FICTION / Mystery & Detective / Women Sleuths

Address all correspondence to:
Fireship Press, LLC
P.O. Box 68412
Tucson, AZ 85737
fireshipinfo@gmail.com

Or visit our website at:
www.fireshippress.com

DEDICATION

I dedicate *Under the Influence* to my gorgeous and brilliant wife Susan, the Love of my Life, my Marketing Director, Website Builder and endless inspiration. It was she who inspired this new venture. When we met twenty-five years ago, we didn't have a clue the wild ride that we were in for, but we took the 'leap of faith' and jumped in with both feet. I have never had a day of regret. And although occasionally our life is still chaotic, I wouldn't miss a day of it for the world. I look forward to getting old together, although that will be a long, long time from now, and spending eternity together thereafter. I will Love You forever.

Under the
INFLUENCE

A Point Pleasant Beach / Cordelia Corbett Mystery · Book 1

J. T. Kunkel

Cortero
An Imprint of FIRESHIP PRESS

CHAPTER ONE

May 2021

"I'm not going in," I muttered under my breath to no one in particular as I stood momentarily paralyzed outside of St. Peter's Roman Catholic Church in Point Pleasant Beach, New Jersey. I'd recently learned from the Borough of Point Pleasant Beach's website their tagline was, *A Historic Past and a Vibrant Future.* I chuckled to myself, "A vibrant future indeed!" remembering Grace and Frankie's Adult-oriented company name on my favorite Netflix show to binge-watch when I had nothing else to do, which these days seemed to be most of the time.

Suddenly, spanked out of my daydream, my older sister Katie had sneaked up behind me, her auburn hair identical to mine shining in the sun. "Come on, Cord; you can't stand out here all day. You know what Gram would have said."

We both recited it together, "Time's a-wastin', no time for pastin.'"

"What does that even mean?" I asked. I wiped a sudden tear from my eye. "Now, we can't even ask her."

She shook her head. "I don't know. She made it up as she went along, like pretty much everything she said and did. She was an amazing lady.

Now, let's go celebrate her life." She motioned behind her. "Come on, guys." Erin, four and Shannon, two obeyed immediately, followed by her downtrodden husband Jack. She snapped the whip. "Come on, Jack, we want a good seat."

He gathered up the girls. "Yes, my love. We're coming."

I felt sorry for him, such a nice guy but no match for Katie. No man seemed to be a match for Katie.

Three rows from the front, I spotted Lily, my younger sister, her husband Rory, and their toddlers, Finn, three and Dylan, almost two. They had their hands full. Lily mouthed, "Help," as we approached their pew. Collin ran from one end of the pew to the other. Finn attempted to vault over the back of it. Rory nearly allowed him to, seconds before I grabbed the boy.

The chapel pews were nearly full, and we would have been out of luck had Lily not saved the whole row. I tried not to stare at the casket where Catherine Carrie McDougal Corbett was laid out. The lighting made her look so angelic; I thought she might rise and fly among us at any point.

I glanced down slightly to see my parents Liam and Orania 'Rani' Corbett in the front row. Their heads appeared to be bowed in prayer, but odds were they were discussing what they'd be serving when everyone came to the house after the service. My dad wasn't much for sentimentality. Besides, my Gram had finally succumbed after suffering from lung cancer for five years, so it seemed as much a relief as a shock to most of the family. Unfortunately for me, I sat firmly in the camp who thought she'd never die.

⁓:⁓

By 'the house,' I hadn't meant their house in New Rochelle, New York, where we all grew up, trying to replicate the Dick Van Dyke Show in the 1960's videos my dad ordered on DVD from God knows where, but my Gram's house at 105 Trenton Avenue in Point Pleasant Beach. It was a hundred-year-old five-bedroom, three-bath bungalow, two blocks from the beach, backing up to Little Silver Lake. One of my earliest memories is sitting in the backyard with my Grampa, dangling our feet in the water, fishing for nothing.

It felt strange with my parents in charge at Gram's house, because that was never allowed while she lived. She'd be shooing them out of the kitchen, reminding them that her grandparents built this house, the first generation from Galway, Ireland. They would come back from the dead if they messed with her. I smiled at the notion that my Gram brought me up, never to forget I had the heart and soul of a Galway girl. I reckoned I never would.

~:~

I wondered how long I had been daydreaming when I heard my dad finish his sentence with "...the reading of her last will and testament."

Lily plunked down next to me on the floor within a couple of seconds. She chuckled. "They never did have enough chairs in this place. And Gram always said...." We repeated it together, "Those closest to the floor can sit on it."

She threw her arm around me. "How come you haven't come by in a while? I miss you, girl."

I smiled. "Well, the last time I did, it took me three weeks to get all the Play Dough out of my hair."

She hit my arm. "You lie so bad. That never takes me more than three days." She realized, "It's that guy. Didn't he dump you?"

I nodded. "Yes, Corbin."

She shook it off. "Aw, he had a stupid name anyway. Besides, he wasn't your type. You need to find someone who adores you, not someone who's too busy to take you to lunch because he's on the squash court with his accountant." She thought of something else. "So, what are you doing about your apartment? Doesn't your lease run out next month?"

I groaned. "Yes, and it's driving me crazy. I love living in the Village, but what's the point now that I lost my job at Goldman Sachs?" I rolled my eyes. "I'm thinking about a career move. I want to start my own company."

She nearly jumped off the floor. "That's so great! I'm happy to hear you want to get off Wall Street. You were never suited to that. What do you want to do?"

I scratched my head as I tried to come up with something clever. "Um, something un-Wall Streetish."

Lily hugged me. "I'm worried about you, Cord. I think you are depressed."

I defended myself. "Well, of course I'm depressed. Gram just died. Isn't that one of the stages of grieving?"

Katie sat on my other side, ignoring the fact that Lily and I were having a moment. Subtlety not being her best quality, she whispered loudly, "So, what do you think the big secret is with this will reading? Doesn't she just sell the house, and we divide the money equally? I figure it's worth about a million and a half. And don't you think Mom and Dad should be considered one household like the rest of us?"

I thought about it. "Oh, I don't know, Kate. I thought that since they are the next generation, they will inherit whatever there is, and maybe we'll inherit the leftovers when they die."

She considered that concept. "No. What's the point of that? They might live another thirty years. They're barely sixty. Dad can still run five miles a day when he wants to. He's far too healthy."

Lily and I stared at her.

Finally, my mom and dad came out of the kitchen, which sat by itself, segregated in the rear of the house with the living room in the front, typical of a turn-of-the-century bungalow. If they knew what Gram had written in the document, they weren't giving it away. They stood by the natural stone fireplace and called everyone to their attention. Looking around, I remembered how dark this living room used to be when it was all-natural wood, but Gram had it all updated when Grampa died, having it sheet-rocked and painting most of it white, bringing it into this century. Had I owned this house, I would have removed the wall between the kitchen and the living room, making it one huge space on the first floor, but what did I know?

Before starting, my dad waited for everyone to quiet down. Several of my aunts, uncles, and cousins were there, so probably thirty people were waiting for the outcome of the reading. I seemed to be the only one with little interest. After all the build-up, I figured my mom and dad would get anything significant.

Dad loved the stage and seemed to relish the moment. "I'd like to thank you all for coming today. As you may know, my mother was very specific in her wishes that no one is sad in the event of her death. I know this is a difficult task for many of us, but we continue to try."

He pulled a document from a file folder. "There is one particular section that she requested I read for the first time when we are all together, so I am doing as she wished." He looked up and smiled. "Or I know she will come back and make my life miserable."

My mom said, "Get on with it, Liam."

He started reading. "My loving family, if this is being read to you by Liam, then I have finally passed. First, let me tell you that I loved you all dearly, and I will miss each and every one of you, especially you, my darling son. I look forward to the day we meet again in heaven."

His voice cracked, and he wiped a tear from his eye.

He waited a few seconds to compose himself, then continued. "As most of you know, I am a huge proponent of housing, and I have spent much of my life fighting homelessness. It is very important to me that my close heirs become homeowners, so I have decided to contribute in this way. If any of my grandchildren are not homeowners at the point that I pass, I am passing the deed and ownership of this property on to them. There is only one condition. They must live in this house and agree never to sell it. They must then agree to make the same stipulation in their will."

He paused and looked around the room. No one said a word.

He continued. "In the event that all of the grandchildren are already homeowners, then the property will be sold, and the proceeds donated to sheltertheworld.org. If multiple grandchildren do not own a house, they may share the house until the point that one remaining is the sole owner, or they may share for life, but it may not be sold. The rest of the document may be read in private and shared later. There is nothing unusual in it."

He stopped and asked, "Does anyone have any questions?"

Katie asked, "Does anyone have a lighter?"

My mom jumped in immediately. "No, we don't have a lighter, and burning the will isn't going to solve anything. The attorney has copies."

Katie looked serious. "I'm not talking about for the will. I'm talking about the house. There's still time to get the insurance money. At that point, the house is a moot issue."

Lily raised her hand. Dad pointed at her, ignoring Katie's question completely. She asked, "Can this will be contested? I'm not sure she was of sound mind when she did this."

Katie spoke again. "How can you two be so cool? You're impacted more than we are. You were her immediate heirs. Doesn't this tick you off in the least?"

My dad spoke quietly. "We knew what she'd put in there all along. We had that conversation many times. Mom's death was never a part of our retirement plan. We knew she would never want the house sold, and we had no desire to live here." Then he turned to me. "Sweetheart, you're the only daughter we haven't heard from. I'd love to hear your reaction."

I hadn't had much time to absorb the fact that my life had been completely turned upside down in the course of a few seconds. On the other hand, I had to admit that I was ready for a change, so why not this one? I realized everyone in the room stared at me. I had no choice but to speak.

"I loved Gram with all my heart. I don't think it's a coincidence that I spent more time here both as a kid and as an adult than either of you did."

I motioned to Lily and Katie. I smiled to have found my voice. "Gram and I had a special bond. I somehow feel that it was written in the stars that I should be the keeper of 105 Trenton Avenue. Yes. I'll do it."

Katie stood up and walked out, yelling behind her, "Jack, grab the kids. We're leaving."

CHAPTER TWO

A few days later, I packed boxes in my apartment in Greenwich Village at Mac Dougal Alley and Waverly Place. Normally, Katie and Lily would be here helping me, but they were still adjusting to the fact that their slacker sister now had a million-dollar net worth. At the same time, they struggled to make the mortgage payments on their multi-million-dollar houses in Westchester County, New York.

It still seemed surreal. I felt good that at least my parents didn't feel any kind of way about it. They were still in my corner or at least didn't resent me. My sisters, especially Katie, might take a while to come around.

It only took me a few hours to pack everything I owned and move it from my furnished apartment into my 1991 Jeep Wrangler. I thought it would be fun to own a car born the same year I was. Although sometimes, it made me jealous, my car had more energy than I did. I needed a new life, and moving to Point Pleasant Beach might be the only way to get it.

~:~

I arrived at my new home in the morning on Wednesday, June 9th. I decided to sleep in the back bedroom because I had always slept there before Gram died. It felt the most natural, and since I hadn't moved any furniture, the bed felt like it always had, soft but firm and secure.

I woke at seven by a Facetime call, surprisingly, Katie and Lily. I rubbed the sleep from my eyes, wondering if I saw right. The last I knew, they weren't speaking to me.

Katie yelled, "Wake up, sleepyhead! It's the first day of the rest of your life. You should be out running on the beach or strolling on the sand for shells, something other than sleeping."

I stretched and yawned. I wasn't letting them off the hook. "Hey, I thought you weren't speaking to me."

Lily took over, likely to be more convincing. "Can you ever forgive us, Cord? We got a little caught up in the moment. What matters to us is that you are happy, and getting you out of the city made a huge difference. When we thought about it, we realized how perfect it was. And now we're going to say it together."

They counted down. "Three, two, one. We're sorry!"

I sat up in bed. "You're forgiven. If you guys can forgive me for eating the goldfish, I can forgive you for this."

Katie said, "Aww, poor Goldie. She never knew what hit her."

I scratched my head and asked, "Hey, Kate, what are you doing at Lil's house anyway?"

She scrunched up her face. "I couldn't deal with Jack another second. If he kissed up to me one more time, I thought I would throw up. Why doesn't he have a backbone? Just once, I wish he'd say 'no' or tell me to shut up."

I wasn't sure what to say. "He is a nice guy. He surely doesn't deserve you." I wondered if she'd get my meaning.

Katie looked a little confused. "Thanks."

I clarified without clarifying. "You know what I mean."

She let it drop. She had something else on her mind. "So, what's your plan, Cord? What are you going to do when you grow up?"

I wasn't comfortable with where this conversation seemed to be going. My mom and dad had pretty much given up on it and had probably resorted to prayer that my ambitious side would kick in at some point.

But at thirty, I wondered if even they were giving up. I jumped out of bed, wishing I could leave my iPhone there, and headed for the bathroom. I started brushing my teeth with my Sonicare, trying to drown her out.

I could barely hear her trying to yell over the buzz. "Cord, Cord, Cord. Cord, hey Cord!"

I momentarily stopped brushing. "Sorry, I'm brushing my teeth."

She yelled, "Stop that! You're trying to drown me out."

I agreed. "Okay, I am. But that's because I don't want to hear the same old lecture about how I need to be like you. I'll never be like you."

She tried a different approach. "Okay, you don't have to be like me. How about Lily? You could be more like her."

I felt like I might scream. "No! I'm not going to be like either of you. I came down here so I could be myself. I never fit in, in New York City. I never even liked the Village that much. I hated Wall Street. You know the last thing I did that I really loved?"

Lily sat on the edge of her seat. "No, Sweetheart. What?"

"Right here in Point Pleasant Beach, right after I turned sixteen, when I spent that summer with Gram working at Kohr's Frozen Custard since 1923, not to be confused with Kohr's The Original Frozen Custard since 1919, or Original Kohr Brothers Frozen Custard also since 1919."

Katie responded, "That's a lot of Kohrs. I'm not even going to ask why there are so many, but what did you like about it? I'd absolutely hate serving screaming kids ice cream cones all day, every day. I think we have a basic personality difference."

I stared at her in disbelief that she might be just discovering this. "Ya, think? If you're a Type A personality, I'm a Type Z."

She tried to convince me. "We're not that different. We used to all dress as the same thing on Halloween every year."

I laughed. "We used to wear the same pajamas on Christmas Eve, too, but that didn't make us Santa Claus."

Lily broke in. "So, now that you're back in Point, you're going to get a job at Kohr's? Tell me you're not. They called that a *summer* job for a reason. You do it for a summer to get it out of your system."

I smiled dreamily. "When I think how simple life was back then, it makes me long to go back. I don't think it would be so bad, even if I did it while I got my bearings. I could make a few bucks, get a feel for the place again. I'm sure a lot has changed in fourteen years."

Katie quipped. "Well, there were a lot less tattoos back then, I can guarantee that."

I shook my head. "Don't get me started about tattoos. Remember in elementary school when Bobby Smith accused me of having one."

Lily laughed. "Well, you didn't have to punch him, Cord."

I was incensed. "He looked up my skirt, for God's sake. I should have done a lot worse."

Katie chuckled. "You were also nine and had snow pants on."

I smiled. "It's the principle of the thing."

Lily cackled. "I bet you wouldn't mind now if Robert Smith, Esquire, took a peek these days. He's gotten really cute, and he's available again, I hear."

I couldn't believe it. "Don't tell me the quarterback and the prom queen got divorced. Do tell!"

Katie had the dirt. "Here's what I heard. He got so tired of her flipping her hair with her 'Valley Girl' voice that he started spending all of his time at work, including nights and weekends. So, she filed for divorce on the grounds of abandonment." Kate seemed to be enjoying this. "Well, since he is an attorney, not wanting to be outdone, he countersued on the grounds of cruel and inhuman treatment, something about fingernails on a chalkboard."

I finished brushing my teeth. "Hey, guys, unless you are getting in the shower with me, I'd better go."

Lily laughed. "Well, it wouldn't be the first time. Remember when mom tried to save hot water and shoved us all in the shower at the same time?"

I complained. "Yes, I always got water in my ears."

Katie concluded the call. "So, all we got out of this call is that you're going to try and get back your summer job from fourteen years ago. How are we going to report that to Mom?"

I couldn't believe it. "Mom put you up to this?" Then I thought about it and understood. "Oh, I get it now. She probably wanted to make us all get along again. She didn't really care about the outcome of the call.

Besides, she wouldn't care if I got my summer job back as long as I didn't go back to Wall Street."

Lily took control of the conversation. "Okay, Cord, you go shower then get that job at Kohr's. You're going to need money coming in eventually. I get that you have no mortgage, but the property taxes on that place have to be at least a thousand a month, so it's not like you're going to be living for free."

I wasn't worried. "It's not like I didn't save any of my Goldman Sachs money. I've got a decent stash, but you're right. I don't want to drain it." I started to take off my pajamas.

Katie complained, "You realize we're still here, right?"

I chuckled. "I figured I'd have to do something to get rid of you two. I'll talk to you later." I hung up and turned on the shower. I had a big day ahead of me.

CHAPTER THREE

I decided not to overdress for my unscheduled interview. I saw on Kohr's Facebook page that they were accepting applications, so I had all I needed to know. I seemed to be a shoo-in. I felt pretty sure that I could beat out the high school and college kids I'd be competing with. I was a touch overqualified, but I felt pretty sure they would take what they could get with today's job market. I wondered what they paid. I'd heard convenience stores were paying upwards of twenty dollars an hour due to the job market; people were simply dropping out of the market completely or sitting at home collecting unemployment, exceeding what they ever made working. The world had gone insane.

I opted for a one-piece black floral romper with black gladiator sandals, perfect for the beach but professional enough for an interview. Besides, if any cute guys were on the beach, I looked hot enough to get a few looks. Hey, being single, no one in my life could complain about guys looking at me. I got so tired of that after a while. I always thought it was fine if they looked but didn't touch. Most of the guys I had been with didn't share that philosophy. I felt relieved to be alone.

I signed on to their Facebook site to see if Kohr's Frozen Custard posted their manager's name on their home page, so I'd know who to ask for. Nothing came up when I clicked on the 'About' link. I figured, though, whoever ran the place was probably a distant relative of Archie Kohr, the original purchaser of the first ice cream machine in the Kohr family, located at their dairy farm in York, Pennsylvania, back in 1917. I learned when I worked there that eventually they relocated to the Jersey shore in 1919, creating all three Kohr Frozen Custard companies still in business today.

When I worked there fourteen years ago, Sally Kohr McIntosh ran it, a great-granddaughter of Elton Kohr, Archie's younger brother. According to Sally, Elton split from his brothers in 1923 to start the Point Pleasant Beach Kohr's. He never expanded his part of the business beyond that location, even though the other brothers expanded into Maryland, Delaware, and Virginia.

It only took seven minutes to walk from the house to Kohr's. I couldn't quite call it *my* house yet. I wondered if I'd ever be able to think of it as anything but Gram's house. I started thinking about what to say when I got there, when suddenly I arrived. The Chippy's Fresh French Fries down the boardwalk smelled tantalizing. They made me feel right at home. I can't count the number of times I had lunch there when I worked at Kohr's. We complimented one another perfectly as neighbors on the boardwalk. They provided lunch or dinner, and we provided dessert. Sure, they sold funnel cakes, but who didn't prefer ice cream when push came to shove?

I got a pit in my stomach as I approached Kohr's. What if I'd made a huge mistake? What if they hated me? What if they laughed in my face? I decided to face my fears. When I went to the counter, there appeared to be a middle-aged woman working in the back, preparing for the day. When she turned around, I wasn't sure, but it looked like an older version of Sally Kohr McIntosh, still here after all these years. She was around twenty-five when I worked here, so that would make her nearly forty now. This had to be her.

I asked, "Sally, is that you?"

She nearly jumped over the counter. "Oh my God, Cordelia Corbett, Jewel of the Sea, as I live and breathe."

I couldn't believe she still remembered what my name meant in Gaelic.

She thought about hugging me over the counter but then glanced around at several of her employees and backed off. She'd probably reprimanded them for doing something similar. She asked, "So, what are you doing with yourself?"

She set me up perfectly. "I'm looking for a job. I'm hoping you have one for me. I recently inherited my Gram's house, so I'm living down here now."

She looked at me with wide eyes. "You're kidding me. I just posted an Assistant Manager position on Indeed. And I don't need to interview you. You were one of my star employees. If you want the job, it's yours."

I couldn't believe it. "Are you still the manager?"

She laughed. "Well, kind of. I own the place now. I'm technically manager, too, but I've been looking for someone a little more mature than most of the employees that run through here. I can't believe you walked in here today. This is a miracle." She looked around. "You're not an ex-con or anything, are you?"

I laughed. "God, no. I just got fired from my last job, but it just wasn't a good fit."

She finally reached across the counter, defying her initial reluctance. "Then, give me a hug, girl. This is the best day I've had in a while." We hugged.

I got chills at the coincidence of our timing. "I feel the same way, Sally."

Sally smiled broadly. "Hey, it's early; let's go for a walk down the beach and catch up. I thought about opening early, because I got here and had nothing better to do, but we won't start getting any real customers for a couple of hours. One of the kids is due in any minute so they can finish opening."

I agreed and waited while she closed up the front. Within a few minutes, she came outside, hugging me for real. She held me at arm's length. "Wow, you've really filled out. You were such a skinny kid."

I looked down, wondering if she had called me fat. I realized she meant that I'd matured in the chest area. "Oh, you mean these. Yeah, they swooped in during the fall after I worked here. Thank God. I didn't think I'd have anything to speak of, being a touch of a late bloomer. Too bad they waited so long. I could probably have gotten Tommy Peterson to look at me when he worked here."

She shook her head as we headed down the boardwalk. "Well, if that's what it took to get Tommy to look, you were better off without him. That's something I've learned in my thirty-nine years."

We passed all the familiar sights. We walked through Jenkinson's South. As far as I could tell, they still owned most of the boardwalk. We eventually got to the end of it and the motel zone. We decided to stop at the Food Shack, a charming spot that included waterfront dining, a bathhouse with showers, and a gift shop. It had something for everyone. The food tasted excellent, too. I had the Lifesaver; an open-faced English muffin topped with avocado, tomato, and two eggs, an amazing combination. Sally had the lobster omelet which, besides the obvious, included asparagus and cheese. It looked delicious.

As we finished our meals, I asked, "So Sally, can I ask you something?"

She nodded as she wiped her mouth with her napkin. "Sure, Hon, anything."

I wasn't quite sure how to word it. "What are you still doing here?"

She appeared to wince slightly at my question. I guessed I could have been more sensitive in how I worded it.

I started to apologize, "I'm sorry, Sally, I—"

She interrupted me. "No, there's nothing for you to apologize for. We all make choices. Some of them are good and some, well, not so good. And, for the most part, this wasn't a bad one. But I did meet a guy. His name is Dieter. The whole Kohr family emigrated from North Germany, so it's no wonder I fell for a German guy. Well, he came over here on a foreign exchange program, and we started dating. I knew there wasn't a future in it, that he'd eventually be going back to Europe, but I didn't know when.

"Well, a month after my dad died, and I had just purchased the business, he asked me to go back with him. I had to tell him that I couldn't. It broke my heart, Cordelia. I told myself I'd move on, that everything would be okay, but I've never gotten over him."

I wondered, "So, your last name isn't German; it's Irish. Where did that come from?"

She smiled. "That's from my dad. He's the only known Irishman in the Kohr clan. It's probably why I took to you so quickly. He is second-generation and speaks with a bit of a brogue, handed down from his *very* Irish father." She laughed. "My mom was nearly disowned for not marrying German. It was quite a scandal. That's one of the reasons I have Kohr in my name. They agreed that even though she married a MacIntosh, the Kohr name would remain prominent, German and Irish indelibly standing together forever."

I nodded. "I can understand that. We still have strong pressure to marry Irish, even though my parents pretend to play it down. Evidently, my sisters Katie and Lily got the memo because they married Jack Murphy and Rory Finnegan. However, they couldn't quite get there and actually change their last names, keeping the Corbett name cleanly intact. They will always be Corbetts, through and through." Before we left, I headed to the ladies' room then met Sally at the cash register.

As we paid the check, I heard a scream coming from the rear of the building toward the location of the bathhouse. A young woman came running out of the bathhouse yelling, "Oh my God, there's a dead woman in the shower."

And my career as an amateur sleuth officially began.

CHAPTER FOUR

Everyone froze, seemingly not knowing what to do, so I yelled to Sally to call 911 as I ran into the women's shower room. A woman around my age lay naked on the shower floor, with blood running down the drain, reminiscent of the movie from 1960, except this showed in living color. She couldn't have been dead long, because she had bled heavily, and the blood was very fresh, but there wasn't any question that she was dead when I took her pulse.

I rolled her on her back and started CPR, which I had learned as a girl scout but had never actually performed on a human until now. When I saw her face, I felt a glint of recognition. I knew her from somewhere. I even felt like we'd been friends at one time. I put that thought aside as I tried to save her life.

Sally had connected with the 911 operator. She tried to stay calm. "Cordelia, what's the address of this place?"

I said between breaths, "How many Food Shacks with bathhouses can there be on Point Pleasant Beach?"

She repeated that to the 911 operator, who continued to ask her for the address.

I yelled, "Go ask the cashier. You can go through there." I pointed to the bathroom, which I could tell from its location was shared by the restaurant and the bathhouse.

She ran out the restroom door. I got the feeling she wanted an excuse to leave. This seemed like it might be hopeless, but I wasn't a medical expert. I'd been doing CPR for at least five minutes.

I was getting exhausted. I yelled, hoping someone outside could hear me. "Is there anyone out there that knows CPR?"

A male voice responded. "Well, I do, but I'm not supposed to go in there."

I said sarcastically, "A woman is dying in here. I don't think she'll mind." I watched the drain. "We need someone to stop the bleeding while someone else does the CPR."

He finally came in, rather than talking over the concrete walls. I was pleased to see a far cuter redheaded guy about my age than I expected based on his voice. He immediately took over the CPR. "I've done this several times. I'm a hockey coach, so we've had a few incidents."

I smiled as I grabbed a towel hanging off the hook nearby, and put compression on the wound, which appeared to be a gunshot, at least to my untrained eye. I admired his technique. "You really know what you are doing. I wish you'd gotten here earlier."

He didn't have the time or the air to respond but glanced appreciatively in my direction. We went on this way for another ten minutes when we finally heard sirens. Within a few minutes, two EMTs descended on the scene and took over, requesting quite sternly that we back off and leave the lifesaving to them.

We walked outside, where Sally sat on the beach with her arms wrapped around her legs. I introduced my friend. Sally, this is my life-saving friend; um, I have no idea what your name is."

She stood up, then backed up slowly, saying, "You do realize that you are both covered with blood?"

I looked down at my brand-new romper, then looked at his jeans and white tee shirt. It wasn't a good look.

He decided not to shake hands. "Hi, my name is Sean McPherson."

Sally gave me a 'He's cute, *and* he's Irish' look.

I laughed and poked her. "Cut it out."

He looked totally confused. "What's going on here that I don't know about."

I decided I'd better introduce myself. "Hi, I don't think we've been properly introduced. I'm Cordelia Corbett."

Sally smiled. "I'm Sally Kohr McIntosh."

He shook both of our hands. "I wish we all could have met under happier circumstances."

I nodded. "I know. It was horrible."

He agreed. "I'm a Psychologist if you want to talk about it sometime. Business has been down lately so I have some openings." He smiled. "It does give me more time to spend on the beach, though, so it's not all bad." He looked me up and down; I imagined he might be trying to figure out what I looked like if I wasn't covered with blood. Finally, he asked, "Do you live around here, Cordelia?"

I nodded. "As a matter of fact, I do. I live over on Trenton Avenue, backing up to Little Silver Lake."

He smiled. "We're practically neighbors. I live on Laurel Court, just off the lake. I've probably run by your house a thousand times."

I shook my head. "Well, technically, you ran past my Gram's house. I recently moved there. Last night happened to be my first night." I drew Sally into the conversation. "And Sally here, is my new boss. There's a lot happening in my life."

I realized another life stood in the balance twenty feet away, and we were disregarding her. I decided I'd better check. "Hey, I'm going to check on the poor woman in the shower. I'll be right back."

Sean said, "I'll stay right here."

I didn't want to bother the EMTs as they had made it clear that we weren't welcome in their realm. I peeked around the corner to find them strapping the woman on a rolling stretcher, covered completely with a couple of sheets. I asked, "Is she—"

The one pushing the stretcher said, "I'm sorry. She's gone. Thank you for assisting. From what we saw, you couldn't have done anything more."

I felt heartbroken but not shocked, and happy I tried to save her. I asked, "Where are the police? Have they been here?"

He said, "Yes, I think they are questioning people in the restaurant. They were here until a couple of minutes ago."

I thanked him and headed for the restaurant. I saw a couple of cops chatting with the cashier. I figured it might be a good time to get their attention. The cashier said, "You can sit anywhere."

I smiled. "Actually, I wanted to talk to the police."

One of them said to me, "I can talk to you. Officer Jones can finish up here with Connie."

I nodded and said, "Thank you so much."

He asked, "Would you like to go outside?"

I agreed. "That would be good. I'd rather be outside getting a little fresh air."

We walked toward the boardwalk. He asked, "What can I do for you?"

I wasn't sure where to start. "Well, as you can probably see, I had been trying to revive that poor woman in the shower. I'm very sorry she didn't make it."

He acknowledged me. "We appreciate that you jumped in and took over before the EMTs arrived. We don't often see that these days."

I smiled. "Thank you. I've never done that before, but something about it felt right." I tried to gather my thoughts. "What happens now? How will you solve the murder?"

He chuckled. "Oh, it's pretty much out of my hands once I file my report. Then, the Investigative Division will take over."

I knew this would be his standard answer. "So, what does that mean?" I looked at his badge. "Can I call you Phillip?"

He smiled. "Phil is fine. It means in English that one of our two detectives will take the case and start investigating. They will come down here and start snooping around, asking questions, seeing if anyone saw anything, that sort of thing. They'll be responsible for gathering any DNA testing if applicable. I'm not sure that's going to be possible in this case, considering the woman died in the shower with the water running." He looked me in the eye. "I know this might seem kind of awkward, but I need your clothes."

I laughed. "Wow, I knew cops in this town moved fast, but that's a little faster than I'm willing to go right now."

He reddened. "I'm sorry. I'm mean for evidence. You are covered with it. I'm going to need everything. Can I follow you home?"

I smiled. "Phil, I do think you're cute. I really do, but like to date a few times first."

He didn't seem to know what to say, which was my goal. "No, I mean I just need to gather evidence."

I chuckled. "Oh, is that what they call it now?"

I hesitated a few more seconds, watching him suffer, then let him off the hook. "It's fine, Phil. I was just giving you a hard time. I'd be happy to strip down for you."

He avoided my gaze. "Well, Ma'am, Officer Anne Clarke will escort you home. He handed me a Haz-Mat suit. "Put this on. You can use your own room to change in. She just needs your clothes."

I winked. "Oh, darn." I decided to change the subject. "Is there anything else you can tell me about what will happen after this?"

As we walked to Clarke's squad car, Phil considered whether there might be any other details that he could share with me. "This will be a high-profile case because we don't get many homicides. There were only nine crimes that could be categorized as violent last year, including domestic disputes. The last homicide here happened in 2015 in the Apartments on Trenton Avenue. It turned out a guy came on to his next-door neighbor and paid the ultimate price."

I donned the hazmat suit and climbed into Clarke's patrol car.

I thought back as we neared the house. "I remember that murder in 2015. It was shocking to everyone in the area. You can stop at the next house on the left. My Gram lived here. Stuff like that doesn't happen here. I live in what was her house now."

Clarke acknowledged, "Oh, I hope that doesn't mean that she passed away."

I nodded. "Yes, last week. It's been quite an adjustment for the family, but she had a full life, and she wanted us to celebrate it, so that's what we're trying to do."

She nodded as we got out of the car. "Good for you. I lost my grandmother last year, and it's still hard to talk about it." She followed me in the kitchen door and handed me a large paper bag. "Put everything in here. That includes your underwear, socks and shoes…oh, and the Haz Mat suit."

I headed upstairs, yelling behind me, "I'll be right back. You said you needed everything. Right?"

She yelled behind me. "Yes. Everything."

I followed my strip down with a super brief shower, but I didn't want to make her wait, so I hurried and came down carrying the paper bag filled with everything I'd been wearing.

"So, who should I call if I have information about or want to assist with the case?"

She looked confused. "Well, if you have more information, you can give it to me now."

I insisted. "Well, what if I think of something later?"

She pulled out a card as we got back in the squad car. "Here is my number, and on the back is listed our other extensions. She took out a pen. I'll write down the detectives' names. It could be one or both of these. Detective Raymond Gardner of the Ocean County Prosecutor's Office and Detective Clint Daniels at the Point Pleasant Beach Police Department." She commented, "I'd personally start with Detective Daniels, because we tend to be closer to the action than the Prosecutor's Office, but that's up to you."

I nodded. "Makes sense to me. Thank you for that information. I'll give him a call if I think of anything else."

Back at the Food Shack, we parted and shook hands, and she headed back into the restaurant to meet her partner.

CHAPTER FIVE

I walked back out to the beach to find Sally. She sat alone, staring at the water. I sat down next to her. I asked, "What happened to Sean?"

She handed me a card. "He had to go home with another cop, but he asked me to give you this."

He'd handed her his business card with a note written on the back. "Cordelia, I enjoyed meeting you today. I'd like to see you again, perhaps under less bloody conditions. Yours, Sean."

We both sat, staring at the waves breaking over the shore for a while before either of us spoke.

Finally, she said, "Life is very fleeting. A woman comes to the beach, expecting to get home like any normal day, and ends up dead. What is wrong with this world?"

I corrected her. "This wasn't just any woman. I knew her."

She gave me a questioning look. "You did? From here?"

I thought about it. "I don't know."

She stood up. "I guess you'll figure it out, but we'd better get back so I can open up. God knows if Shelby ever showed. Kids these days."

I wondered, "Is that Shelby Irons?"

She looked at me with amazement. "Yes, how did you know?" She brushed the sand from her pants. I followed suit, and we headed north toward the boardwalk.

I smiled as we walked. "She lives right next door, and I thought I remembered Gram telling me she worked at Kohr's. Small world. Now we can be besties. What is she, seventeen? I can relive my teen years through her. Do you have any cute high school guys working there that she'd probably like to date? I can watch them negotiate teen dating vicariously."

She nodded. "As usual, we have the stud of the football team, Billy Fordham. I don't know why they always end up working for me. They give me nothing but heartache, but I always hire them. I know that Shelby has her eye on him, but he seems to be after another girl named Terri Thompson. But she doesn't seem to give him the time of day; at least that's what he says to his buddies. Isn't high school always the same? I try to stay out of it all as much as I can."

I shook my head. "I've got my work cut out for me as Assistant Manager, I can tell already. You must have a nerdy guy who's going to fall for me immediately and act like a puppy-dog around me. It's inevitable."

She chuckled. "Oh, yeah. That's Aaron Blizinski. You'll have your hands full there. Puberty has met its match in you, I can tell you right now. You'd better cover those up." She pointed at my breasts.

I laughed. "Do we have uniforms or anything?"

She shook her head. "No, that idea died several years ago. We couldn't get the high school girls to wear the ones we used. Then we had a contest, which resulted in all sorts of ideas from fifties car hop outfits to bodysuits. It quickly got out of control, so we dropped the idea completely."

I smiled. "Darn, why don't we wear the white shirts and the plaid skirts? I loved those. They were simple and tasteful."

She agreed. "We're from a different era. Kids today march to a different drummer."

Before long, we'd made it back to Kohr's. We asked, "So, when do you want to start, Cordelia? It can be as soon as you'd like."

I thought about it. "How about tomorrow morning. Today's been a little crazy. I need to catch my breath just a touch, but I promise I'll be ready to roll tomorrow."

She hugged me before she went in the side door. She waved. "See you tomorrow. This is going to be great."

I agreed. "Can't wait. I'll see you then."

~:~

A part of me wanted to walk further up the beach, but my mind was such a mess; I didn't have it in me. The combination of the run-in with the shadow of death and the redheaded and attractive Irish Sean McPherson.

When I got home, I brought up the Patch News Website on my laptop, where I found out most of the local dirt. As luck would have it, they had posted a picture of the victim of today's murder, although she looked considerably better than she had when I'd last seen her, and even more familiar. Through an article posted within the past fifteen minutes by Patricia Miller, I determined that her name was Rachel Lynne Gaston, and she hailed from Easton, Pennsylvania. She worked as a Social Media Influencer with millions of followers on Twitter, Instagram, Facebook, LinkedIn, and TikTok. Her opinion alone had spawned multiple products and ensured dozens of New York Times Best Sellers.

According to family members, she headed to Point Pleasant Beach for a brief vacation and a little rest and relaxation before her busy summer season kicked in. She had traveled alone and stayed at the Windswept Motel, steps away from the Food Shack where she'd been shot and left to bleed to death in the bathhouse attached to the building. The article provided the same contact information that Officer Phil had given to me.

I felt like I was getting closer to solving the mystery of who this woman was. The Rachel Lynne sounded familiar, but the Gaston didn't. I felt like I knew her from Point Pleasant Beach. I concentrated hard on that face and tried to picture it fourteen years younger. I was convinced I had known her when I spent the summer with my Gram when I was sixteen.

I tried out names. Rachel Lynne Redding, Rachel Lynne Reddling, Rachel Lynne Reddy. I was so close, but none of those worked. Then, it came to me. Rachel Lynne Redmond. She started that summer as my best friend, the granddaughter of one of my Gram's closest friends, and we ended the summer mortal enemies because she stole my first real boyfriend, Bobby Freeman. I vowed I would never speak to her again, and I never had. And now she was dead.

I felt like I needed to know more about what she'd been doing since then. I signed onto Rachel's Facebook page. The first thing I noticed was how active she had been on social media. She treated it like a full-time job. She posted nearly every day, and she constantly friended new people. She updated her location when she went anywhere.

I jumped onto her Twitter Page and noticed that she made an effort to Tweet multiple times per day. She liked to get people to respond and often Tweeted several times on the same topic, making her opinion very clear. She did similar things on the other sites.

I noticed a dangerous trend. While everything appeared to be good on the surface, she treaded consistently in dangerous territory when people disagreed with her. Over time, she became more belligerent and opinionated, and it didn't seem that all appeared well in her world. I wondered if she felt threatened or in danger. I couldn't help but wonder if her Internet world had gotten out of control, and she'd been swallowed up by it.

I stared at her profile picture—Rachel Lynne Gaston, formerly Redmond, young, smart, educated, beautiful, dead.

I did a broader Internet search of her, looking for earlier background information. Rachel was age thirty, exactly my age, born in 1991, like me. Born and raised in Easton, PA. Her father, a life-long employee of Binney and Smith, now known just as Crayola. She attended Easton Area High School and graduated with honors in 2009. She married her high school sweetheart, attended Lafayette College, and got a Bachelor of Arts in Film and Media Studies.

At one time, it had been her goal to become an actress, and she'd been very active in both school and community theatre, but when her father died suddenly right before her college graduation, she divorced and moved back into the family home, but kept her married name, Gaston.

She started a blog soon after graduating from school and used that to build the following that she has today. Today, as a social media influencer, her seal of approval has become nearly the equivalent of being approved by Oprah. At the time of her death, she'd been working with Netflix on a reality series similar to Shark Tank, where people pitched their ideas and products to her, and she either decided to support it with her massive network or not. Unfortunately, her untimely death would make that just a dream she had.

After reading her blog, it felt like I almost knew her as a grown woman, and I felt even worse about her death. I felt drawn to the case and stared at her picture on the screen. It looked like she was pleading with me to help her. I couldn't explain it; it was just a feeling. I felt guilty for how she and I ended our friendship over petty jealousy as sixteen-year-olds.

I stood and went into the bathroom, trying to forget how horrible I felt. I immediately stripped down and jumped in the shower. The hot water running down my skin helped to soothe my frayed nerves. Why couldn't I let the police take care of her case? Why did I feel compelled to solve Rachel's murder? It felt strange to me, but I had no doubt that I needed to do it. Did I feel like I could absolve myself from the guilt of a soured friendship from fourteen years ago?

As I dried my hair in my robe, I decided to Zoom call Lily. We were very connected, far more than Katie and me. So, I thought she might have a helpful perspective, even though I might have to yell over two energetic toddlers. I decided to take the chance. She usually had her laptop on.

She came on the screen almost immediately, looking unusually unfrazzled. She said, "Hey, girl, why are you still in your robe. Don't tell me you just got up?"

I shook my head. "No. I'll tell you all about it, but first, tell me why it's so peaceful there."

She spoke quietly and showed me crossed fingers. "Collin is watching Disney Plus, and Connor is napping. Had you called a half-hour ago, you would have experienced one of our typical pre-nap meltdowns, but you were lucky enough to miss it. So, I was catching up on my Facebook and my email. What's up?"

I didn't want to shock her, but I jumped right in. "There was a murder today at the bathhouse behind the Food Shack, a woman I knew from my childhood, from Pennsylvania, in the showers. I tried to administer CPR, but she didn't make it. Do you remember Rachel Lynne Redmond?"

She gasped. "Oh my God! I think I do. I can't believe you did that. Are you okay? That sounds unusually heroic of you. I'm really proud of you, Cord. I wonder if you should see someone now. Couldn't you get PTSD or something?"

I waved her off. She couldn't help but think about what she'd do had it been her in that situation. Empathy wasn't a strong suit in our family. I tried working on it with them. Katie probably would never get it, but Lily still had some hope. I said, "I'm fine. But I need your opinion on something."

She nodded, looking like a million dollars as she always did, but with concern on her beautiful face. She might be the only stay-at-home mom of two toddlers I knew who dressed for success every day, did her hair and nails daily and, quite frankly, looked more professional than most of my friends who were working from home, in sweatpants and tee shirts.

Today she sported a white button-up blouse under an open black cardigan sweater, with a gold dolphin necklace and matching earrings. She looked like she probably would go back to practicing law, which she was doing when Collin was born. While she put her law career on hold, she and Rory understood she'd get back to it when the kids 'stabilized,' whatever that meant. Something told me that she dressed this way to not so subtly communicate to Rory that she was going back to work sooner than later, but he wasn't getting the message, at least so far.

I wasn't sure where to start. "Okay, you already acknowledged that me jumping in and doing CPR on this woman in the bathhouse might have been a little out of character. Well, since then, I've been obsessed with her case, like she has chosen me, is begging me, to solve it. I've been on her personal website, and I feel like her picture is imploring me to help her."

She probably thought I had lost it but wasn't ready to commit. "Just who was this woman again. Her name did sound familiar?"

I minimized zoom so that I could see Rachel's blog site. "She used to visit her Grandmother in Point Pleasant Beach. I got to know her that summer I spent with Gram. She was my best friend until she stole a guy I dated, and then I hated her. We didn't speak at all after that. Then as an adult she became a social media influencer. She lived in Easton, Pennsylvania, right on the Jersey border. She started as a blogger but had gotten so many followers that many companies, from Amazon to Tesla, had used her to test products. She has become very influential and new product developers are bending over backward to develop relationships with her to ensure a smooth product launch."

She nodded. "Wow. I had no idea. What a gig. All she had to do is sit in her house and give the thumbs-up or thumbs-down, and she gets a pay-off."

I agreed. "Yes, it seems pretty sweet, but it came with a downside. There seemed to be increasing pressure to approve new products and lots of anger emanating from those who were rejected. You could see that on her social media sites. Some of it got downright ugly."

She had a worried look on her face. I wasn't sure where it came from. Finally, she spilled. "Is this a guilt thing because you ended up hating each other, or do you feel like your life isn't exciting enough, Cord? Because I can offer up a ton of real-life right here with my two monsters any time."

I smiled. "No thanks. That might be too much excitement for me." I almost forgot. "Hey, I didn't tell you. I went to get my old job back at Kohr's, and Sally owns the place now. She offered me a job as Assistant Manager."

She stood up in front of the laptop. "No way! I can't believe you waited this long to tell me that! That is so great! When do you start?"

I suddenly realized I wasn't close to ready. I felt horrified. I saw all the color run out of my already white redheaded, freckled Irish face, "Um, tomorrow morning."

She chuckled. "Wow, you don't look nearly as excited as you should."

I felt panicky. "Yeah, I've been concentrating so much on this case, I'd nearly forgotten I need to be ready to show up at work tomorrow morning. And I'm not just an ice-cream-cone-filling-slacker anymore. I'm responsible for what other employees do. What was I thinking? I've never managed anyone before."

She tried her most soothing voice, realizing that I was going off the deep end. "You'll be fine. You've worked on Wall Street and lived in New York City. We're talking about an ice cream shop in Point here."

That didn't help. "Yes, and I got fired from Wall Street. Epic fail. Thanks for reminding me. I'd be living on the street if Gram hadn't died and left me her house."

She looked at me sternly. "You wouldn't be living on the street. You'd be living with Rory and me and taking care of the kids while I went back to work." Suddenly she realized what she had said. "Oops, I guess we hadn't discussed that with you."

I suddenly realized what she'd said. "So, you had it all planned out, that I couldn't possibly fend for myself, and that you'd have to take me in like a homeless person on the street. Thanks for the faith in me." I couldn't stay on. "I have to go." I exited from Zoom.

CHAPTER SIX

Sometimes, family was more than I could stomach. They all acted like they had my best interest at heart, with Lily scheming to get back to work, using the pretense of helping me out. The fact remained that while Lily was a good mom, she didn't have the temperament to stay home with her kids, and the whole family recognized it.

Katie made no pretense about having no interest in stay-at-home-parenting and immediately brought in a live-in Au Pair as soon as she could when her firstborn came into the world so that she could go back to work. I had to admit, though, her girls were amazingly well-behaved as a result. At the same time, Lily's boys were completely out of control.

I guessed I made a mistake confiding my newly acquired interest in becoming an amateur sleuth to Lily when I didn't even understand my compulsion myself. I just knew that I had to help this woman. So, I jumped back on Rachel's webpage to learn more. I sensed her frustration before she left town to take her final vacation. And while she didn't specifically let her followers know where she headed, she didn't turn off her location, either. Anyone following her on Facebook knew she'd been in Point as of yesterday. Hindsight is twenty-twenty, but that wasn't very smart on her part if she felt threatened.

I decided that I needed to go back to The Food Shack to get any fresh impressions from the staff before they faded. Still, I wasn't sure why. I just knew that I needed to. Besides, I loved the food there, and I felt hungry. I only had a three-block walk from my house to the Food Shack, so I took off, feeling refreshed and motivated to get the truth.

Sometimes people are more open in a casual conversation than they are with the police. I counted on that as I found an empty table near the window. I recognized the waitress, Maureen, from earlier, so I knew she'd been working when Rachel's body was discovered.

She brought me a glass of water and a menu. "Hi, do you know what you want, or do you need a minute?"

I wasn't sure how to engage her. I tried to be casual. "Hey, lots of craziness here today. A woman died here earlier?"

She glanced around nervously. "Yes, I'm not supposed to talk about it, but it was horrible. I just came in, and I often change for work in the bathhouse, so I'm the one who discovered her."

I couldn't believe my luck. "Did you see anyone else around, like anyone running away or anything?"

She looked at me funny. "You're not a cop, are you?"

I laughed. "God, no. I work at Kohr's. I just wondered. Since I heard she got shot, I figured the killer had to be close by and in the ladies' showers, so it could have been obvious to anyone paying close attention that someone may have been rushing out of the bathhouse about that time."

She thought about it. "Yeah, I guess you're right. I didn't see anybody coming out of the bathhouse."

I wondered. "How about in the parking lot? Did you see anyone getting into a vehicle to leave when you were coming in?"

She thought back. "Let me think. I wasn't paying that close attention. There are always people coming and going."

I implored her. "Think hard. This could be really important."

She asked again. "You sure you're not a cop?"

I smiled. "No, but I have no problem helping them. Sometimes these cases go cold really fast, and there's no way to reconstruct what went on after the fact, after people's memories have grown fuzzy. Did you ever watch Cold Case? Such a great show."

She laughed. "Yes, now I binge-watch it on A & E. It's so good." She thought back. "Wait a minute. I remember something that might be important. As I pulled into the parking lot, there was a red convertible; I'm pretty sure it had a horse emblem on the back of it because it nearly backed into me, quite close, at a pretty high rate of speed. I had to hit my horn, or he would have hit me. I gave him a gesture out the window, which he returned to me out his roof."

I thought about it. "That had to be a Mustang. Wow, that might be really important. Did you see the guy at all?"

She shook her head. "No, just his hand." She glanced at the woman standing at the cash register. "Sorry, I've got to get back to work. Just signal me when you decide what you want to eat."

I agreed. "Okay, Maureen. Thank you so much."

She rushed away.

I studied the menu and, after a couple of minutes, called her back to the table. "I think I'll have the Fresh Fish Sandwich and a side of Crabby Fries."

She smiled. "Good choice." She commented, "Hey, it doesn't seem fair that you know my name, but I don't know yours."

I extended my hand. "I'm Cordelia Corbett. It's nice to meet you."

She smiled like we were long lost friends. "My full name is Maureen Applegate. But my friends call me Mo." She shook my hand.

I smiled. "Nice to meet you Mo. I'm sure I'll be seeing you around. I recently moved down here from New York City. I inherited my Gram's house. I worked at Kohr's at sixteen, so I got my summer job back, plus they made me Assistant Manager." I whispered, "I hope I can handle it. Kids today can be a little challenging."

She laughed. "I know. I work with a bunch of them. Nice to meet you, Cordelia."

I took my hand back. "My friends call me 'Cord,' so you qualify."

She smiled broadly. "How nice, Cord then. I made a friend today. I live on Metedeconk on Parker Avenue with my ten-year-old daughter Brooke. I've worked here for ten years. I love it."

I had one more question. "You didn't see the license plate on that Mustang Convertible, did you? Even the state would be helpful."

She thought back. "It definitely wasn't New Jersey. It might have been Pennsylvania. Aren't they blue on the top, white in the middle, and yellow on the bottom?"

I nodded. "That's great. Did you tell the police any of this?"

She shook her head. "No. You had a way of making me remember things that they didn't. Maybe you missed your calling."

I thought about it. "Thank you, Maureen. I'll let them know you said that."

She looked at her pad. "Hey, I'd better get your order put in, or you'll be here all day."

I laughed. "That's okay. I don't start work until tomorrow." I pushed my luck. "Was there anyone else who might have seen anything this morning?"

She hesitated a second. "You might want to speak to Jackie. She came in about the same time I did, and I know the police took her statement, too. We haven't had a chance to talk; it's been such a crazy day. And we don't actually see eye to eye."

I nodded. "Thanks, Maureen."

She started toward the kitchen but doubled back. "Call me 'Mo.' If we're going to be friends, it has to work both ways."

I agreed. "Okay, Mo. Thank you so much."

She chuckled. "Don't thank me until you get your food. That's what I'm supposed to be here for." She took off for the kitchen.

I searched name tags as waitresses rushed back and forth between the kitchen and the dining room and finally spotted Jackie. She was a tiny thing, probably about my age. She couldn't have been a hundred pounds soaking wet. She had short brown hair that hung down across her face about half the time when she didn't fling it back with a motion that seemed to have become as natural as breathing to her. Her arms were covered with tattoos, and she had a butterfly on her neck. I wondered how I would get a moment to ask her a few questions, when she stepped outside and lit a cigarette. I took the opportunity to follow her.

She looked at me suspiciously as I approached. "Hi, Jackie, my name is Cordelia Corbett. Can I have a few words with you?"

She hesitated as she took a drag off her Lucky Strike non-filter. This woman seemed very hardcore. "I don't have much time. I'm grabbing a cigarette between orders."

I smiled patiently. "Well, this won't take long. I wondered what you saw this morning around the murder of the woman in the bathhouse."

She looked me up and down. "Are you an undercover cop?"

I shook my head. "Oh no, not at all. I'm a concerned citizen, making sure the police get it right. You know how short-staffed they are these days with the defunding going on?"

She glared at me. "Oh, I see. So, you're one of those Conservative Trumpers trying to make sure the country goes to hell. Well, I don't want any."

I smiled. "Oh, no, nothing like that. I'm not affiliated with any political party. I'm just trying to make sure that the police have all the information they need to solve this case, so it doesn't end up cold."

She brightened. "I love that show. I watched ten episodes yesterday on my day off."

I figured I had her. "And you wouldn't want this to end up on the show, would you?"

Even she had to admit, "No. Her family deserves to know what happened."

I asked, "On your way in this morning, did you see anything that drew your attention? I think you may have arrived right after Rachel got shot." I figured adding a name to make her less anonymous couldn't hurt.

She nodded. "Yes, I've been thinking since I spoke to the cops, a guy ran like a bat out of hell from near the bathhouse to the parking lot. He jumped in a red convertible and streaked out of here."

I nodded. "That's the guy that nearly backed into Mo's car as she pulled in."

She gave me a questioning look. "Oh, I had no idea. We haven't had a chance to compare notes. We're not all that close, to be honest. I don't think she likes my kind."

I gave her my two cents. "Oh, I don't know. I met her today, but she seemed pretty open-minded to me."

She stomped out her cigarette. "Sorry, I'd like to chat all day, but customers await. I hope I helped."

I followed her into the restaurant. "Yes, you did. Thanks." I found that my food had been delivered already but wasn't cold, thankfully.

About halfway through my meal, Mo returned and asked, "Did you get anything from Jackie?"

I nodded. "Sounds like she saw the Mustang guy running to the car. He's definitely a suspect." I wasn't sure if I should say anything. "And friend to friend, she doesn't think you 'like her kind.'"

She looked at me blankly. "She said that? I barely know her."

I nodded. "Exactly. She believes that you have purposely excluded her from your circle of friends because you don't think she measures up."

She smiled a frustrated smile and shook her head. "Now, isn't that ironic, when all this time I thought she had avoided me because I might be too prissy or too straight."

I agreed. "It's not surprising. In college, my last year, I found out that a couple of girls that I thought were my friends couldn't stand me. It's easy to talk past one another and never really know what the other is saying or feeling. Sometimes, we need to take it a step deeper to really get to where we need to be. And sometimes, it's too late. I guess you two have an opportunity here, and you can either take it or squander it. But at least you've identified it, and you've both acknowledged it."

She laughed. "Are you sure that you don't have psychology training? Whether you do or you don't, you're going to make a great Assistant Manager at Kohr's, and I guarantee you'll use all those skills and more." She thought about what I said. "I'll make a point of talking to Jackie about her perception of me and how I've treated her. I think there is still time to turn this around. I don't dislike her. I just don't know her. So, I'm certainly willing to get to know her, and I hope she's willing to do the same.

I smiled. "I hope she is too. You seem like nice people to me, so this could be a win for both of you."

CHAPTER SEVEN

When I left the Food Shack, I decided to head to the Windswept Motel, which was the next building down the beach. Since this might be my last day not working for a while, and I had no idea what my work schedule was, I figured I could knock this out while still on the beach.

I walked to the front desk and encountered a girl in her early twenties. According to her nametag, she was Amanda.

I smiled and started my spiel. "Hi, my name is Cordelia Corbett." Now that I got here, I realized I hadn't prepared what I would say. "Do you have a guest here by the name of Rachel Lynne Gaston?"

She smiled and moved closer to the counter, whispering, "Well, I'm sworn to secrecy because she's here, traveling incognito, but, yes, she's here. She's probably the most famous guest we've ever had. We hope she gives us a 'thumbs-up.' That could really put us on the map."

I hated to burst her bubble, so I figured I'd ask a few more questions. "Was she traveling alone, or did she share a room?"

She continued whispering. "Well, she traveled alone, officially, but a real hot guy searched her out this morning, so I wondered if they had planned to hook up." She chuckled. "I almost gave him my address by

43

mistake, if you know what I mean."

I smiled. "So, he was quite a looker?"

She nodded. "He looked like that blonde *Dukes of Hazzard* guy my grandmother used to be in love with."

I wondered, "Did you give him her room number?"

She shook her head. "No, that's against policy, especially with someone as famous as she is. But she wasn't there anyway. I knew that she had headed to the beach, so I let him know.

I felt terrible having to tell her the next part. I almost left and let her figure it out for herself, but that wasn't very kind, and then I might end up looking like a suspect myself. I looked her in the eye. "I hate to have to break it to you this way, but Rachel is dead."

She looked confused. "No, she's not. I saw her this morning, a few hours ago."

I filled in the details. "Someone found her shot to death in a shower stall in the bathhouse at The Food Shack."

She gasped, "Oh my God. Do they know who did it?"

I actually hadn't spoken to the police but guessed they didn't. "I don't think they do, so I'm investigating a bit on my own, which I'll share with the police department."

She asked the obvious question. "Why?"

I wasn't sure I could explain it. "Because I think Rachel would have wanted me to."

She looked at me like I had gone a bit crazy. "Did you know Rachel?"

I nodded my head. "I knew her when we were very young. We kind of lost touch."

She seemed to be getting angry. "Then, how could you possibly know what she would have wanted?"

I understood her frustration because I couldn't explain it either. "I can't explain it. It's just a feeling."

She backed away from the counter and said more loudly than anything she had said yet. "I think you need to get out of here. Now."

I figured I had worn out my welcome, but I had one more question. "Did you see the car this guy drove?"

She pointed to the door. "I don't know. It was red, I think."

~:~

I decided to talk to the police today before starting my walk home, even though I'd already spoken to Phil earlier. The Point Pleasant Beach Police Department was four blocks down New York Avenue and a ten-minute walk.

I practiced my speech as I walked. I realized that Detective Clint Daniels wasn't likely to be any more receptive to my interference in this case than Amanda at the motel had been, but I had to try, for Rachel's sake. I actually knew very little about the police or police work in general. Still, I assumed that they were a very tight-knit group who liked to do their work internally without much input from civilians like myself. So, if I got a result resembling anything different than that, I'd be one step ahead of the game.

I had butterflies when I approached the reception desk in the front of a relatively non-descript office-like building with a small sign in the front: Point Pleasant Beach Police Department. I asked Megan, the front desk Receptionist, if Detective Clint Daniels was available.

She responded with a heavy North Jersey accent. "Can I tell him who's cawling?"

I responded politely. "Yes, my name is Cordelia Corbett."

She seemed to have a script. "Will he know what this is in regawds to?"

I tried to stay positive. "No, but I am here about the Rachel Lynne Gaston murder."

She spoke into the phone, then to me. "He will be with you momentarily. Please be seated, and he will come get you."

Within a few minutes, a plainclothes detective, probably around forty, with a full head of curly dark brown hair and a friendly face, came out of a significant metal door leading to the back to retrieve me. He reached out his hand. "Ms. Corbett, I presume."

I stood and shook his hand. "Yes, you presume correctly. Nice to meet you, sir."

He smiled as he led me back through the metal door to what I assumed was normally utilized as an interrogation room. He said, "So, what can I do for you? I wasn't expecting anyone with information on the Gaston case this soon. We posted the contact information a couple of hours ago."

I confessed. "Well, I was actually at the scene this morning right after it happened. Officer Valente gave me your contact information."

He smiled. "Leave it to good old Phil. He brings me the prettiest ladies. I'm not even sure how he does it. It just seems to work out that way. Do you have any information about the case?"

I knew I was blushing several shades of red. I struggled with where to start. "I spoke to several people at The Food Shack this afternoon, and they remembered something they didn't report to the officers this morning."

He took out a notepad. "Okay, shoot." He already seemed kind of annoyed that I had inserted myself in what he believed to be his case.

I tried to sound confident. "According to two waitresses who came into work right about the time of the murder, a man left in a red Ford Mustang convertible with Pennsylvania plates at a high rate of speed. He was seen moments earlier, running from the whereabouts of the bathhouse where Rachel had been shot."

He seemed interested. "Do you have an idea who this gentleman might be?"

I had a theory. "Well, I don't, but Rachel had been under increased pressure by customers and prospective customers to rate their products highly. She had gotten threatening remarks on her blog site and several of her social media sites from people whose products hadn't fared so well under her scrutiny."

He considered my theory. "So, you think someone whose product that she gave a thumbs-down to on social media could have been so upset that he killed her?"

It sounded to me like he doubted it. "Yes, that's exactly what I think. Some of the comments on Facebook and other sites were marginally threatening. Some of these people are desperate. They've put their life savings into these products, and they see her as their possible savior or the devil, depending on how she rates them. I could see a crazy person confronting her, threatening to kill her if she doesn't change her rating, her refusing, and bam, she's dead."

He chuckled to himself. "Well, I appreciate you coming in with your theories, Darlin'. Now, if you'll leave the police work to us, we'll all be a lot happier. Is there anything else I can do for you today?"

I asked, "So, to be clear, when I solve the case, you don't want to know about it?"

He looked at me with an amused smile. "Surprise me in court."

I stood, ready to go. "I plan to."

~:~

It only took less than fifteen minutes to walk home, but I still felt boiling mad. It seemed like I had been disregarded and dismissed. I don't think it was coincidental that he called me 'pretty' initially. He wanted to disarm me, to bring me down to his level. I should have recognized his typical male tactics. Okay, so he wasn't bad looking in his own way; he seemed like a chauvinist through and through. I felt like the women's movement had been set back fifty years by the time I left the Police Station.

My anger might have shown slightly as I answered the phone when Katie called around four. All I said was, "Yes?"

She reacted immediately. "That's how you answer the phone when your loving sister calls? What is going on with you, *Cordless?*"

I wasn't in the mood to be made fun of. "Don't call me that, *Kitty Cat*." We had all made up nonsensical affectionate names for our siblings during adolescence. Lily's was *Lolita*. Of course, mine seemed to me to be the worst.

She softened her voice. "Okay, so what's up? Didn't you get the job?"

I couldn't believe how far behind she'd fallen in the news department. I filled her in about my job, the murder, my investigation after the murder, and my unfortunate encounter with Detective Daniels.

She laughed. "You remind me of Vivian, my Au Pair. I give her one day a week off, and she gets in more mischief than I get into during the whole rest of the week. Good thing you two don't cross paths. You'd be dangerous together."

It wasn't that I resented being compared to a twenty-three-year-old Au Pair whose most difficult decision in the day is which park to take the girls but, well, okay, I had to admit I did resent it. "Katie, this wasn't mischief. This is a murder we're talking about. Someone died. They lost their life. They won't be going home to their family. Dead. Done. Kaput."

She tried again. "Yes, Cordelia, I get it, but it wasn't someone we knew. So, as sorry as I am for her family and friends, I'm not going to let it ruin my day. And congratulations on getting the job."

I stood there with my mouth open, wondering how someone related to my mom and my Gram, two of the most feeling and empathetic women I knew, could be as unfeeling and obtuse as Katie. I couldn't continue this conversation. I finally said, "Hey, I've got a thing. Can we talk later?" And before she could respond, I hung up.

It wasn't even dinner time yet, and I felt completely spent. I couldn't go to bed, because I would just lay there and stare at the ceiling. I'd worry about starting my job tomorrow, about Rachel and why she died, about being disregarded by the too good looking for his own good Detective Daniels, and about why I suddenly felt the need to become an amateur sleuth in the first place. I never had any interest in the past. When I thought about it, starting a new job was the least of my worries.

CHAPTER EIGHT

I jumped on my laptop, hoping to find out more about Rachel's social life. I wondered if I could figure out whether the guy with the red Mustang had been a friend, a lover, or someone who needed her approval rating. Just a color, make, and model of a car and possibly a state wasn't a lot to go on.

I wasn't sure where to start, so I went to the Social Media pages of anyone who appeared to have an open dispute with Rachel. People were not shy about arguing or letting her know that they believed she'd gotten it wrong. It seemed the more money they stood to lose, or conversely, the more money they stood not to make due to her rejection, the more adamant and desperate they appeared.

I searched well into the night for anyone with an ax to grind with Rachel, and who showed photos of themselves in a red car of any type. They were few and far between, and even when I found one, they were never convertibles or Mustangs. Perhaps Detective Daniels had a point. This line of suspects appeared futile.

I started to question my original theory of who shot Rachel. Perhaps it wasn't the guy in the red Mustang. Maybe, as Amanda had assumed, he was a friend of Rachel's, and he went looking for her on the beach. Maybe when he found out that she'd been shot, he took off in a panic, thinking that he might be considered a suspect. Or perhaps he never found her because she got shot in the bathhouse, and he took off in anger, feeling rejected.

Maybe I needed to go back to the scene of the crime and question other witnesses. Perhaps other possible suspects were seen running up or down the beach from the front of the restaurant. I only spoke to people who were in the back near the bathhouse.

I sat back in my chair, wondering why I did this at all. I'd already faced rejection from a motel front desk clerk, antagonism from a detective, and complete misunderstanding from my sister. I got absolutely nothing out of this, except maybe the feeling I was making up for my petty jealousy all those years ago, so why did I continue?

Almost immediately, the answer came to me: because it's the right thing to do. The strange thing was, I could hear the answer in my Gram's voice. Then it hit me. I couldn't understand why I had felt so different at the restaurant when I heard the woman scream, why I jumped into action, why I performed CPR even though I had never done it before. These were all changes that had come over me since moving into Gram's house. I'd never thought of going back to work at Kohr's until, yes, until I moved into Gram's house. I'd never spoken to so many new people and made so many new friends in twenty-four hours as I had in this one, the first twenty-four hours I'd lived in Gram's house. My heart jumped at this revelation.

⌒⋰∾

I arrived at Kohr's Frozen Custard at 9 a.m. sharp on Thursday. Sally had already worked for an hour on getting the store opened. She nearly jumped out of her skin when she saw me. "Oh, thank God you're here, Cord. I had nightmares all night that you had second thoughts." She thought for a minute. "How much do I need to review? Do you remember how to set up the front? Not much has changed over the years. We have a few more products, but you'll pick that up fast."

I glanced at the cash registers. "The registers are the same. I can't

50

believe you aren't accepting credit cards yet. How are you getting away with that?"

She laughed. "Yes, we are one of the last cash holdouts on the boardwalk. It will be a sad day when we finally give in. I can imagine the day when we don't accept cash at all. I don't think it's far off."

I agreed. "A lot of fast-food chains aren't accepting cash. I imagine it won't be long before our society is totally cashless."

She changed the subject. "So, how are you doing after yesterday? I know that had to be a lot to handle, especially on your first day in a new town."

I smiled. "Oh, I'm fine. Some funny things are going on with me, though. I'll tell you about it later."

She nodded. "You'd better. I'm so happy you're here. And not as an Assistant Manager, as a friend. You've grown and changed a lot. It suddenly seems like we are a bit closer in age, and you are what I need in my life right now."

I agreed. "I feel the same way, Sally. I felt it as soon as we reconnected."

I asked, "So, who's working today? Am I going to have to run interference?"

She checked the schedule. "Yes, Shelby Irons, your next-door neighbor, and Billy Fordham, Mister Oblivious. So, you will have your hands full with teen hormones. It'll be a great way to break you in."

I rolled my eyes. "I can hardly wait. It'll be like reliving my high school years vicariously."

⁓:⁓

We spent the next couple of hours separately but in sync, getting the ice cream stand ready to open. We opened at 11 a.m. and would stay open until Midnight. I had forgotten they stayed open so late, I guessed, because there was a legal limit as to how late I could work at sixteen. Now, the sky's the limit. How nice for me.

About halfway through the day, I asked, "Hey, Sally, we never talked about what my hours would be. I trust that I'm not working 9 a.m. to Midnight seven days a week."

She laughed. "Oh, yeah. Well, I wish I could have you all that time, but I realize you might burn out quickly. So, here's my plan. Mondays and Tuesdays are the quietest days, so I'll be on-call those days, but I'll run with my most trusted staff with no manager, so you'll be off. Then, Tuesdays through Sunday, you and I will alternate between the 9 to 5 and the 4 to Midnight shift every other day. So, you and I can overlap for an hour a day if we need to communicate about anything."

I waited on a customer while I absorbed what she told me. I wasn't thrilled about losing my weekends, but at least I would get two days in a row off. Although they wouldn't correspond with anyone else's. I smiled and handed the customer two ice cream cones. "That'll be nine dollars even."

She whined. "Why don't you take credit cards? I hate carrying cash. You are the last reason in town to have cash. I hate it."

I smiled sweetly. "I'll pass your concerns on to our owner, who is a member of the Kohr family and takes every complaint very seriously."

She nodded, licking the cones so they wouldn't drip. "That would be great. Thank you."

I shouted back to Sally. "Another cash complainer. I think it might be time to bring this place into the two thousand and tens. You seriously are at least ten years behind the times. I remember people asking about credit cards when I worked here fourteen years ago. But, not like this. It's like almost every customer now."

She nodded. "I know I have to pull the trigger soon. I hoped to get through this season. I took a hit last year with the crowds down. But it's not quite so bad this year, so maybe I'll bite the bullet. I'll bet that volume will go up to offset the cost. I hate cash as much as the next person. I avoid places that take cash."

I smiled. "Can I tell people that we will be taking credit cards soon? They will be so happy."

She nodded. "Sure, why not. We can always use the good PR." She remembered our last conversation. "Anyway, if you're ready, we can start that schedule tomorrow. You can work 9 to 5, and I'll work 4 to Midnight, then Saturday, you can work 4 to Midnight, and I'll work 9 to 5, and we'll keep alternating. Deal?"

I agreed. "Sure, why not? I like change, so not having the same schedule every day is perfect for me."

Sally looked around. "Hey, what happened to Billy and Shelby?"

I chuckled. "Oh, they are working on straightening out the walk-in freezer."

She grinned. "You didn't put two sex-starved teens in a tiny freezer together. Did you? Tell me they're not making out in there right now."

I nodded. "That's the plan. I hope they got it. They needed a little push. She reminds me so much of me at that age. I couldn't resist."

She put her arm around me. "I think I could learn to love you, Cord Corbett." She looked at the counter behind me. "It looks like you have a visitor. Maybe you'd like to take a break."

I turned around to see Sean McPherson standing at the counter. I went over to wait on him. "Well, what can I get you, sir?"

He flashed a twenty. "I have to get an orange and vanilla twist and whatever the lady will have."

I smiled. "Well, let's make that two, then. I'll be right out to join you."

CHAPTER NINE

I stepped out of the employee exit, and momentarily, I had freedom. The sun felt hot, so we walked up the boardwalk toward Jenkinson's, where there were usually a couple of empty tables. Technically, you weren't supposed to use them unless you were a customer, but over the years, we had reached an agreement that they wouldn't hassle our customers, and we'd give their employees all the free ice cream they could eat. It had been an unspoken gentleman's agreement that seemed to work for years.

Sean smiled as he sat across from me. "I wondered if you'd think I might be being too bold, coming to visit you at work and all."

I touched his hand, which wasn't altogether unpleasant, and smiled back. "I'm glad you did. Yesterday turned out to be such a crazy day, and I honestly wasn't sure I'd see you again. When you meet someone while performing CPR, almost anything can happen as a result."

He nodded. "Yes, I suppose it can. I had to really convince myself to come down here. Dealing with rejection isn't my best quality. There's no telling how many little kids I might have knocked down in my wake had you said 'no' to my offer of a cone."

I threw my head back for dramatic effect. "Well, good thing I didn't then, isn't it?" I looked at him across the table. "You know what I like best about you, Sean?"

He thought for a second. "Honestly, I don't have a clue."

I thought about reconsidering my answer, hoping it didn't hurt his feelings. I warned him in advance. "Well, it's not so much a personal trait as a background."

He seemed to hang on my every word, which felt very nice and a quality I hadn't noticed until now. "Oh? I guess it would be hard to be offended by it, then."

I smiled weakly, "Well, that's a good way to look at it." I took a deep breath, then let it out. "Well, in all honesty, it's the fact that you are so obviously of Irish descent. I wouldn't have to explain to my parents why I've brought home another annoyingly Italian-, German-, Spanish-, or God-forbid African American. I always feel like I'm starting at the bottom of the hill and trying to work my way up before I even get in the door with the poor guy."

He thought for a minute. "Well, I would have preferred that it be a trait that I could actually control, but I'm willing to work with it. If I have something that gives me a step up to dating you compared to other guys, I'm all in."

I felt myself blushing. Sometimes I hated my snow-white skin. "Wow, we're talking about dating already, and all we've done together is attempt to save a woman's life. That's a pretty big leap, isn't it?" I winked, trying to look coy.

He got a serious look on his face. "Oh, I don't know, Cordelia. Didn't you feel like we kind of bonded, working together toward a mutual cause? And even though we didn't succeed in saving her life, we did our best, and we stood up for what is right."

I couldn't argue. "You're right, of course. I already feel like I know you. You have a real familiarity about you. Do you know what I mean, Sean?"

He nodded, looking me straight in the eye. "I have to say; you're the most interesting woman I've met in quite a while. It's amazing that you just moved here and that you live so close to me. I don't believe any of these things are coincidences."

I thought back to this morning. "Do you want to hear something really weird?"

He nodded. "Sure, I like to hear your voice."

I struggled to stay on track, hoping he didn't mean my voice was weird. "Thank you. That's sweet. But listen to this. I told you that I moved into my Gram's house because she died earlier this week, right?"

He agreed. "Yes, you did."

I continued, "Well, strange things have been happening to me since I moved into her house."

He looked concerned. "What kind of things? Are you okay?"

I smiled. "Yes, I'm fine. It's sweet of you to be worried about me like that. I could get used to this." I wondered if I should really be sharing my feelings with a guy I barely knew, but uncharacteristically, they were flowing right out of me, where normally I would have been far more reserved. This seemed to be another example of what I'd been trying to explain to him. "That's what I'm talking about right there. Until I moved into my Gram's house, I never would have said that to you. I might have thought it, but I would never have said it."

He seemed curious. "Oh? What other things have you done since you moved that you wouldn't have before?"

I thought about it. "Well, I've been obsessed with Rachel Lynne Gaston's death. I've been interviewing witnesses. I visited the Police Department. I've been spending endless hours on the Internet studying who she'd become as a person and why this might have happened to her. I feel a connection to her that I can't explain. I don't know if I told you this, but I knew her as a kid and we were best friends at one point, then had a falling out that I feel responsible for. Maybe that's partially why I feel compelled to solve her murder."

He didn't seem as interested in that as I was. "Well, or it could be because you were right there when she died. That will probably fade."

I argued. "There were a ton of people around when she died. Take you, for instance. I don't see you getting all obsessed with her death. You've pretty much moved on with your life, to the point where you're seriously considering dating me. And, believe me, I'm flattered. But you, and everyone else who was there, except me, has moved on with their lives, but mine has stopped. I even told Detective Daniels at the Police Department that I would solve this case and surprise him in court. Why would I have said that?"

He tried again to change the subject. "I'd really like to focus on you and me."

Suddenly, I felt like he might be pressuring me into something I didn't want to do. It wasn't a good feeling. I spoke. "You know what, Sean, maybe this wasn't such a great idea. You seem like a nice guy and all, but I don't think the timing is going to work for me." I stood up and walked back toward the boardwalk.

I heard him say behind me. "Cordelia, wait."

Tears welled up in my eyes as I approached Kohr's. I couldn't possibly go back in there crying. I walked right past the counter while Sally waited on a customer. I felt that she saw me but didn't comment. I wondered if she saw how upset I looked. This felt so embarrassing. I never wore my heart on my sleeve like this. At least not until I moved to Point Pleasant Beach and my Gram's house.

~:~

Within ten minutes, I had gotten my composure back and resumed work. My two love birds were coming out of the freezer as I arrived. I smiled at Shelby and asked, "Everything all straight in there?"

She gave Billy a look. "It sure is, Miss Corbett."

I punched her lightly on the arm. "Please, call me Cordelia. Cord would even be better. I'm not that old. God, Miss Corbett makes me sound like an ancient substitute teacher that you are planning on putting rabbit ears behind the next time she walks up the aisle between your desks. I am not that person. I'm the fun Assistant Manager who assigns you to straighten the walk-in freezer, knowing full well you're going to spend most of your time in there making out."

They both looked at me with the innocence of Jesus. Billy pled first. "Oh, no, Miss, I mean Cord, we would never do that. We don't even like each other *that* way. Right, Shelby?"

She took the baton. "God, no. Billy's like a brother to me. We were making sure that freezer ended up being spic and span."

I smiled and put one arm around each of them as if I might tell them a story. I hated to burst their bubble, and yet, it would be so much fun. "Let me share something that I learned today that I had no idea of when I worked here at your age." I paused for effect, then spilled the beans. I started real quietly. "Security cameras. They are everywhere. You can't get away from them. So, if you think you're being clever, sneaking away for a cigarette, or something more potent. Or if you think you're going to get away with a little smooch here or a little feel there." I hesitated again. Then said loud enough to startle them. "You're not!"

Shelby's face went ashen. "Are you going to tell my mom?"

I smiled. "God, no. I'm telling you for your own good before something happens that you don't want an audience for."

She covered her face. "It already did."

I glared at Billy. "My God, Billy, don't you have a girlfriend?"

I realized that my attempt to play cupid had completely backfired, and I had to accept the blame for all of this. And it seemed so unlike me. I never meddled in other people's love lives. But you know who it seemed like? My Gram. This was getting scary.

CHAPTER TEN

Sally ended up sending me home a little after seven. I figured she felt sorry for me, considering I'd had a disastrous first date and a horrible matchmaking experience, and sent my next-door neighbor home crying a couple of hours before I left. Poor Shelby. How could she not have known that Billy had a girlfriend? I even knew Billy had a girlfriend. So, why had I been so determined to set them up?

I had too much running through my mind. I decided to get back to investigating Rachel Lynne Gaston's death. When I brought up her website, I did a double-take. Between the last time I had visited and now, the whole world had heard about her death. There was a tremendous amount of activity on the site, people mourning her death, supporting one another as they tried to deal with the senseless death of yet another young woman in this country, and several people talking just to get attention, with little interest in Rachel.

I took a special interest in that group, wondering if anyone could be twisted enough to cause someone's death in order to get attention. I figured this might be as good a place as any to search for young men with red Mustang convertibles. I hadn't had much luck previously, but maybe my luck had changed.

I went through them one by one, searching for pictures that might give me a clue. After a couple of hours, I spotted it, a red Mustang convertible. Since I never actually saw the car, I couldn't guarantee this was the one in the parking lot behind the bathhouse right after Rachel died, but it could be. I checked the rear license plate: Pennsylvania.

My heart started beating more quickly. I checked the name. John Michael Owens. He hailed from Nazareth, Pennsylvania. I looked it up on Apple Maps, only ten miles from Easton. My gut told me he knew Rachel personally. So, why was he on her site pretending that he didn't? Was he covering his tracks? Now that I had a name, I knew I could find this guy. He had no place to hide. The Internet can be your best friend or your worst enemy.

I hit a link to go to this guy's Instagram page. He had tons of pictures of his car, around town in Nazareth, and at the Jersey shore: Long Branch, Asbury Park, Seaside Heights, Surf City, Beach Haven, Brigantine, Atlantic City, Strathmere, Sea Isle City, Avalon, Stone Harbor, Wildwood, and Cape May. Why hadn't he posted any photos of Point Pleasant Beach? It seemed to be the only one he missed. Or had he just removed it?

I had to find this guy. I looked online for the cheapest of those people finder programs that you can use once and cancel immediately thereafter. I found one for a dollar and searched his name. Within fifteen minutes, I had a full report of most recent addresses, relatives, email addresses, phone numbers, places of employment, schools, and all sorts of other information I didn't need.

I found out he was single and twenty-nine years old, never married, and had no children. He had never lived anywhere but Nazareth, Pennsylvania, and worked there at a local garage. I also obtained his most likely address and cell phone number. I wondered what I would say if I called him. How could I get him to admit he'd been in Point Pleasant Beach?

Before I did anything rash based solely on a hunch, I decided that I'd call Mo from the diner. She told me that she hadn't seen him at all, only his hand, but sometimes you see more than you think you do.

Then it struck me that Jackie, the other waitress, had actually seen him running from the Bathhouse to his vehicle. She'd be an even better witness. I'd exchanged contact information with Mo, but not Jackie, but she hadn't been quite as cooperative. I wondered if Mo had taken to heart my comment that Jackie felt like she looked down on her.

I took a chance and dialed Mo's number. I wanted to reconnect with my new friend sooner than later anyway. She answered on the first ring. "Cord, I can't believe you are calling me right now. Guess who's here with me."

I took a wild guess. "Jackie?"

She sounded astonished. "How did you know? That's amazing."

I laughed. "Well, I think she's our only mutual acquaintance."

It sounded like they were hitting it off. "Hey, do you want to stop over? My daughter just went to bed, and we're having a couple of glasses of wine."

This sounded perfect. "Absolutely. I have something I needed both of your input on, so your timing is great."

She gave me her address, then laughed, "Metedeconk isn't that big. The biggest mistake people make is driving onto and off the peninsula without realizing it by taking a right on Princeton Avenue, and they miss fourth street. Then they end up in Windward and never find our little community."

I felt confident. "I use the Waze app on my iPhone now and rarely get lost these days. Plus, I always know where the cops are."

She sounded interested. "You'll have to show me that. I'm always getting lost."

I could hear Jackie chattering in the background. It sounded like they had really hit it off. It felt good that I had helped to repair their communication breakdown. That seemed so unlike me until I moved into Gram's house.

I grabbed my laptop and headed out to the car. According to Waze, the five-mile trip would take eleven minutes. I tried to organize my thoughts. I knew that most people seemed to think I'd gone a bit over the top when it came to my interest in Rachel Lynne Gaston's death. I wasn't even sure how to explain it. I just knew I had to do it. It went hand in hand with several other unexplainable personality changes I'd experienced since moving into my Gram's house. I wondered if I should see a therapist or a priest specializing in ghostly possession. Or maybe I had been so close to my Gram that I felt closer to her now that I lived in her house.

I pulled into Mo's driveway at 549 Parker Avenue, wondering what to expect. I didn't know these two well, and I felt a little nervous.

As soon as I pulled in, they both came out with wine glasses in hand, but these weren't your typical, traditional, stemmed wine glasses, but serious glasses meant for consuming significant amounts of wine. They had to be at least twenty-four ounces. I wondered if Mo had sleeping facilities because I had a hunch driving home wasn't going to be an option. Happily, though, I didn't need to be at work until 4 p.m. tomorrow, so I had a lot of flexibility.

As soon as I got out of my Jeep, they both hugged me, which I hadn't expected, especially Jackie, who had not even appeared to like me, much less want to hug me the last time we met. She handed me a full glass of white wine and smiled. "You are way behind, girl. That's why we had to meet you out here with a glass. Time is a wastin'."

The three of us went back toward the house, arm in arm. It had been a long time, forever actually, since I'd had close girlfriends other than my sisters. It felt great to be in exciting and unchartered territory. I knew I had my Gram to thank.

As soon as we got near the house, I realized I had forgotten my laptop. I said, "Hold on a minute. I need to get your opinion on something."

They looked at me suspiciously when I came in with my computer. Jackie said, "Oh, no, you aren't going to take depositions now, are you?" They both burst out laughing. I wondered what number bottle of wine they were on. The two empties on the kitchen counter answered my question.

I set up my laptop on the kitchen counter. "Okay, girls, this will be pretty painless. I'm trying to identify the guy in the red Mustang, and maybe the car itself."

Mo rolled her eyes. She said to Jackie. "See, I told you she's obsessed with this." She put her arm around me. "You need to get a life, Cordy. Do you have a boyfriend?"

I smiled sadly. "Well, I thought I did, but I think I blew it yesterday. He didn't seem very supportive. I figured if I had that feeling on the first date, what would happen after the tenth date, or after we were living together, or married?"

Jackie said, "Whoa, girl, slow down. You're already thinking about getting married on your first date? That might be a problem. And what wasn't he being supportive about?"

I thought back to our conversation. "Well, I wanted to talk about this case, and he wanted to talk about us. He seemed a little self-centered."

Mo took a long drink of wine. "You are really dragging our party down, Cordy. You need to apologize to Sean the next time you see him."

I smiled. "How did you know I meant Sean?"

She nudged me. "I have a way of knowing things, Cordy. Can I call you Cordy? I really like it. Please, please, please, please, please."

I'd never liked being called 'Cordy,' but she acted so sweetly about it, I couldn't say 'no.' I put my arm around her, trying to be more likable. It seemed like I'd been failing so far. "Of course, Mo. I'd love that." I figured this might be as good a time as any to reel her in. "Now, can you look at this for ten seconds, and I'll leave you alone about it for the rest of the night."

I motioned Jackie over. "And Jackie, it's even more important for you because you were an eye-witness."

She rolled her eyes. "It's about that woman again, isn't it? When will it all end?"

Mo said softly. "Let's do it for Cordy. She said she'd leave us alone after this. Right Cordy?" She started to slur her words slightly. I wished I could catch up with her. I needed a good buzz about now.

I sat down at my laptop, and they stood behind me. I navigated to John Michael Owens' Instagram page and scrolled through pictures.

Mo gasped, "There's the car. I'd know it anywhere." She looked closely. "Hey, can you magnify that bumper?" There appeared to be a small sticker on the right side of the bumper. When I focused in on it, we could read it. It read: 'Don't mess with me, little girl.' She suddenly got very quiet. "I've been having nightmares about this bumper sticker. I had no idea where I'd seen it before. Now I know why."

Jackie stared at the screen. "Let me see this guy. I want to know if I can remember him." She put her hands on my shoulders. "You're getting me hooked on this, Cord. And I didn't think anyone could."

I knew I had a very clear picture of him on the beach that I'd seen the other day. I brought it up on the screen and enlarged it.

Jackie nearly jumped up and down. "That's him. That's him." She downed her wine. "Do you think he killed her? We have to call the police."

I put up my hand. "Whoa, not so fast. I'm not handing this to them. You have no idea how rude Detective Daniels was to me. He's getting nothing until I say he gets it, and then he might not even get it."

Mo had an idea. "Hey, where does this John guy with the Mustang live?"

I gave them the bad news. "In Nazareth, Pennsylvania. It's about a hundred miles from here."

She wasn't giving up. "Still no reason we can't give him a visit. That's less than two hours."

I felt like we had changed roles. "How come you two wanted nothing to do with this before, and now all of a sudden, you are gung-ho?"

Jackie answered, "Because now we are a part of it. It's not just you. I know I saw that guy. If he's the murderer, and we all work together to bring him to justice, that will be so cool."

The idea started to grow on me. "That *would* be better than me having to do it alone."

Mo agreed. "Of course, it would. I'll grab the girl next door to watch Brooke while we're gone."

I jumped up. "Okay, I'll get the Jeep started."

CHAPTER ELEVEN

According to my report, he lived at 137 Victory Lane in Nazareth, Pennsylvania. Considering the apparent size of this guy's ego, his address, Victory Lane, wasn't surprising. However, the house was surprisingly modest when we arrived. We checked the address three times before descending on the property.

Mo and Jackie had brought a couple more bottles of wine with them and polished them off during our hour and a half drive despite my warnings of police checkpoints on I-78. I felt as sober as the night. I still hadn't settled on what to say, but hoped it would come to me.

We boldly walked to the front door and knocked.

The guy in the picture opened the door. He seemed surprised to see three relatively young and attractive women. He asked, "What can I do for you ladies?"

I asked, "Are you, John Michael Owens?"

He nodded and smiled. "I am. And you are?"

I jumped in. "We are three concerned citizens. Were you in Point Pleasant Beach earlier this week?"

The smile flew from his face faster than a gaggle of geese flying south for the winter. He thought fast. "Now, why would I be in New Jersey? I've got a job here."

I agreed. "Yes, you do. You work at Murante Auto Repair, and I can easily ask them if you were off earlier this week."

He gritted his teeth. "Okay. Just what is this about?"

Mo swayed a little. "We think you know what this is about."

Jackie nodded. "Yeah, we think you know what this is about."

I wondered why I'd decided to bring two drunk girls with me. I continued the thought. "Right after Rachel Lynne Gaston died, you were observed leaving the area at a high rate of speed. Care to explain that?"

It surprised me when he looked up and down the street, then motioned us inside. I wasn't completely sure we were safe, but he seemed relieved now that he had been outed. He motioned toward a large couch. "Please sit down. Would you like anything to drink?"

We all declined. I asked, "So? What's going on?"

He pulled up a chair in front of us. "You're right. I did go to Point Pleasant Beach. I had set up an appointment to meet with Rachel Lynne. I have a product that she had downright panned, and she just about killed my sales. I wanted to meet with her to convince her to give it another chance."

I wondered, "She only lived ten miles from you. Why did you drive over a hundred miles to meet with her when you could have waited until she got back and met here in Easton?"

He sat back in the chair. "We were supposed to meet at Pop's Kitchen, just off of I-78 in Easton, but she suddenly decided she had to get out of town. Her trip to Point Pleasant Beach turned out to be a last-minute change of plans. When she canceled our meeting, I asked if we could reschedule down there. She agreed, so we planned to meet at The Food Shack."

Mo got his meaning immediately. "So, you were the reason she came to The Food Shack in the first place. Even if you didn't kill her, you may be responsible for her death. That's where she died, right?"

A tear ran down his cheek. "I can't believe she's dead. I only wanted to talk to her. I needed to talk to her. She's the only person who can help me. Now, she's gone."

I felt sorry for him in a way, but his grief seemed more directed at his product and his finances than her. I nodded a touch sarcastically in his direction. "I'm sure you'll recover. But I'm pretty sure that she won't." I thought about it further. "Are you positive you didn't have the meeting, but you were unable to convince her to change the rating of your product, so you killed her?"

He stood and started pacing the room. "That's exactly why I left. I figured if anyone knew I had an appointment to meet her, they would assume I killed her. I panicked. I had to get out of there before anyone saw me." He looked at the three of us. "Evidently, someone saw me."

I nodded. "You don't exactly have the least noticeable car in the world." I thought about his story. Parts of it seemed believable, and he didn't appear to be lying. "So, if you didn't kill her, who did? Before you bolted, did you see anyone acting suspiciously?"

Jackie looked disappointed. "You mean he didn't do it?"

I shook my head. "I'm thinking not."

He smiled. "Oh, bless you. Would you testify on my behalf? The cops have been sniffing around here. I think it's a matter of time before they arrest me."

I repeated my question. "John, this could be a matter of life or death. Did you see anything suspicious near the bathhouse? She was shot in the bathhouse and left to bleed to death in the shower."

He commented, "I guess she must have gone to the beach and didn't think she'd have time to go back to her motel before our meeting."

I felt suddenly suspicious again. "Do you know what motel she stayed in?" Of course, he did; Amanda at the front desk told me he asked for her room number.

He looked away. "Um, yeah, I guess so."

I raised my voice. "John, listen to me. If this is going to work, you need to tell us the truth, the whole truth, and nothing but the truth. If you start lying or withholding details, you are going to be toast."

He looked ashamed. "Okay, I got down there early and came up with a plan. I thought maybe I could intercept her before she left for The Food Shack. I knew there were a couple of motels at that end of the beach, and I figured if she would be meeting me at The Food Shack, she'd probably be staying at one of them. I knew what her car looked like because I followed her to her vehicle once after an event in Atlantic City."

I shook my head. "So, you've stalked her before. And I'm supposed to believe that you didn't kill her? That is getting harder, to be honest."

He could barely look at me. "Well, once I found her car, I thought if I got her room number and caught her before she left for the beach, we could meet in her room instead. The way I envisioned it: I could seduce her, then everything would be good forever after that. She'd have to support my product if we fell in love. Right? She was a beautiful woman. I would have been attracted to her whether she had social media influence or not. I was ready to take a chance."

Jackie took over to summarize. "So, we're supposed to believe that you were meeting her down here, but when you got to the meeting site, she had already died. But hours earlier, you tried to track down her motel room with the intent of having sex with her so that she would give your product a thumbs up, and you could live happily ever after. Do I have that right?"

He nodded. "Except, it sounds really bad when you say it."

I looked at Mo and Jackie. "I don't know about you two, but I have to sleep on this one." I looked back at John. "At the beginning, you almost had me. It sounded like a definite case of mistaken identity, that you were in the wrong place at the wrong time. But the fact that you sought to track her down to do God-knows-what after you had already secured an appointment with her really bothers me. "It speaks to character. It speaks to intent. If you were prepared to put on a complete scam on Rachel and assault her for the good of your product, how do we know that you are not lying to us now?"

He threw his hands up. "You don't."

I agreed. "Exactly. We don't. We honestly don't know what to think of you.

We stood and walked out.

~::~

The girls both slept most of the way back to Mo's house. It gave me nearly two hours of solitude to think. I tried to wrap my head around our visit with John Michael Owens. Had we spent a half-hour with a psychopathic killer or one more victim of Rachel Lynne Gaston's thumbs down?

The clock had nearly struck midnight by the time we pulled into Mo's driveway. I had planned on having drunk a ton of wine by now and having to sleep it off before driving home, but since that wasn't the case, I decided to call it a night after tucking the other two in and sending the girl next door home.

This had been good practice, staying up late. I needed it because I would be working until midnight alternating days, starting tomorrow. The good news being that I could sleep as late as I wanted tonight in anticipation of working late tomorrow night.

When I settled into bed, I thought about our strange night with the man I would have sworn was the killer before I met him. Now, I didn't know, but my gut said he didn't have it in him. When his first instinct was to bring us into his home rather than send us away, it seemed to me that he didn't kill Rachel. Would that come back to bite me later? I had no idea, but I would go with it for now until he proved me wrong.

CHAPTER 12

It felt so nice to sleep naturally until I awoke without an alarm. Something can be said for working four to midnight alternating days. Working nine to five on the days after I worked until midnight the night before might not be quite as pleasant, but the upside would be this, luxuriating in bed for as long as I felt like it on the opposite days.

I glanced at my watch after turning over and going back to sleep several times. It said ten after ten. It felt sinful but blessed at the same time. I thought back on last night and the success of sharing a two-hundred-mile round trip with my two new friends. The reality that I had made two new friends and rekindled a more mature relationship with my old boss, now that we were both fourteen years older and wiser, made my move to Point Pleasant Beach seem so right. I'd never had many friends, so having three felt nothing short of amazing.

As I stretched in bed, I debated my next move with Sean. I wondered if I'd completely blown my chance with him or if I'd get an opportunity to make our last encounter up to him, perhaps in a big way. He was right. I was obsessing about Rachel Lynne Gaston. And I certainly wasn't going to drop the case, but there was a time and a place for everything. He didn't need to hear about it all day, every day.

I decided to take a chance. I dialed his number on my iPhone. He picked up immediately. I thought that might be a good sign. I heard a smile in his voice. "To what do I owe the pleasure of this call, Cordelia? I wasn't quite sure I'd hear from you again."

I chuckled. "Um, about that. Can I get a free pass? I had been really stressing over my first day at work or sweating in front of a really cute guy? I don't know. You can pick whatever explanation for my extremely rude behavior works for you. Then you can decide if you can forgive me."

He sounded ever cheerful. "I have already forgiven you. I thought I'd show up later at Kohr's and try again. I'm a glutton for punishment."

I cooed. "How'd you like to come over for breakfast? I'm serving?"

I thought I heard him breathing hard. He asked, "You're talking about food, right?"

I chuckled with a Simon Cowell accent. "You are a naughty one, aren't you? Of course, I'm talking about food. What else? Are pancakes and eggs okay?"

He laughed lightly. "I'll be right over."

I immediately jumped out of bed and into the shower, realizing that I had invited a man I barely knew to my house for breakfast, and I wasn't even out of bed yet. He seemed like a nice enough guy, but staying in bed would clearly give him the wrong message, especially after my slightly suggestive telephone call.

By the time he rang the bell, I was fully dressed and had begun cooking to my heart's delight. It felt good, though, to have a man watch me adoringly while I scrambled eggs and flipped pancakes.

As we ate, he asked, "So, what happened the other day? It seemed like we were having a pretty good time, and then you were gone. I sat there for a while, hoping you'd come back."

I wasn't sure how deep to go with my explanation. "Oh, it's been a while since I've been in a relationship, and a few ghosts were haunting me. It's kind of hard to explain." Truer words were never spoken. "I'm glad that you forgave me. I guess dating a psychologist has its perks."

He nodded. "It probably has its downsides, too. I probably over-analyze. I'm working on going with the flow a little more." He leaned across the table and kissed me.

I had to admit; it wasn't totally unpleasant. I blushed. "Wow, that came from out of the blue."

He stared into my eyes with his very blue ones. "I like you, Cordelia. I'm not going to lie about that. I know I haven't known you long. Okay, it's been less than a week, but I believe that I'm falling in love with you."

I looked at him with a combination of shock, amusement, and disbelief. "What? You don't even know me. You haven't even seen me without make-up. Admittedly, I hardly wear any, but that's not the point. You haven't seen me at my worst. Well, maybe yesterday, it might have been close. But, anyway, you can't love me yet. That's a big deal. That takes time, monumental amounts of time. So, I want you to shove that back in until there's been plenty of it. And I know you didn't tell me that you loved me, but you said that you're falling in love with me, and that's way too much, too soon. You're a therapist. You should know that."

He watched me argue with myself like watching a rally in a tennis match. Finally, he responded. "Yes, I am a therapist, and I always tell my patients to be honest. So, that's what I'm doing. I could have waited, and maybe that would have been the best thing, but this felt real. I'm sorry if it doesn't fit in with your best-laid plans."

I bit my lip. "I don't know if I can date a therapist. I'm used to being with guys who wouldn't know a feeling if they fell over it. This might be too much; I don't know. It feels dangerous. Strangely appealing but dangerous at the same time. I don't know if that's good or bad or why I'm talking so much or so fast. I feel like if I fill the air, then you won't have time to talk, and you won't say anything else that I can't handle."

He opened his mouth again, and much to my chagrin, said, "You're incredibly beautiful."

I looked away. "No, no, no, no. Don't even think about going there. Don't tell me you think you are falling in love with me, then tell me I'm beautiful. That's not fair."

He chuckled. "I'm just telling you how I feel. How can that be wrong?"

I thought about it. "Oh, that can be wrong. That can be wrong on so many levels; I can't even name them. How you feel may have nothing to do with anything. It may be how you feel today, this morning, or how you feel this hour or this minute. It may have nothing to do with how you might feel tomorrow, or next week or next year."

He stared at me with those eyes. "I know this is something that's not going to fade in a day, or a week, or even a year. I haven't had this feeling in quite a while, or maybe this exact feeling, ever. When I see your white skin and red hair, it ignites something deep in me, something that feels like it's been ignited from generations of passion. I've been waiting for you my whole life, Cordelia Corbett. I'm not going to let you go now."

I wasn't prepared for this. I had hoped for a long, slow courtship, starting as friends, moving on to good friends, then best friends, then special friends, then perhaps lovers, but that whole process could take years as far as I knew. I wanted to savor the moment, not to jump into anything or rush through it. I wondered if I would catch up, or even if I should. I smiled sympathetically.

"I don't know, Sean. You are very sweet, but I'm not sure I can accelerate to your speed any time soon, and I would feel too guilty if I tried to slow you down to where I am."

He seemed truly interested in where I was. "Please share where you are, Cordelia. It's the only way I'll ever know."

The way he said 'Cordelia' made the corners of my mouth turn up. I couldn't help it. "I want walks in the park, hand in hand. I want bonfires on cool fall evenings. I want bike rides in the spring. I want to run down to the waves and run back before they catch us. I want to ride horseback, motorbikes, snowmobiles, jet skis, and things I can't even think of right now. I want to travel together, to the Grand Canyon, the desert, the plains, the West Coast, the Bayou, the Great Lakes, to Alaska, Hawaii, Canada, Ireland of course, Europe, the Middle East, South Africa, Southeast Asia, Australia, South America, to other places I've always wanted to go, but never dared to go."

He inquired politely, "And when do you want to fall in love?"

I felt frustrated. "No one should ever know the answer to that question. Love should happen when it happens, and that should be the most special, memorable experience of our lives and something we should cherish forever. We should be able to relive that moment for as long as we live. If we can't, then it isn't real." I stared into those eyes. "Do you see now why you can't be falling in love with me?"

He sat back in his chair and responded to my concerns, "I don't think we are as far apart as we appear to be. The fact that we are having this conversation means that we are heading in the same direction. We're both looking toward the future, and isn't that where we should be? And who knows? Just because I'm falling in love, I haven't put a time frame on it either. That could be this week, next month, or next year. I don't know. I know I'm falling. I haven't fallen."

A tear ran down my cheek. I couldn't tell if it was a tear of joy or sadness, just a stray tear. I didn't know what to say, so I said, "Thank you, Sean. I think you are slowing down for me without making it sound that way, and that's really sweet. I hope it works out."

⁓⁚⁓

We spent the rest of the morning eating and sharing stories of our childhoods, which couldn't have been more different. I had a storybook childhood in New Rochelle with an older and a younger sister, perfect parents, a perfect home, and perfect grandparents. There seemed to be no reason for me to be floundering in my life at thirty. In theory, I should be the most well-adjusted person on earth.

On the other hand, Sean had an emotionally abusive, alcoholic mother and a physically abusive father who left when he turned six. If anyone should have been messed up, it should have been him, yet he seemed successful, well-adjusted, and emotionally balanced. However, he had never been married at nearly forty, so I wondered about that. Did he have a fear of commitment? Would he be everything he seemed to be once I got to know him? These were all questions I would eventually get answered, but I chose to enjoy the ride for now.

CHAPTER THIRTEEN

Sean left around noon. He had to prepare for his first appointment of the day, which he had remotely at 12:30. Telehealth had revolutionized the therapy business, allowing psychologists to access patients from a much broader geographic region, as long as they were covered by insurance the therapist accepted. In theory, if you accepted Blue Cross, you could see patients from anywhere in the country if they had a phone or a computer. While it wasn't quite that simple, the future might be.

But for Sean, it at least meant that he could meet with his existing patients in the comfort of his own home and theirs. Most patients preferred remote visits to travel, and he made accommodations for the few that didn't.

As I pondered the life of a therapist, a knock came on my front door. I glanced through the window and saw a teenage girl with black shoulder-length hair through the small smoked-glass window. I couldn't place her, figuring she might be selling something. When I opened it, it surprised me to find Shelby, my employee from next door, standing in front of me with tears streaming down her cheeks.

I couldn't imagine what she might be doing here, but then I

remembered everything that had transpired at Kohr's and wondered what had happened at home as a result. I said, "Please, come in, Shelby." I put my arm around her and led her to the couch, sitting down next to her.

She sniffled for a while as she composed herself. Finally, she began. "Cordelia, my parents threw me out of the house. I don't have anywhere to go."

I sat there in shock. I couldn't imagine parents throwing their own daughter out on the street. "Why? What happened?"

After a few minutes, she could finally speak. "Well, things have gone from bad to worse since you saw me last. Not like it wasn't humiliating enough when you caught Billy and me in the freezer. After he got home, he told Terri Thompson, and she spread it all around the school. Somehow it got back to his parents who called my parents who blamed me for corrupting their darling son."

I sat there with my mouth open, which I knew looked rude, but I couldn't think of anything intelligent to say.

She touched my arm. "Now, Miss Corbett, I mean Cord, this wasn't my first time, I'll admit that, but he was the aggressor here, so I certainly didn't corrupt him."

I felt immediate relief that I wasn't responsible for her virginity.

She struggled with the next part. "My mom is so mad. When she found out I'd been intimate with my last boyfriend, she made me promise to wait until I got married before I ever did it again. So, bottom line, I'm on the street. Can I stay here?"

I wasn't prepared for that. I had no idea how her parents would react if I got in the middle of their family crisis. I wondered if they knew how I contributed to Shelby and Billy being alone in the freezer. I figured I'd better say something. I looked into her deep brown eyes, her black-haired bangs nearly covering them. "Shelby, are you sure that's a good idea? I don't want your parents to see me as a part of the problem. I am a brand-new neighbor. What if they hate me?"

She wasn't letting up. More tears streamed down her cheeks. "Please, Cord. I have nowhere else to go."

I couldn't put her out on the street. "Okay, but let's think about it as temporary."

She hugged me. "Oh, thank you so much. You are the best."

I held her at arm's length. "You do know that I'm going to have to call your mom, though?"

She half-smiled. "Can't you wait a few hours to make her suffer?"

I nodded. "Yes, I can do that."

We high fived.

I took her upstairs. I realized I'd have to address something that I'd been avoiding since I moved here, and maybe it would be for the best. While there were technically three bedrooms upstairs, the two rear bedrooms were nested, so you had to go through one to get to the other, common among houses built around 1900. There were a couple of small ones on the main floor, but they were being used as an office and a storage room.

I told Shelby, "You'll take the rear guest room that I've been using since I moved in this week, because I'd been used to using it all these years when I visited my Gram. I'll move to the front room."

She asked, "Oh, are you sure I'm not putting you out."

I insisted. "I needed a push to move to the master bedroom. You were just that push."

She smiled and hugged me. "This is going to be so much fun. I'm glad you said yes."

I smiled, rolling my eyes. "I hope I don't live to regret it." I wondered, "Hey, do you work tonight?"

She nodded. "Yes, four to midnight."

I laughed. "Me too. I'll have to call your mom from the store. I don't want to do it quite yet. I'll give her something to worry about. Does she know you're working?"

She shook her head. "No, she doesn't know my schedule. She'll think I'm out walking the streets or with Billy. I didn't want to get him involved in this mess. Besides, I don't even know if I officially want him as a boyfriend. Now that I can have him, he's not anywhere near as appealing. Do you know that feeling?"

I had to admit I did. "Yes, I've been there. Sometimes, the mystique just goes away."

She hit my arm. "Exactly! How come you understand that, and my mom doesn't? You are so cool."

I laughed. "Just how old is your mom? She can't be that old."

She counted on her fingers. "She's thirty-six."

I nodded. "That's only six years older than I am. Actually, she and I should be more peers than you and I. How come you and I see eye to eye?"

She thought about it. "She's old for her age. Even her siblings call her a killjoy. And she is one. My dad is more understanding. He doesn't dare to cross her."

I looked at her. "You didn't even bring a suitcase of clothes with you, did you? What do you plan on wearing to school?"

She reddened. "I hoped I could borrow something. We are about the same size; except I don't have your bust."

I sent her to the closet. "Feel free to try on anything in there."

~:~

About twenty minutes later, she came downstairs in an outfit I didn't even remember, which I felt sure looked far better on her than it had on me—white shorts, a blue tank top, and matching blue sandals. I turned her around. "That's adorable on you. I could never pull that off. I'd look like I was trying too hard. You look completely natural and confident."

She looked in the full-length mirror standing in the living room and commented, "I *do* look pretty good if I do say so myself. I never looked this good in my clothes. Maybe we should switch off more often." Then she hugged me again. "But seriously, thank you for making me feel at home. I know you could have easily sent me away. You have no idea how much I appreciate it."

I begged her, "Don't make me regret it, Shelby. I have a feeling there may be a lot you're not telling me that led to your departure. Now, I respect your privacy, so I want you to respect me enough to be honest. That's all I ask of you."

She agreed. "You're right, but it's been mostly mom and daughter stuff. Part of the problem is that I'm eighteen, and I've been threatening to move out since my birthday. I guess she called my bluff."

I felt relieved. "Oh, now that makes more sense. I'm happier to have you here under those circumstances. At least the police won't be showing up in the middle of the night accusing me of kidnapping."

She chuckled. "She's not that crazy." Then, she thought about it. "Well, come to think about a few of the things she did before I turned eighteen, yes, she is." She smiled. "Now that you know I'm eighteen, do you have to call my mom?"

I thought about it. "Well, not legally. But I still think it's the right thing to do. If I had a daughter, I'd want to know where she is regardless of her age."

She seemed satisfied. "I guess I would too. But definitely call from work, in case she decides to come storming over here, neither of us will be home."

I agreed. "Yes, I'm not in the mood for a confrontation. This is not my battle. I'm happy to give you a place to stay, but I honestly don't want to take sides. I'm pretty sure if I heard all of your mom's side, I could find something to support."

~:~

We hopped in the Jeep a few hours later to head to work. I preferred to walk, but I thought walking right past Shelby's house might be a little over the top. This thing could resolve itself in a day, a week, a month, but right now, I had no idea, and I didn't want any unnecessary trouble with her mom. I didn't even know if I was doing the right thing, but had this happened to me at her age, I'd probably have wished for someone to step in and take me under their wing. She needed a little support and guidance, and the least I could do is offer her that.

CHAPTER FOURTEEN

I'd nearly forgotten the craziness of pre-summer Friday nights at Kohr's. We never stopped and had lines up the boardwalk all night. The wonderful thing was, I had no time to think about anything. Sure, my life had improved immeasurably since moving to Point Pleasant Beach.

But with my new life came new responsibilities. As I lay in my new bed after work, which seemed far more comfortable than my old bed, I ticked them off in my head. Rachel Lynn Gaston was still my primary responsibility. I vowed to find her killer, and I would. When I found John Michael Owens, I hoped that I had found him, but my gut said 'no.' So, I had to keep looking.

I had two new friends, Mo and Jackie. They could down wine like no one I had ever met, but I liked them a lot. I had a feeling the three of us would have amazing misadventures, the kinds of which I hadn't even dreamed. I loved most that they hadn't even liked one another until I brought them together. That made me feel special.

Then, I thought about my new job. I felt like I'd been sandwiched between generations. Sally Kohr McIntosh used to be my manager, and she had seemed so old at twenty-five when I was sixteen. Now she is a peer at thirty-nine, and we were working on a solid friendship. And the newest addition to my household is Shelby Irons, just twelve years my junior. I imagined we could develop a friendship over time if her mother allowed us to after we filled her in on where she was staying. Work had been too busy, and we never called. Or maybe I had just avoided it for now.

And finally, Sean McPherson, could I call him my new boyfriend, and did I even want to if I could? Despite how sweet Sean treated me, I found myself on guard a good portion of the time. I couldn't even put my finger on the reason why. He certainly could be described as a handsome, kind, sweet, successful, well-educated guy, and yet a part of me questioned his sincerity. It seemed almost like he pushed too hard, like he had a goal, and he did his best to hold back, but sometimes he failed.

Or maybe that was the old me talking. The old me constantly questioned and doubted, thinking I wasn't good enough, smart enough, or pretty enough. The objective me knew different. She knew that *I* had been the valedictorian of my high school class, not Katie or Lily, that *I* had been voted 'girl most likely to succeed' by my senior class, not Katie or Lily, that when I looked at pictures of the three of us together, I knew *I* was the prettiest, hands down, not Katie or Lily.

So why had they been running rings around me in life until I moved into Gram's house? I couldn't explain it, but it wasn't happening anymore. Not now, not ever.

I decided to shut off my mind at 1 a.m. since I had to work at 9. That only gave me seven hours to sleep.

~:~

Saturday's business activity nearly eclipsed Friday night's, which suited me fine because I didn't have time to think. About mid-afternoon, when things slowed down for the first time, I walked up to get the next customer's order, and he said, "What a surprise to see a pretty lady at the ice cream shop." I momentarily drew a blank when I looked up to see a handsome man with curly brown hair, holding the hand of a five-year-old boy.

Finally, it hit me. "Detective Daniels, I didn't know you were—"

He smiled with a smile that made my knees weak. "A widower? Yes, I assumed you knew I was unattached by how shamelessly I flirted with you the day you came into the office."

I felt so confused. I thought he had been talking down to me. All I could think of to say was, "Oh, well, then, can I take your order?"

He refused to give up. "I'd like two orange and vanilla twist cones, one large and one small." Then he commented. "You seem to have a lot of staff back there. Maybe you could join us. I'd love for you to meet Josh."

Shelby had been watching all of this unfold. She whispered, "No problem, Cord, I'll be happy to step in. You go."

I wasn't even sure why I suddenly felt drawn to this man who had been so rude and condescending to me the other day, but I was. His presence felt suddenly like a magnet, and I, like metal. I whispered to Shelby. "Thanks, I think."

He and his adorable little boy stood eating ice cream cones on the boardwalk when I walked out to meet them. The detective said, "Josh, this is Miss Corbett."

Josh stuck out his sticky, ice cream-covered hand and smiled. "Nice to meet you, Miss Corbett."

I shook it anyway, smiled, and responded, "Oh, you can call me Cord. All my friends do."

He looked confused. "You mean like a power cord?"

I nodded. "Yes, I suppose I do. It's short for Cordelia, but that's a mouthful."

The detective stepped in. "Can I call you Cord?"

I thought about it. "I think that's premature, Detective."

He smiled. "Well, in the interest of moving that forward, please call me Clint."

I reddened at his attempt at familiarity. I wasn't even sure I didn't hate this guy, much less, like him. "I'm not sure I'm ready for that, either."

He nodded. "I see this is going to be a challenge. And I like a challenge."

Josh asked his dad, "What's a challenge, Daddy?"

He explained, "That's when something or someone doesn't come easy, but it's almost always worth it in the end."

Josh whispered to his dad, "She's really nice and very pretty, Daddy. I like her."

I tousled his hair. "I like you too, Josh. I'm so glad I got to meet you. You might be your daddy's best quality."

He then got slightly more serious. "We did look into your concern about the guy with the Mustang and found some interesting stuff. He's on our radar now. We're not sure what to think."

I tried to sound casual. "Oh, John Michael Owens? That's so yesterday's news. A couple of friends and I went out to visit him in Nazareth. When all is said and done, I'm pretty sure he's not our man."

Clint looked very concerned. "Cord, you need to be careful. You never know what you might be getting into when you show up at someone's door."

His concern touched me. "I agree, Clint. We probably got a little bit lucky. We can talk separately about this. I'll stop by the station if that's okay."

He looked relieved. "That would be great. Drop-in, and I'll try to free myself up, or calling in advance would be even better."

I nodded. "I'll call. Do I have your cell?" He asked for my number and texted me his. I touched his hand and felt an unexpected jolt of electricity. "Thanks, Clint. I think we'll both be better off working together." I headed back to work. I was calling him Clint!

They waved. I looked back and waved, wondering why I felt so comfortable with them. I'd have to figure that out later.

I grabbed Shelby when I got inside. "Girl, we've got to call your mom. She must be worried sick by now."

She looked like she had been more than dreading it.

I said, "Give me her cell number. We can't avoid it forever. Maybe it won't go as badly as you think it will."

Shelby gave me the number, looking physically ill as I dialed the phone.

Her mother picked up immediately. I tried to sound friendly. "Mrs. Irons, this is Cordelia Corbett from next door. I wanted to let you know that Shelby is staying here with me."

She hesitated briefly, and I hoped that it might not be so bad. Then she lit into me. "Well, it's about time you called. You have a lot of nerve harboring our little girl. Just who do you think you are? First, you allow her to be sexually assaulted at her place of employment, and then you have the nerve to take her in without my knowledge or consent. I've been worried sick. I've been this close to calling the police. You're damned lucky that I didn't have you put in jail."

I wanted to argue that their *little girl* wasn't a minor, but I figured I'd better keep my mouth shut.

She took a breath, so I said, "Well, I didn't want you to worry. Thanks, Bye." I had no idea if half the police department would be lined up in front of my house when I got home or if I'd have to deal directly with the mother, but at least I did what I thought best.

Shelby seemed encouraged, "That didn't sound too bad, at least from this end."

I wasn't sure how much to share. "Oh, she's pretty mad, but maybe now that she's vented and knows where you are, she can start to calm down." I hoped so anyway. I felt pretty sure she'd had an excruciating couple of days.

She wanted details. "So, what did she say?"

I interpreted, "Well, it mostly had to do with her displeasure with me for taking you in and for allowing you and Billy to, well, you know, in the first place. I think deep down she knows that we all shared in the blame for what happened, including her, but she had a laser focus on me right now, and if that works to get her past this, I was fine with it."

She hugged me. "Thanks for everything, Cord. You're a good friend. You don't seem old at all."

I laughed. "When you're my age, you'll see how young thirty really is."

Just then, Sally arrived for the midnight shift and seemed excited to be at work. "Hey, how's everyone doing? I'm so thrilled at how smoothly things have gone since we hired you, Cord. I haven't gotten one angry employee or customer call. I think that's a record."

Sally had a small office in the back. She asked Shelby, "Shel, can you cover the front while Cord and I talk for a few minutes?"

The girl smiled and responded, "No problem. I'm almost out of here, so I'd be happy to cover." She realized what she had said. "Of course, I'd be happy to at any time." Rather than putting her foot in her mouth again, she headed to the front to wait on customers.

Sally sat at her desk, and I sat in a small chair in front of her. She asked, "So, first, is there anything work-wise that we need to talk about? It seems like things are going pretty smoothly."

I nodded. I hadn't even thought about it much. but it seemed to run like a well-oiled machine. I couldn't take credit; it was all Sally. I let her know. "Yes, you have a great operation here. I did nothing but babysit for the most part and clean stuff."

She disagreed. "You are a stabilizing force with the staff. They all love you, and even though nine years doesn't seem like that much, you are bridging the generation gap. I don't understand them the way that you do."

I didn't want to take credit, but she might have been somewhat right. "I really enjoy working with them. They are good kids."

She laughed, "And what's this about Shelby moving in with you? I'm not sure I even want to know."

I smiled. "All I can say is thank God she's eighteen, or I'd be in big trouble. I called the mother to let her know where she was, and she sounded kind of crazy. I don't think I'd like to meet her in a dark alley or in the side yard between houses, for that matter."

She thought for a second. "Okay, enough about this place and our cast of characters. One reason I gave us both the same days off is selfish on my part. I hoped that we could spend a little time together. The fact is you seem to have a way more interesting life than I do, so I'd love to hang out with you."

She looked me in the eye. "I guess this is my awkward, high-schoolish way to ask if you'll be my friend. I haven't had many, okay any, friends that have lasted more than a couple of months since I graduated high school. I'm lonely."

I stood and reached across her desk to hug her. "We are two peas in a pod, Sally. Until this past week, I've been in the same place you were, but something happened to me when I moved to my Gram's house. I can't explain it, but it felt like my life told me enough is enough. I decided to go for it. You were already a part of my master plan. Of course, I'll be your friend. I already decided that days ago."

She looked relieved. "I'm so glad. I thought you might already be deeply entrenched with that guy Sean and not have time for me."

I wondered. "Hey, I just struck up a friendship with Mo and Jackie, a couple of waitresses at the Food Shack; how about inviting them over? They demonstrated the other day a real ability to polish off wine bottles. They're just getting to know one another, too, so the timing is nearly perfect."

She beamed. "That would be great. Maybe we can start a wine gang."

I agreed. "I can use a bunch of women to talk to. I'm so confused about men right now."

Sally chuckled. "At least you've got men to be confused about."

I had to say it. "It's a decision, Sally. Once I changed my attitude and decided to live my life, men started coming out of the woodwork. I'm a little afraid to go into public right now for fear of another attractive man crossing my path. It's the strangest thing."

She complained. "I never go anywhere where I could even meet men."

I questioned that. "So, you never go to the grocery store? You never go get gas in your car? You never go to the pharmacy to pick up a prescription? You never go downtown to pay a parking ticket? You see where I'm going with this, right?"

She nodded. "I think so."

I explained. "There's a whole world out there that most of us are missing because we have our noses buried in our phones. When's the last time you smiled and made eye contact with anyone? I don't care if they were male or female. It seldom happens anymore because we're too busy reading a text or composing a Facebook post. Life is passing us by."

I had an idea. "Let's get together on Monday evening, so neither of us has to work the morning shift the next day. Between now and then, I want you to strike up a conversation with at least ten people in the course of everyday life. This is for practice, so it can be anyone, men or women, children even, I don't care. Just someone to get you in the practice of noticing those around you. And I want you to keep track so you can report back the details, what you said to whom, how they reacted, stuff like that."

She smiled nervously. "I guess I can do that, although I don't quite see the point. Even if I don't have my phone out, nearly everyone else will."

I smiled confidently and replied, "Just humor me."

CHAPTER FIFTEEN

With work, time flew by. Before Monday came, I had decided to clean the house within an inch of its life. My Gram kept the house very neat but wasn't much of a cleaner. She fluffed pillows and straightened books on shelves, but when it came to dusting, scrubbing, polishing, scouring, sanitizing, or any related words, she would rather die.

It was downright scary what I found underneath furniture, the refrigerator, and the washer and dryer. By the time my three wine-drinking friends were due in an hour, I had to quit to get myself in order, knowing I still had probably another full day of cleaning before the house passed my white glove test.

When Mo and Jackie arrived with a couple of cases of wine, I knew they were serious. Jackie bragged as they carried them in. "We went to Working Dog Winery in Hightstown over the weekend, and we bought a case of everything we liked. We didn't want to let you guys down." She stuck out her hand to Sally and grinned. "You must be Sally. We're so happy you invited us. Two weeks ago, all of us were sitting at home. Isn't life amazing?"

Sally agreed. "You can be sure I'll be toasting Cord's Gram, who I can't help but feel had a hand in all this." Despite being a devout German Protestant, she looked up to the sky and crossed herself.

I hadn't quite put it together as succinctly as Sally did. I smiled. "Wow, Sally, and you're not even aware of all the other weird stuff that's happened to me since my Gram passed. I feel like a different person in so many ways. Two weeks ago, I lived in Greenwich Village, in a drab furnished apartment, unemployed, depressed, praying for one friend. Now I have three friends, and two men who seem to both want me. I don't quite get it, but I'm not going to fight it." I looked over at Sally, who hadn't said much since she arrived but had a grin pasted on her face. I asked her directly, "Now, what is up with you, Cheshire Cat?"

She folded her hands in her lap. "Cord, I met somebody special. I took your advice and paid attention to the outside world everywhere I went. I went to Stop and Shop on Sunday, and a guy and I reached for the same bottle of milk, and our eyes met, and we laughed and started talking. We've been inseparable ever since."

Mo overheard the story and reacted. "Wow, I want to hear that advice."

I felt honored that suddenly my advice was so highly regarded. "It's something I've noticed since moving into Gram's house that seems to be working for me."

Sally insisted. "Don't be so modest. You are really on to something here. I've been lonely so long, I had nearly given up, and in one day, you changed my life."

I disagreed. "I didn't change your life, Sally. You did."

She pointed to the 'No Limits' message on the front of her tee-shirt. "I've had this tee-shirt for at least five years, but I've never worn it until today. It never resonated with me until now. You are magic."

I thought about my new life. "I don't know. Maybe you're right. If so, I give all the credit to my Gram." I wanted to keep the focus on Sally. "So, tell us all about him."

Everyone gathered around, wine glasses in hand. She savored the moment. "His name is Jim. He's a once married, once divorced high school teacher, no kids. He's lived his whole life in Point. He was only married for five years in his twenties, they got a divorce as a matter of course, and they parted the closest of friends." She laughed. "Wasn't there an ancient song that had those lyrics?"

Mo agreed. "Yeah, that old guy that plays the Garden every month and sells out. That Piano Man guy. Oh, what's his name. He wasn't bad. He's got those eyes that bug out, though. It drives me crazy when they have him on close-up video. Billy something, I think. My mom made me go with her to see him last year."

I wanted to bring the conversation back to Sally. "So, tell us more about Jim. Where's he teach?"

She didn't even need to think. "Right here in Point Pleasant Beach. He's a math teacher. He also loves the beach. He loves to snow ski in the winter. He plays guitar. He volunteers at his church. He seems like an all-around good guy."

Jackie asked, "Is he a good kisser?"

Mo gasped. "Jackie, we don't even know if they've kissed yet."

Jackie argued. "Based on the look in her eyes, they have at least kissed." She asked Sally, "Am I right?"

She grinned sheepishly. "Yes, he's a great kisser." She didn't expound further.

Mo couldn't wait to hear. "So, what is this magic that changed Sally's life in one day?"

I thought about it and said, 'I'm not sure I'm responsible for any magic, just repeating a little common sense handed down from my Gram. She always told us to 'put down your phone and enjoy the scenery,' whenever we were with her. And maybe there is something to her advice, but I can hardly take credit for it."

Sally protested. "Well, Cord, that wasn't exactly what you challenged me with now, is it? You challenged me to strike up a conversation with ten people I didn't know between Saturday and tonight's party. And look what happened on Sunday. And, I have to tell you, it wasn't comfortable for me. It didn't come naturally for me at all, and I cursed you up one side and down the other until I met Jim, and then a lightbulb went off. If you stay in your comfort zone, you'll stay exactly where you are, lonely and miserable. That's what you taught me." She spoke to Mo and Jackie. "Look what Cordelia has already done for you two. You were co-workers who barely gave one another the time of day until you met her, and suddenly you are best friends. Do you think that's a coincidence? I certainly don't."

Jackie gave Mo a meaningful hug, then jumped in. "I'm willing to try talking to ten people. I think the four of us should meet here every Monday night and discuss our progress. Sally, if a beauty like you can find a man using that technique in one day, it shouldn't take Mo or me more than a week."

Maureen hit Jackie on the arm. "Thanks a lot, Jackie. I think I'm pretty hot still."

I decided to intervene. "Whoa, everybody. We're all fine. It's not like our looks are going to scare anybody away. This isn't so much about what's outside, though. This is about what's inside. We need to open up our eyes and our souls and let people in. They will respond. I guarantee it, not because of how we look, but because of who we are." I made a prediction. "I'll bet by three months from today; we'll have at least doubled the size of our women's wine-drinking group, and we will all have men in our lives if we choose to."

Mo responded first. "I like the sound of that. I want choices, not being so desperate that I jump at the first guy who asks me out in a year. I want to be able to size up my options and, most of all, I want to say 'no' as much as 'yes.' These days, if a guy can speak English and has a car, I'm all in. That's a pretty low bar."

Jackie agreed. "I'm with you. I've met most of my men in pretty low bars. Drinkers don't make good men. Meeting someone anywhere else has to be a good idea."

Sally announced, "I declare our newly formed group be called, 'No Longer Desperate Winers.'"

We all high-fived and poured more wine.

~:~

We were all still awake when Shelby came home after her late shift at 12:15 a.m.

I invited her to meet my friends. "Shelby, meet Mo and Jackie."

Jackie shook her hand. "I remember you. You used to come into the Food Shack with your mom."

Shelby looked impressed. "Wow, I'm amazed that you remembered."

Jackie chuckled. "It's not necessarily a good thing. Your mom had a reputation for being the worst tipper on the East Coast. We used to toss a coin to see who didn't have to serve her. And it wasn't only because she didn't tip; she always complained about the food. It made us wonder why she ever ate there; you would have thought she hated the food, but no, she came back week after week."

Shelby didn't seem at all offended. "Oh, that's how she is. There are a ton of restaurants in the city where we've been asked not to come back. She doesn't seem to care; she just keeps doing it." She then said politely, "It's been so nice to meet you ladies, but I had better get to bed. I have school tomorrow."

Everyone said, "Goodnight."

Mo said after she had gone upstairs, "That's so nice of you to take her in when her mom threw her out of the house. Do you know how many people, in times like this, say that they would love to help but come up with an excuse for why they can't do it? You are the real deal, Cordelia Corbett."

I blushed at the compliment. It amazed me that not only did I have all these new friends, but also how complimentary they were of me, and that they credited me for their new outlook on life and relationships. I felt a bit guilty, knowing that I had nothing to do with it. It felt more like divine intervention, or some sort of intervention that I couldn't explain.

CHAPTER SIXTEEN

I woke up the next morning around nine and jumped on my laptop and Patch News for Point Pleasant and vicinity. I couldn't believe the article I read by Karen Wall. A homeless man sleeping on the beach, whose name had been withheld pending notification of next of kin, was being held in connection with the Rachel Lynne Gaston murder at the Food Shack last week. Several witnesses had identified him as a man who had been seen speaking to Ms. Gaston less than an hour before she died. Any information regarding this case should be reported to Detective Clint Daniels at the Point Pleasant Beach Police Department or Detective Raymond Gardner of the Ocean County Prosecutor's Office.

I slammed my laptop shut. "How could he have not told me this when I saw him? This didn't just come up today. Does he think I'm some sort of patsy?" I asked out loud to a bunch of sleeping beauties. They had all decided to camp out on my bedroom floor, and we talked and laughed until at least 3 a.m.

Sally's eyes shuttered open, and she stretched and yawned. "In all fairness, didn't you tell Clint you were going to stop by the Police Station?"

I hated to admit it. "Yes, I guess you could have interpreted it that way."

She kept that thread. "So, maybe he tried to keep you in the loop, but you didn't hold up your end of the bargain."

My head hurt. "God, I hate it when you're right, but you might be. I guess if they had a suspect, they couldn't hold off forever on arresting him as a courtesy to me." I wondered why I felt so awful. I thought about it. "I guess it hurts my feelings that he didn't give me a call on my cell phone to fill me in. I thought we had that kind of relationship."

Mo, who I thought must still be sleeping, picked up on that immediately. "That kind of relationship with whom? I feel like I've missed something here. I thought you were hot and heavy with that Sean guy, the therapist."

I wanted to shove the words back in. "Yeah, I didn't mean relationship the way it came out. I met a detective working on the Rachel case, and we decided to work together instead of at odds. That's it."

Jackie added, "And he's really cute, right?"

I reddened. "Okay, he's not bad, and he's got the most adorable five-year-old son. He's a widower."

Sally couldn't help herself. "And he's everything that Sean isn't. He gets under your skin, but you also can't stop thinking about him. He makes you angry, but he also brings out a passion in you that you've never felt before."

I stared at her in disbelief, as if she had read my mind. I didn't know what to say. "How could you possibly—"

She clarified, "Because that's who Jim is to me. During my first few hours with him, I wanted to strangle him. I wanted to put the cover back on Pandora's Box. But the more we talked, the more I realized I needed to run to him, not away from him. It's tremendously frightening, almost like looking at your future and seeing your whole life flash before you, the wonderful and the horrible.

"But, once I realized who he was for me, I thanked God and decided I was ready for the ride of my life. I don't know if Clint is that person for you, Cord, but I get the feeling Sean is the safe, boring, Irish guy you can take home to the family. But how bored will you be in a year, five years, or ten years? You need to ask yourself that before it gets too far."

I couldn't stop staring at Sally. "When did you get so smart and intuitive? It seems like last week, you had less of a clue about relationships than almost anyone I knew."

She smiled. "Maybe the same way you changed almost overnight. I just slept in your Gram's house."

At least I wasn't as angry at Clint now that I'd spoken to Sally, so I figured I'd call him to get an update now that I had an attitude adjustment. I hit his speed dial.

"He answered on the first ring. "God don't tell me that hit the news yet. I've been in meetings all morning and meant to call you as soon as I had a second free."

I smiled. "Good morning to you, too. Well, I'm happy to hear that you had good intentions. My Gram used to say that the road to hell is paved with them, but we don't have to talk about that now. Can I come by later, and maybe you can fill me in? I had planned on speaking with the other waitresses at the Food Shack that I didn't get a chance to speak to them last week unless you've already done that."

He responded. "We only spoke to the ones who came forward with information the day of the shooting. We've been a little short-staffed and haven't done a follow-up visit."

I smiled. "Perfect. I'll go down there later this morning and drop by and see you around lunchtime."

He sounded excited to see me. "It's a date then." Then, he retracted it. "Well, not a date date. You know what I mean."

~:~

I headed over to the Food Shack about ten, hoping it wasn't too busy. Jackie and Mo told me they had heard their co-workers, Riley and Samantha, talking about the shooting last week and thought it might be worth speaking with them. They were both working the day Rachel died and may have seen something.

I found a table as soon as I arrived and perused the menu, even though I knew it pretty well. A cute girl in her early twenties came to take my drink order, Riley, according to her nametag. I said, "I'll have a cup of coffee, but before you go, I heard they arrested a guy that hangs around the beach for the murder last week. Have you heard anything about that?"

She looked around like she might be talking out of school. "Well, I walk up the beach every day to work, and there's this creepy guy who's been sleeping there almost every day for a couple of weeks. I told the police about him. Maybe he's the one. I don't even feel safe on our own beach anymore. It's sad."

I asked, "Did you see him the day of the murder?"

She looked around again as if her manager might be watching. "Yes, I saw him talking to that woman who got killed. I didn't hear anything they were saying, but I thought it was strange."

I nodded. "Thank you, Riley." I wrote down my name and number on a napkin. "If you think of anything else that might be helpful to solving the case, let me know."

She stuffed it in her apron. "Are you an undercover cop or something?"

I smiled. "No, I'm a concerned citizen."

She looked uneasy. "You should talk to Sam then." She pointed at the waitress at a table across the restaurant. She swears that she saw that homeless guy talking to another man the same day as the murder, and he had something in his hand, maybe a gun. She didn't get a chance to talk to the police."

I asked, "Could you send her over to talk to me when she gets a chance?"

She bit her lip. "Well, I don't know. Our manager is giving us a hard time about taking breaks to talk about the murder. She says that it's time for all of us to move on. I'll see what I can do, though."

I nodded. "Okay, I understand. But if she can even just for a second, that would be great."

She remembered something. "Hey, I think she has a break after this customer. I'll send her to your table then. I know she'll be excited to tell her story, because she wants it told but is afraid to go to the police station."

I had taken too much of her time. "Thanks, I'll have a cheddar cheese omelet."

She scratched something on her notepad and left for the kitchen.

As I waited for my order, I wondered why the police hadn't spoken to this girl. And why had no one else, at least that I knew of, reported seeing anyone talking to this guy? Who was he, and why had Rachel been talking to him? There were lots of questions but not many answers.

I ate my omelet, pondering the questions when Samantha came to sit with me. She stuck out her hand, and I shook it. She asked, "Hey, aren't you Mo and Jackie's friend? They've done nothing but rave about you since they met you."

I smiled. "That's so nice to hear. I really love them. They've been such a wonderful addition to my life."

She whispered, "You must be some kind of miracle worker. Before they met you, they hated each other, which made it really uncomfortable working with them. We used to pray for them to be tolerant of each other one day, but for them to be best friends is more than we ever hoped for. How did you do it?"

It surprised me to hear that they hated each other. "Well, I think I just opened up their ears and their hearts a little bit. It's amazing what you can accomplish when you do that."

She looked me in the eye. "Do you think you could do the same thing for Riley and me? I always feel like she is talking to the other girls behind my back. I just want to be her friend. I have nothing against her, but I think I come off as not liking her because I don't think she likes me."

I thought about it. "Here's what I would do, Samantha. Sit down with Riley and tell her how you are feeling. Let her know that you want to be friends and that maybe you could start over. Take responsibility for her feeling that maybe you don't like her and that you might have been talking past one another. You'll be surprised when you take responsibility for the problem, how quickly she jumps in and takes responsibility for her part."

She stared at me with her mouth open. "Really? Okay, I'll try it, but that seems too simple. It has to be harder than that."

I laughed. "That's the amazing thing about human interaction; sometimes, all it takes is for us to act like humans." I didn't want to waste her break. "So, tell me what you saw the day that Rachel Lynn Gaston got killed. It sounds like you may have seen something no one else saw."

She breathed a sigh of relief. "Thank God someone wants to listen. I tried to speak to that police officer, but he seemed too busy with our manager to worry much about what I had to say. Sometimes it's hell being twenty-one, I swear." She rolled her eyes. "Anyway, I sat out front enjoying the weather, on the beach, and I saw a man talking to a homeless guy who's been sleeping out there for the last couple of weeks. I saw him pass something to him. I swear it looked like a gun. I might have been a hundred feet away, but that's what I saw."

I asked, "About what time?"

She thought back. "Oh, I'd say around 7 a.m., and it wasn't less than an hour later when that woman showed up dead in the showers. Can it be a coincidence? I don't think so."

I smiled. "That could be really helpful. I saw online that they brought a guy, who was likely that homeless man, in for questioning, so knowing that a third party had given him a gun will be really helpful. Can you describe what the other man looked like?"

She looked up, evidently trying to reconstruct his image. "He had a bathing suit with a terry cover-up including a hood so that I couldn't see his face or his hair color or anything. It seemed almost as if he was hiding."

I nodded. "He may have been. It wouldn't be surprising. Could you tell his height, skin color, anything?"

She nodded. "He might have been a little taller than the homeless guy and definitely white. I can't place why, but I wouldn't say he was super young, maybe late thirties, early forties based on his energy level."

I smiled. "That's great information, Samantha. I'll be talking to the police later today, so I'll relay it to them."

She stood up and shook my hand. "Please call me 'Sam.' Even if Riley and I never see eye to eye, I consider you a friend, so it's been a great day either way." She retreated to the kitchen.

Within a few minutes, Riley came with my check. She asked, "Did Samantha give you everything you needed?"

I nodded and said, "Yes, and I think she has something for you, too."

She looked at me with questioning eyes but said only, "Oh?" as she retreated to the kitchen.

CHAPTER SEVENTEEN

I would gain five hundred pounds if I continued eating on this path. I just finished a late breakfast at the Food Shack, and now Clint expected me for an early lunch. I'd have to eat something, but I didn't need anything after my omelet. Based on the location of the Police Department and the Borough Offices on New Jersey Avenue, I figured that we'd end up either at Jersey Mike's or John and Elaine's. I didn't care either way since I didn't plan on eating much.

I waited patiently in the lobby for Clint as I took notes on my phone from my conversations with Riley and Sam. They were nice girls, and I hoped they worked out their differences. That seemed to be something I'd become good at, and I was still assessing why. Most of my new friends attributed it to my Gram, and they probably weren't wrong.

Suddenly my phone rang with a Facetime call from Lily's phone. I wasn't sure how long Clint would be, so I took it. It surprised me to see Lily and Katie in tandem again. I wondered what I had done now to rate an intervention.

Of course, Katie spoke first. "What is going on with you, Cord? From Mom no less, we hear that you are hanging out with a whole new crowd, *and* you have a *high school girl* living with you. Oh my God, Cord, have you lost your mind? We turn our backs for a minute, and all hell breaks loose."

I had had enough of these two, and I nearly pushed the red button. "You know what? It gets worse. I am working on solving a murder that happened here in Point, and I'm at the Police Department to meet with a detective right now, so, if you'll excuse me, I have better things to do than listen to your closed-minded drivel." I hung up the phone. I nearly high-fived myself as Clint came from the back.

He commented. "Wow, you look happy."

I grinned. "I told my sisters off." I thought about it. "Long overdue."

He smiled. "I guess that's a good thing. You'll have to tell me about it, and your visit to the Food Shack. You're becoming quite a regular there, I understand."

I wasn't quite sure what he referred to, so I figured I'd agree. "Yes, I guess you could say that. The food there is excellent, and I've made a few friends recently among the staff."

As we headed toward the door, he asked, "John and Elaine's or Jersey Mike's?"

At least, I'd guessed right about the lunch choices. I responded, "Let's do John and Elaine's. It probably won't be as crazy, and you can usually find a table tucked away to have a conversation."

He agreed. "Besides, I'm not really in the mood for a sub."

I nodded. "I love their subs, but I ate breakfast while at the Food Shack, so I'm going to have something light anyway."

Clint's mouth watered at the talk of food. "I didn't have breakfast, so I think I'll have mine now since they specialize in it."

We sat at a small booth next to a window. That had been my Gram's favorite table. She and Elaine had become fast friends years ago when Gram moved here. I wondered if she was still around, when she strolled out of the kitchen, not looking a day older than when I had last seen her, at least ten years ago.

She rushed over to the table and hugged me. "Cordelia, I was so sorry to hear about your grandmother. I couldn't bring myself to go to the funeral, but I'm sure she understood. I've been struggling with my own issues the last couple of years, so I may be seeing her again sooner than later."

I wasn't sure how to respond to that. "Well, I hope you are with us down here a long while."

She didn't expound and turned to Clint. "Hello, Detective. I didn't know you two knew one another. Is this something for the town rumor mill?"

He smiled. "Well, I think we are here strictly on business, but you'll have to ask the pretty lady."

I blushed a thousand shades of red. I wished he would stop doing that, but I loved it at the same time. I tried to sound non-committal. "We'll talk, Elaine. I don't want to give away any secrets." I winked.

She headed back toward the kitchen. "Okay, I'll take that as a definite 'maybe.'"

After she left, he gave me a questioning look, not asking anything further about our personal situation, shifting to business. "So, what did you find out this morning?"

First, I had a few questions. "So, who is this guy who's been sleeping on the beach for a couple of weeks leading up to Rachel Lynne's death? Do you still have him in custody?"

He seemed to be deciding how much to tell me, then came clean. "Well, his name is Martin William Raven. His last known address is in Browns Mills. His last known employer was the Joint Base McGuire Dix Lakehurst Fire Department. According to his station commander, he went AWOL about three months ago, and nobody had heard from him since until he surfaced on the beach at Point Pleasant."

I wondered, "So, what evidence do you have tying him to Rachel Lynne's murder?"

He looked me in the eye. "Well, to be honest, right now, much of it is circumstantial, or you might even call it politically motivated. Citizens are not happy that homeless people are suddenly turning up on the beach, but there isn't much we can do about the problem. Sure, we can keep them in a holding cell for a night or two, but that doesn't solve the problem, and with the economy as it is, it's getting worse."

I looked at him like he might be crazy. "So, that's what you've got on this guy? The mayor called up the Police Chief and ordered him to clean up the beach, so you grabbed this guy as a suspect?"

He looked embarrassed. "Well, it's not quite that bad. If you spoke to Riley, you know that Rachel had been spotted talking to him less than an hour before her death. So, we've got that."

I nodded. "Yeah, but that's not much. She could have been trying to help him, or he could have been asking for her help. A conversation proves nothing." I wondered. "So, what's his story? How did he go from being a first responder living in suburban Jersey to living on our beach?"

He sat back after we gave the waitress our orders, his Crab cakes Benedict, and mine a Bacon, Lettuce, and Tomato sandwich, not on the menu, but something Elaine would usually be willing to whip up for me.

He gave me a little background. "Most of the guys who are career firefighters tied into the military bases are ex-military themselves, many of them diagnosed or undiagnosed PTSD or other battle-related disorders. Martin was no exception. He served in the Army in Iraq and Afghanistan and settled in Jersey when he returned, like a lot of his buddies."

I listened intently, "I had no idea."

He nodded. "Most people don't. So, anyway, about four months ago, one of the firefighters, a guy who saved Martin's life in Iraq, lost his life battling a blaze. Martin didn't take it well. He blamed himself for not being able to save him from the fire. He started calling in sick quite a bit, then stopped showing up at all. He stopped answering his cell phone and then disappeared. His cell phone went dead; he withdrew from social media, he stopped paying his mortgage, and literally fell off the face of the earth as far as his friends and co-workers were concerned. He had no known family."

He smiled sadly. "At least a couple of his co-workers have come to see him since we took him into custody, and his spirits have improved a little. He seemed despondent when we picked him up."

I asked the obvious question. "So, do you think this guy is capable of killing anyone? And even if he is, why would he kill Rachel?"

He thought about it. "I don't know. There's a lot that mental health professionals don't even know about PTSD. Maybe he lost it."

I thought about it. "Doesn't make any sense to me."

He remembered my meetings. "So, you met with someone we hadn't spoken to. What did she have to say?"

I wasn't quite ready to move on, but I would circle back if I needed to. "Oh, yes, her name is Samantha Rollings, a nice girl. She said that she saw, granted it might have been from a hundred feet, a man talking to Martin and handing him a gun."

He sat there with his mouth open momentarily. I was happy his food wasn't delivered yet. He answered, "What? How come I haven't heard that until now? That's explosive. That could be the nail in Martin's coffin or his salvation, depending on what that gun means."

I nodded. "I'm still struggling to figure out what it means, especially in light of what you told me about Martin. He is likely an excellent marksman and is not likely highly sensitive to the concept of killing someone, at least in the abstract. Do you think someone paid him off to kill Rachel? I don't know how it could be his salvation, though."

He explained. "Well, we originally arrested Martin thinking if he did this, that he acted alone, maybe with robbery as a motive. But if someone else was involved, perhaps he was a secondary player, carrying out someone else's wishes. To some judges, that could mean the difference between first-degree murder and second-degree manslaughter if he was coerced or threatened."

I felt sure of one thing. "I want to meet him, Clint. How much longer do you think you can hold him? Is he actually under arrest or being held as a suspect?"

He shifted nervously in the booth. "We haven't pulled the trigger yet. The judge is balking, saying that we don't have enough evidence. We may have to set him free as soon as today."

I wondered, "How about this new information about the gun?"

He thought about it. "Do you think Samantha would sign a statement?"

I rolled my eyes. "Come on now. She's the one who came to me. She couldn't understand why the police didn't seek her out. The cop at the restaurant seemed more interested in talking to her manager, she said, who hadn't seen anything."

He pounded the table. "I have a feeling I know who the cop is and who the manager is. It all makes sense to me. It's not right, but it makes sense."

I didn't even want to know. I chuckled. "Sometimes less is better."

CHAPTER EIGHTEEN

We decided to meet the next morning, since I worked the four to midnight shift on Wednesday. I started working on questions to ask Martin in the morning as I walked home from the Police Station. I loved living where I could walk nearly anywhere I had to go.

After our extended lunch, a strategy meeting at Clint's office, and my walk home, it was nearly three by the time I got home. I hadn't expected to see Lily or Katie's vehicles parked in the driveway. I guess they figured they would attempt it in person if they couldn't harass me by Facetime. They chose the wrong day to mess with me.

They sat quietly on the couch when I arrived, no doubt plotting their intervention for hours. They immediately jumped up, came over, and hugged me in a show of fake sisterly solidarity. I wanted to throw up. They had better tread lightly and remember whose property they were treading on. It wasn't Gram's any longer, much to their chagrin.

Katie motioned for me to sit on the love seat facing them. "So, we thought it would be great to catch up. We never get together anymore."

I snickered. "This doesn't have anything to do with the fact that I hung up on you earlier?"

She responded more quietly than Katie normally could. "Of course, that's why we're here, Cord. We're worried about you. You're doing out-of-character things like that."

I couldn't believe it. "So, you're going to use the same conversation we just had as an excuse for the very intervention that was so ridiculous in the first place and caused the conversation in the second? That's precious." I felt myself getting angry.

Lily sat knee to knee on the love seat and took my hand. "Cordelia, you need to listen. We are worried about you. When we see you going off the rails, it's our responsibility as sisters to help you onto the right track. When we hear that you are hanging out drinking wine with waitresses, ice cream people, and God knows who else, I think we have a right to question your judgment. And to hear that you've taken one of them into your own home. What are you doing to Gram's legacy, starting a commune?"

I fumed as Katie took over. "And we were thrilled when we heard that you'd found a therapist to date. Now that's sensible, and he's even Irish, so we thought, good for you. But rumors are now you're after a cop? Jesus begumdrops, Cordelia cantankerous Corbett, when you finally start to get it right, you screw it up. A cop? Come on now. You were raised better than that."

I felt proud that I hadn't lashed back at either of them yet and found strength coming from my Gram. I took a deep breath and pondered my response, knowing it would leave them speechless. "I'm saddened that you could utter the words you just did in the house where Catherine Carrie McDougal Corbett spent most of her life. If you even listened to one word Gram said, you know that compassion and opening up your heart were the words that she lived by. She didn't care what you did for a living, how much money you made, what religion you practiced, or the color of your skin. That is why she became one of the most well-respected women in this community.

"So, for you two to come in here with your small-minded attitudes, suggesting that I need an intervention, I suggest that you are the ones who need to look within. And until you can adjust your hearts, do not return to this house. If you have nothing else, I wish you a good day."

I opened the front door and escorted them out with their mouths hanging open before they could say a word.

They stood outside talking for ten minutes before finally getting in their respective vehicles and departing. Cordelia one, meddling sisters zero. I felt so great; I wanted to run around the house yelling, "I win, I win, I win, I win." But I didn't think that would be ladylike, so I sat on the couch, reflecting on what had just happened.

I thought about how they had looked down their noses at me when I decided to go back to Kohr's to work. I had to face it. They were shallow snobs, and we had nothing in common, and the more I changed, the less we had in common. If they weren't willing to come along with me, we might not ever see eye to eye again. It seemed sad in a way, but I felt better about myself than I ever had.

After they left, I sat on the steps to the front porch, enjoying the beautiful late Spring Day on the Jersey shore. I felt like the luckiest woman alive to live within a few steps of the beach, to have friends, and to feel in control of my life for the first time as an adult. Seconds later, it surprised me to see Sean coming up my street from a distance. I'd avoided a couple of his texts lately, not quite sure how I felt about him these days.

He walked across my lawn, smiling. "Hey, you're not ghosting me, are you?"

We hadn't spoken since Sally had accurately identified my true feelings about Sean somewhat before I had. I didn't know how to let him down easy. I guessed this would be my perfect opportunity. I chuckled. "No, of course not. I've been busy with work, my new friends, and the case."

He tried to suppress a frown but couldn't quite pull it off. "So, you haven't given up on that murder case yet?"

He gave me the opening, and I took it. "Sean, you are a really nice guy." I hesitated.

He gave me a look that said, "Uh-oh."

I continued. "I think we want different things. To be honest, I feel like you want to control me, and I am not in a place in my life where I want to be controlled."

As a therapist, it would be difficult for him to deny that he had controlling tendencies. He nodded. "Okay, that's not the first time I've heard that, but I'm working on it, and I can change."

I smiled. "I don't want to change you, Sean. You should find someone that loves you for who you are, not for who they want you to be or who you are trying to be. That's no way to live."

He offered, "Well, then, can we be friends?"

I thought about it and came up with a definitive answer. "No, Sean. We can't. Goodbye, Sean."

He turned and walked away.

That went better than I thought it would.

~:~

I sat for a while, planning a walk on the beach, when Shelby walked up the street on her way home from school. She grinned as she crossed the lawn. "Cord, I'm so happy you're home alone. I haven't been able to catch you for five minutes."

I agreed. "I know, Shel. I'm so sorry. Do you have any time now, or are you working tonight?"

She shook her head. "Nope. I'm off. You and I close tomorrow; that'll be fun." She flipped her hair. "Hey, wanna take a walk on the beach? It should be perfect out there today. Gimme a sec to change, and I'll be right out."

Within five minutes, we were headed to the beach. We decided to take the forty-minute walk south to Bay Head Beach. Especially this time of year, it wouldn't be crowded, and we could have a bit of alone time catching up. She seemed interested. "So, how'd it go the other night with the wine slugging crew? They seemed heavily into it."

I chuckled. "Yes, Mo and Jackie can consume far more than Sally or I can. It makes for interesting conversation as the evening wears on. They are really fun to be with, though. They rode all the way to Pennsylvania, over a hundred miles, to check out a suspect in the murder case. They didn't have to do that. I thought it was so nice of them. We've gotten to know each other so much better even since then."

She thought of something. "Oh, your sisters were here when I left for school. They didn't seem very happy. How did that go?"

I tried to laugh it off. "Oh, sisters will be sisters. They're not super happy with me right now. They have a certain expectation of me and my life, and I'm not living up to it, so they are disappointed, I guess."

She looked at me seriously. "You aren't going to listen to them, are you? If you want to know what I think, I think they are jealous of you. They've always been able to control you, and now that you have your own life, they don't like it. Well, good for you, Cordelia. It's about time you got out from under their apron strings."

I agreed and smiled. "I feel exactly the same way. I'm glad that you do too. I respect what you think."

She looked at me. "Are you serious, Cord? I'm just a kid. Why would you care what I think?"

I took her hand as we walked. "Because you're smart, independent, you're opinionated, and you've got a lot going for you. You could have folded when your mother tried to reel you in, but you said, 'No, I'm not doing it. I'm doing things my way.' Good for you, Shel. I've got a lot of respect for you."

She said to herself, "Wow, Cordelia Corbett's got a lot of respect for me. Now that's something I can take to the bank."

I laughed. "Well, thanks. I'm not sure how much money you'd get, but I appreciate the sentiment."

Out of nowhere, she hugged me. "You're the best thing that's ever happened to me, Cord."

And I could honestly say, "That goes double for me."

CHAPTER NINETEEN

The next morning, I left for Clint's office a touch shy of 8 a.m. He'd promised me a chance to speak with Martin William Raven, the suspect in the murder investigation.

I sat in Clint's office while he threw questions at me. "So, do you have a plan? We don't usually let a civilian interrogate a suspect."

I smiled. "Hey, you're kind of cute when you're nervous. Are you getting heat from the top over this?"

He made a face that I couldn't interpret and said only, "You let me worry about that."

I asked, "So, are you and I doing this together?"

He shook his head. "Well, not officially. I'll be behind the one-way glass, listening in and watching, and if anything goes awry, I'll be in that room faster than you can say, 'Get your hands off her you—"

I interrupted, "I get it. Will he be restrained?" I started to get nervous myself.

He nodded. "Yes, he will be handcuffed to the table, so he cannot move about the room."

I breathed a bit easier. "Okay, it should be fine then."

Clint added his two cents. "Besides, when I've talked to him, he's always been very calm, so I don't think you are in any danger. These are just precautions." He checked the paperwork in front of him. "Okay, sign this waiver stating that if anything goes wrong, we are not in the least way responsible, and we can move forward."

I signed it and handed it back to him.

We stood and headed to the interrogation room.

He said on the way, "You don't have to do this. We are the professionals. In fact, for your safety, I'd really prefer you didn't. But I'll be there for you if you insist. You do seem to have a way with people, so maybe you can get him to open up. We've gotten nothing substantive from him yet. Without more evidence, we'll probably have to let him go."

Clint led me into the interrogation room. I suddenly wondered what I was doing there. I had no training as a cop. I'd never even read a murder mystery, and suddenly, I was seated face to face with a suspected murderer. I tried desperately to summon my Gram.

Clint said, "Martin, this is Cordelia Corbett. She's working with us on this case and has a few questions for you. We'd appreciate your cooperation." I guessed he figured the less said, the better.

Martin nodded but didn't respond.

I wasn't prepared at all, assuming that my questions would come to me when I saw him, and I wasn't wrong. I asked, "Do you know who Rachel Lynne Gaston is?"

He nodded again. "Yes, she's a very nice lady."

I'd already gotten more than I expected to get, so I moved forward. "Do you remember any details about the day she died?"

He thought about it. "Yes, well, I assume she died that day. The day that man offered me money to kill her."

I remembered Sam's testimony. "Did he give you a gun too?"

He smiled a crooked smile. "Yes, and I took the gun, but not the money."

I felt confused. "You took the gun to kill her, but not the money?"

He raised his voice, "No! No. I didn't say I took the gun to kill her. I took the gun because I'm a collector. It was a Glock 17, a real beauty. So, I took it and buried it in the sand. I never intended to kill the woman."

I had to ask, "So, you moved from a three-bedroom, two-bath ranch house in Browns Mills to live on Point Pleasant Beach, and you refused how much money?"

He tried to remember. "A thousand dollars, I think it was."

I repeated it. "A thousand dollars. Couldn't you have used that money?"

He said matter-of-factly, "Well, anyone can use a thousand dollars, but it's not that I'm poor; I have plenty of money in the bank."

In a way, this made no sense, but I started to get it. "So, when you lost your friend in the fire, you felt like you no longer deserved to live in a house? You ended up here, under the stars, like he's living among the stars somewhere."

He nodded. "You're a smart lady. You remind me of Rachel. We had the same conversation the day she died. She was trying to help me, she said. She tried to convince me to move inside, to a shelter, anywhere. It wasn't until I explained it all to her that she understood and left me alone. She left me with that beautiful smile of hers, only to lose her life. It's ironic that I, of all people, the one she tried to help and connected with, should be accused of her murder."

I needed to tie up a loose end. "So, this guy with the money and the gun, can you identify him?"

He thought about it. "I'm not sure. He wore a hoodie with the hood up, so I only saw a part of his face."

I searched for other attributes. "How about his voice? Anything unusual about that?"

He nodded. "I can't really describe it, but unusual. It wasn't loud. I could barely make the words out over the waves. I guess you might call it scratchy. It wasn't smooth or deep. I'm not sure if I would recognize it if I heard it again, with all the noise in the background."

I had a personal question. "Here's something that I'm curious about. You've been around the block enough times to know that they are recording this interview. Why did you disclose so much to me when you wouldn't tell them anything?"

He winked at me. "That's such an unfair question to ask while the tape is still rolling."

I agreed. "You're right. You had your reasons. Maybe we can talk over coffee sometime."

He smiled. "I'd like that, Cordelia. Thank you for treating me with respect and dignity. That's honestly all I ever wanted."

I nodded. "It's a lesson we all could use a little refresher course on these days."

Just then, Clint came in with keys to the handcuffs and immediately unlocked them. He said to Martin, "I'm going to release you to the Desk Sergeant who will get you your belongings and have you sign a few papers so that you can be on your way. I appreciate your cooperation."

He let him out of the room, and I waited for Clint to return, which he did after a few seconds. I remarked, "My, didn't you turn into Mister Sensitive all of a sudden."

He smirked. "Well, I learned from the best, I suppose. I don't guess you give lessons."

I smiled, "Well, anything for a price."

He gave me a funny look, and I wasn't sure if he might ask me something. Finally, he did. "So, how is that boyfriend of yours doing?"

I didn't realize how excited I'd be to give him this information. "Oh, sadly, we broke up yesterday."

He took my hand in his. "Oh? How sadly?" He pulled me close and kissed me.

I pulled my hand away, whispering, "We're still on camera, aren't we?"

He looked at the two-way mirror. "God, I hope not. Although I've seen worse antics in this station." He whispered, "We'll talk later."

I nodded and winked as we left the room, but it was too late. Several of his co-workers applauded as we came out of the room, and I don't believe it resulted from my brilliant interrogation skills.

Not to be outdone, he bowed, and I curtsied before we crossed the squad room to the exit. It looked like the world found out about Clint and me just about the same time we did, and we were okay with that.

☙⊱

It was nearly time for Shelby to leave for school by the time I got home, and I was flying on air. I'd promised to walk with her today; it only took fifteen minutes. She must have been able to tell I'd come home in a super delicious mood when I drifted dreamily into the house. She remarked,

"Wow, your questioning must have *really* gone well, Cord. You are practically on a cloud."

I couldn't lie, and what would be the point? Laughing, I said, "He kissed me, he kissed me, he kissed me, and I liked it."

She looked confused. "The homeless guy?"

I looked her straight in the eye. "No, follow along here. I dumped Sean yesterday, and I told Clint today, and he kissed me. But this wasn't a 'hi, how do you do' kiss; more like an 'I could have died and gone to heaven, and I would have been okay with that' kiss." I tried to think. "Oh my God, oh my God, oh my God, what does this all mean? What about Josh? Am I going to be his mom? There is so much to think about."

She put on the breaks. "I have to leave in thirty seconds for school. I'll talk you down to earth on the way."

I felt breathless. "Thanks, Shel. You're the best eighteen-year-old I've ever known."

She patted herself on the shoulder. "I know, Cord. Just remember that around Graduation gift time."

We started walking down the street, away from the beach, toward the high school. Shelby looked at me as we walked. "So, he kissed you?"

I wanted to recount it, including every detail. "Yes, I'd finished my interrogation. He had been behind a two-way mirror, listening and recording the interview. So, he came in and asked me how 'my boyfriend' was. Of course, he referred to Sean, not that he had really been my boyfriend, but I knew who he meant. I told Clint that I had broken up with Sean. And Clint didn't waste any time. Right there and then, he kissed me. It wasn't until we left the room that we found out they were still recording in there, so we got a round of applause from his co-workers. He bowed, and I curtsied on the way out."

She hung on my every word. "How exciting! Why doesn't anything like that ever happen to me?"

I laughed. "Well, don't forget the security camera incident."

She gasped. "You didn't ever watch it, did you?"

I hit her arm. "Of course not."

She let out a sigh of relief. "Thank God." She thought about it. "Is it still there? I'd hate to think that someone could chance upon it."

I smiled. "No, the tapes are erased and taped over every three days unless they are manually removed. It's an ancient system. I can't believe they haven't graduated to DVDs yet, much less hard drives, but you're safe."

She returned to the topic at hand. "So, this had to be *some* kiss, I guess. You're already talking about marrying this guy. Maybe you need to back up a little. How did you two leave it?"

I thought about it. "Well, he got a call and had to take off. He offered to drop me, but I wanted to walk. I love to walk. It gives me a chance to think. But, as you can see, I got pretty wound up by the time I got home."

She smiled. "Well, I guess you were still processing. You weren't ready to marry him, so that's good and normal. You like this guy. I could see it the other day when the three of you were eating ice cream cones together. I have to tell you, I saw a connection there, and you just met his son right then?"

I nodded. "Yes, it felt the same for me. I immediately connected with him. And I've never been someone who is a kid magnet. Sure, I like kids. Who doesn't?"

She raised her hand. "I can't say that I do."

I ignored her. "Oh, give it time. You will. You're still a kid yourself. Anyway, this felt different. This is a kid I can see spending my life with."

She looked me in the eye. "This is serious, Cord. You've really thought about this, haven't you? I thought I'd be able to talk you off the cloud, but I don't think it's going to be that easy. I think you're in love."

I rolled my eyes. "Come on, Shel, are you sure? I just met this guy. And sure, I get butterflies in my stomach whenever I think about him, I dream about him whenever I'm not with him, and I wish every minute away, that we're not together, but—" I interrupted myself. "Oh my God, I'm in love."

She nodded. "Well, I can confirm that I've never felt that way about any guy I've been with. The closer I get to a guy, the further away I want to get. Do you have any idea what that means?"

I laughed. "Just that you haven't found the right one. You'll know it when you do. There's nothing you won't do to be with this guy. And he may not be chasing you, and that will drive you even crazier. Don't worry, though; it'll happen, and I hope I'm around to see it."

She looked concerned. "Just where do you think you're going? It's not like you're old."

I smiled. "Well, I didn't mean that exactly. You'll probably be going off to school, and then we won't see each other every day like we do now."

She bit her lip. "I don't know if I'm going to school. My parents have kind of pulled the plug on tuition now that I've moved out of the house."

I made a panicky face. "Oh, I had no idea. Gee, I'd love to kick some in, but I don't have that kind of money."

She punched my arm. "Cord, I am not hinting that I need tuition from you. Don't be a dork. I'm saying that I might not be going to college right now. I might have to save up some money first."

I thought about it. "Well, if Uncle Joe and Aunt Kamala have their way, you'll be able to go to Community College for free, or you can rack up all the student loans you want and never pay them back. What a country, right?"

She put a finger on her chin. "I don't know. Sounds pretty good to me."

I warned her. "Just remember, there is nothing free in this world. *Someone* pays for it. Never forget that."

She didn't respond, so I wasn't sure if she got it, but I felt like she did. "I wouldn't mind working full time at Kohr's while I save money."

I thought about it. "I'll talk to Sally. I'm not sure what size staff she retains during the off season. I'm not sure she can support herself and me on winter ice cream volume. There's not a lot of traffic on the boardwalk in February."

Suddenly, we were six blocks down Trenton Avenue at the high school. She looked apprehensive as we approached the double doors. "Well, I guess this is where I get off."

I hugged her. "Thanks for listening. I'm sure we can work something out on your job situation. Don't worry. I want you to enjoy your last few weeks of school. This should be the time of your life."

She looked at me cross-eyed as she approached the door. "God, I hope not. I have much higher aspirations." She disappeared through the doors, and she was gone.

CHAPTER TWENTY

I had nothing planned for the day until I had to be at work at 4 p.m. for the dreaded midnight shift. Around 10 a.m., I got back to the house. Feeling restless, I knew I couldn't just hang around. I took off toward the beach with no destination in mind.

As soon as I hit the boardwalk, I turned right and headed south. I wasn't sure why, but I felt drawn that way. I walked briskly, with a mission, even though I had no idea what it was. Within a few minutes, I could see the Food Shack on the right, but I didn't stop; I continued.

I remembered that Samantha said Martin had been about a hundred feet to the south when she saw the unidentified man give him the gun. I counted my paces until around a hundred feet from the restaurant. I looked around for anything that might give me a clue as to why I'd been drawn here. I walked in small circles, searching the vegetation on the edge of the beach. Within a few minutes, I saw a stick protruding from the ground, almost like a marker. I started digging in the sand. It looked like it had been recently disturbed.

A few people walked by, gawking at me. I must have looked a little odd in my white capris and pink flamingo blouse, digging in the sand, but I had the determination to find whatever was buried there. Within about five minutes, my fingernails hit something hard. I dug deeper and harder. I dug a wider hole until it measured nearly a foot long, six inches wide, and nearly six inches deep. My fingers were getting tired, and my nails wouldn't be the same for months. Ten minutes later, I had completely unearthed my prize: a revolver.

I didn't know much about guns, but I identified this as a Colt 45 and not the Glock that Martin had described this morning at the police station. And, if he'd been released, where did he go? He'd been hanging around not far from here. I wasn't ready to go home, so I covered the gun over with sand and continued down the beach.

A few hundred yards later, near Elizabeth Avenue, I saw something floating in the water, about ten to fifteen feet from shore. I waded out, and my greatest fears were confirmed, a body. A huge wave came in, carrying it to me, and before the undertow carried it back out, I identified him as Martin William Raven. I waited for the next wave to bring him back in. I tried my best to drag him ashore against the raging current.

Finally, after about fifteen minutes, I had him at a point where the undertow would no longer pull him out. I sat on the beach next to him, exhausted. I knew I couldn't do anything to save him at this point. He had been shot multiple times and had probably taken in a lot of water as well. I pulled my iPhone from my pocket, thankful that I had bought the waterproof cover. I dialed 911.

~:~

As I sat waiting for the first responders, I tried to put the moments together leading up to finding Martin. I wondered if I had seen something that I wasn't aware of as I searched the beach for something unknown. I vaguely remembered someone running up the beach and wondered if that had been the killer, posing as a jogger.

It seemed like hours, waiting for the police to arrive, so it startled me when the squad car and ambulance drove onto the beach near to where I sat. While two EMTs attended to Martin, Officer Ronald Smith from the Point Pleasant Police Department asked me a few questions.

I stood up to give the EMTs a little space. We walked slowly up the beach. He asked, "So what were you doing out here when you found the body?"

I thought about it. "I found myself searching for something, but I didn't know what."

He didn't seem to understand. "Ma'am?"

I tried to explain. "I was drawn out here is the only way I can describe it."

He took notes.

I expounded, "Well, first I was drawn up there where I found the gun."

His attitude suddenly changed. "A gun? You say you found a gun. Where did you find that, and where is it now?"

I led him up and across the beach. "It's up here. I found it buried. I dug it out and left it here." When I got to the place I marked, I pulled it out of the sand. I showed him. "See, here it is."

He freaked. "Drop the weapon. Now."

I dropped the gun, wondering what the big deal was. I looked over at him to see that he had drawn his weapon and said in a very tight and nervous voice. "Hands on your head."

I complied.

He explained, "We will be bringing you for questioning regarding the death of Martin William Raven."

I couldn't believe it. "I don't know what you think you are doing. Do you have any idea who I am? I questioned this suspect in your offices this morning. What is your supervisor's name?"

He seemed unimpressed. "Ma'am, if you aren't supposed to be here, we will figure that out soon enough, but I can't very well ignore that you were found with a dead body and then led me to, perhaps, the murder weapon, now, can I?"

I looked at his badge for a reminder of his name, my frustration boiling over. "Now, Officer Smith, let's think logically here. If I killed him, would I have led you to the murder weapon?"

He laughed. "Oh, you wouldn't believe the stuff we have seen. Murderers lead us to bodies all the time, thinking they are so clever. So, no, reverse psychology doesn't work on us. That may be exactly what you thought. You kill the guy, call 911, then lead us to the murder weapon, and we'd think you were innocent and let you go strolling home. Do you know the odds of finding a body and a gun in two separate places on the beach within minutes of one another and not having anything to do with how they got there? So, we clearly have cause to detain you at this time."

I started to realize I might be in trouble. We were just completing the two-minute ride to the police station. He helped me out of the car. I demanded, "I want to speak to Clint, I mean Detective Daniels."

He led me into the station. "There will be plenty of time for that." He led me to the very interrogation room that Clint had kissed me in this morning. This felt like my worst nightmare. He sat opposite me at what had become an all-too-familiar table. He had a pad in front of him. He asked, "So, why don't we start at the beginning? Go back to where you believe this starts and tell me everything."

I could only tell the truth and hope for the best. I started slowly. "Okay. I met Martin William Raven this morning. I've been working with the Department and doing a bit of investigative work on the Rachel Lynn Gaston case. We made some real breakthroughs this morning, I think. He told me about a man who gave him a gun that he hadn't told the police about previously, and he'd gotten released this morning as a result."

He took notes but didn't comment.

I thought about the rest of my morning. "When I got home, I walked my 'surrogate daughter,' Shelby, to school. When I got home, I felt really restless, so I went for a walk. I felt immediately drawn to the beach. I had no idea why, but I felt compelled to walk to the south. I can't even explain it. I can't say that I've ever felt that way. I ended up digging around and finding the gun. It surprised me to find a Colt revolver, because I thought I would find the Glock 17, 9mm that Martin had described to me. He told me that he had buried it on the beach."

He asked, "So when you found a different gun, what did that make you think?"

I thought about it. "It made me feel like I had missed something, which is why I continued down the beach. Did I expect to find a body? No. But I couldn't say it surprised me either. I can't describe the feeling.

To be honest, even since I moved into my Gram's house a couple of weeks ago, I've been having a lot of feelings that I haven't been able to explain. I would put these in that category."

He seemed to be drawing as opposed to writing notes now. He showed me his drawing of the beach and stick figures. He spoke. "Let me tell you how I see it playing out. You questioned him this morning and became very frustrated that there wasn't enough evidence to hold him because you are sure that he shot Rachel Lynne Gaston, with whom you seem to have an unexplained obsession. You brought a gun with you because you knew he had one. Now, I doubt you shot him and then dragged him to the water. That would have been physically impossible, especially in broad daylight."

I felt exasperated. "Were you here when I interviewed Martin? Because you couldn't have summarized our conversation any more inaccurately. Is this how police work is done? You make up scenarios to fit your arrests and hope the judges and prosecutors buy your speculation? You should be ashamed."

He looked surprised that someone as apparently meek and mild as me could jump down his throat this quickly. He seemed to take it personally. "I'm working with what I have, lady."

I spit back at him. "Then get something else to work with. The interview happened *today*. I'd hope you can find it in your archives."

Just then, the door opened, and Clint walked in. He said to the Officer, "Can I see you for a second?"

Officer Smith glanced at me.

Clint said, "She's not going anywhere, are you, Cordelia?"

I smiled. "No, Sir."

The officer reluctantly left the room with the detective. They stood right outside the door and had what sounded like a heated discussion. I heard little bits and pieces. Officer Smith saying, "She had the body and a gun; what would *you* have done?" Clint responding, "I would have taken her at her word."

They went on like this for a while before both of them came into the room. The officer explained, "You are going to be released under the supervision of Detective Daniels."

The officer left the room.

Clint smirked. "Well, what do we do now? I guess I'll handle any additional questioning personally."

I looked at my watch. "I know what I'm doing. I'm going to work," and walked out.

CHAPTER TWENTY-ONE

It wasn't quite time to go to work, actually right before 1 p.m. when I got home. Shelby had just arrived. School seemed to be winding down for her, so she rarely stayed a full day. She had just finished changing when I walked in.

She asked, "How did your day go, Cord?"

I gave her a funny look. "Well, I found a gun buried on the beach. I found that poor Martin guy dead in the ocean, and I nearly got arrested for it. I might be in jail right now if it weren't for Clint, who saved the day. He took personal responsibility for me."

She nearly jumped up and down. "Wow, that's amazing! Thank God he intervened. Are you going to be okay going to work?"

I nodded. "Yes, I need to stay busy. Sitting around and thinking about it would drive me crazy."

We left for work together. She asked, "So, where were you on the beach when you found the gun?"

I will never forget that. "Probably a hundred feet past the Food Shack. It couldn't have been far from where Sam saw the guy give Martin the gun, but this wasn't that gun. I'm so confused."

She put the scenario together. "And further down the beach, you found Martin?"

I nodded. "Yes, but not too much further."

She looked at me. "What in the world drew you there? Did you want to talk to Martin? You knew that he'd been released. You two had joked about finishing the story when you weren't being recorded, right? Maybe that's all it was. Maybe too much is being made of this pull you felt to go down there. I know what you're thinking. You think your Gram directed you down there."

I nodded. "Of course, I do."

She pleaded with me. "You need to be careful when it comes to the cops. They are far more earth-bound if you know what I mean. 'My dead Gram directed me down to that part of the beach,' probably isn't going to impress most policemen. You were lucky you have a detective who's got the hots for you, but you can't always count on that."

Sometimes I wondered how this eighteen-year-old girl got her wisdom. It was downright weird. And she seemed to get wiser every day.

~:~

I looked up halfway through the shift to see Sean in my line. I swore under my breath. It looked like he'd taken a page out of Clint's book, except he didn't have a cute five-year-old to back it up. He just had an annoying, 'There's nothing you can do about it, I'm a customer,' look on his face. I almost switched lines with Shelby to serve him right, but I thought better of it. I didn't need to put her in the middle of my love life.

He stepped up and ordered a large vanilla and orange twist. I nearly said, "We only twist orange with vanilla," which is what pops into my head every time someone asks for a vanilla and orange or an orange and vanilla twist. All they have to say is, "an orange twist," because we only twist it with vanilla. I think all it means is that I'm facing ice cream burn-out. It happens.

When I handed him his cone and took his cash, he started on me. "So, I heard the police brought you in today. That's horrible. Are you okay? If you ever need to talk, you know where I live."

I smiled, "Yes, I even have your telehealth information should I not

124

be able to get to the office for a consult." I wondered, "Hey, how did you know about this anyway?"

He avoided my stare. "Oh, it's a small town. Everyone knows everything." I could tell he was lying.

I decided to take him up on his offer. "How about right now."

He looked concerned. "Are you sure? You look pretty busy."

I motioned Billy from the back. "Oh, no, it'll be no problem." I knew this guy wasn't telling the truth, and I wanted to figure out why or what about. This might be my only chance. I certainly wasn't going to call him and visit him on his turf. I met him on the boardwalk, eating his ice cream cone.

He smiled, but it seemed fake. "I'm surprised you were willing to talk to me."

I tested him. "Then why did you bother to come all the way down here?"

He didn't look me straight in the eye, another indication of a lie. "It's always a pleasure to see you, Cordelia, you know that." He used my full name. Interesting.

I pressed him. "Okay, so truth. How did you find out the police brought me in today?"

He had to know he couldn't lie. He was a therapist. He dealt with liars all day long. Finally, he confessed. "I saw them putting you in the squad car on the beach. I was on my run. Five miles a day keeps the doctor away."

I asked, "So, why didn't you say that upfront?"

He looked at his feet. "Oh, I don't know. I thought you might be embarrassed. What did they get you for, indecent exposure?"

I glared at him. "You take that back. I am always appropriately covered on the beach unless, of course, a huge wave takes off one half or other of my bikini, but I always stay submerged until things are all put back together again. I'm afraid I'm too modest ever to be arrested for that. I think that might be a little wishful thinking on your part, so shame on you since we are broken up now." I wasn't sure how to get from there to murder. "Actually, they picked me up on suspicion of murder, but it got straightened out quickly by—" then I realized who I was talking to.

"They straightened it out quickly."

He hadn't missed it. "Must be nice to be dating someone on the force. It gives you a few perks, I suppose, like getting you off a murder rap." He appeared to be getting angry.

I denied it. "That's not really true." Although, I said it weakly.

His face reddened. "Oh, come on, Cordelia, you can't tell me if Detective Superman hadn't been pulling strings for you that you'd be here working tonight. You'd still be in there answering questions. Isn't that true?"

I nodded, feeling guilty because I had taken advantage of my relationship with Clint. I said quietly, "Yes, you're right." I couldn't quite fathom why I felt guilty, but I did. And he liked it.

He had an odd half-grin half-frown when he stood up and said as he left, "You'll pay for playing with my emotions, Cordelia. You don't get to do that. I loved you, and you threw me away. You'll pay for that—mark my words."

~:~

I felt badly shaken up when I got back inside the ice cream stand. I momentarily went into Sally's office to right my sails before taking over a line. Who was this guy, and where had he come from? We never dated. We barely, nearly, almost started a relationship that never got off the ground. His anger level for the amount of time we were together was completely over the top. It made me question everything. Was he really a legitimate therapist? And, if he was, why couldn't he better address the very issues he allegedly did with singles and couples every day of his working life?

Shelby saw me sitting in the office looking shell-shocked on the way back from the bathroom and couldn't stop herself from seeing what was going on.

Before she could open her mouth, I cautioned, "Are you sure Billy can handle the front with no help? He doesn't have the same skill set that you and I do."

She laughed. "How's he going to learn? Besides, he's got the bell."

I rolled my eyes. "You know how guys hate to ring the help bell. It's a

126

male thing; admitting they need help isn't their best quality."

She stood fast. "This will only take a minute. Are you all right? You look like someone just shot your dog, and as far as I know, you don't even have one."

I wasn't sure how much to share. We had several relationships to balance. I had the role of her boss, her surrogate mom, and her landlady. Well, okay, she wasn't paying me rent, but you know what I mean. And we were friends. We had struck a delicate balance that I didn't want to ruin. I started slowly. "I haven't seen Sean since we broke up, and it didn't go well. Okay, it went worse than not well. In the end, he threatened me, saying that he loved me and that I would pay for throwing him away."

She looked at me incredulously. "Well, that wasn't very loving, would you say?"

I agreed. "No, I'd call it downright mean and narcissistic. I think this guy is diagnosable. I'm starting to question whether he even works as a therapist." I thought about the conversation. "He also knew firsthand that the police had picked me up. He claimed to be on the beach for his morning run when they took me away. That must have made him happy. I wonder if he came out tonight to gloat."

CHAPTER TWENTY-TWO

When Shelby and I got home at quarter after twelve, Clint sat on the hood of his car, parked in the driveway. He smiled and said, "Evening, ladies."

I corrected him. "It would be so nice if it were evening, but you realize we have to be back at Kohr's by nine tomorrow morning, right?"

Shelby headed toward the side door. "And with that, I'm headed to bed. Good night."

We both said, "Good night."

Then Clint jumped off the car and wrapped me up with a hug. "I thought you might need one of these with the day you had today."

I chuckled. "And it kept on coming at work."

He gave me a questioning look.

I felt near to tears. I couldn't handle anyone being overly empathetic. I probably had an emotional issue. I tried to tell him without crying. "Sean came by work, pretending to be supportive about today's near arrest, and ended up threatening me."

He gritted his teeth. "He's the next one coming in for questioning and we will spare nothing to make sure he tells all. I haven't trusted that guy from day one. I don't know why we haven't brought him in yet."

I jumped in, "Whoa, slow down, Mr. Testosterone. He implied it more than actually threatening me."

He was angry now. "Does that red-headed twit not know that I will cut his—"

I needed to get this under control. I kissed him, and he kissed me back. We both forgot about what's-his-name.

~::~

After work on Thursday, I felt particularly guilty for how I had left my relationship with my sisters the last time I'd seen them. I knew they were trying to help and protect me in their own misguided way and that their actions had been out of love.

I knew that a Facetime call wouldn't do, so I texted them to meet me at Lily's house, even though the hundred-mile drive would take nearly two hours with traffic. That seemed to be their favorite place to Facetime me from, so I figured we might as well meet there in person. We hadn't communicated at all since I threw them out of my house. Since I called the meeting, I hoped they wouldn't try the same strategy they attempted earlier.

I felt encouraged already as they both hugged me when I came in, that we could be ready for a new start. Katie started first as usual. She couldn't help herself. "We're so happy that you decided to get together. We've had time to think since we talked last time, and we might have been a little bit harsh in our reaction to your changes. After all, you are doing really well."

I tried to ignore how she constantly talked down to me. "Well, thank you, Katie. I'm happy that you noticed. I think you two are so used to me being a screw-up, it's taken you a little while to notice that maybe there's actually nothing to worry about right now."

Lily joined in. "I have to admit that watching you move to Point to Gram's house, working at Kohr's seemed like a step backward, but somehow it seems to be working. I wish I had the number of friends that you do. So, I'm going to ask you a favor, and Katie doesn't have to if she doesn't want to. I'd like to join your Monday night wine group. It sounds like a lot of fun. I haven't made any new friends in years."

I laughed. "Be careful what you ask for. We have certain requirements. You may end up with more friends than you know what to do with."

She nodded. "I'm willing to take that chance." She motioned to Katie, who seemed uncharacteristically quiet. "How about you, Kate?"

She had a funny look on her face and finally said, "I'm not sure I'm likable enough. What if I'm the only one who can't make any new friends. That would be so embarrassing."

I hugged her. "Oh, Katie, you have nothing to worry about. If you could stop being so self-protective and open up, people would like you."

She shook her head. "I don't know about that, Cord. I'm not like you. People naturally like you. Why do you think Lily and I stick together so closely? We don't have anyone else. I don't know why we moved to Westchester County. Rye is not a friendly place. I barely have spoken to my next-door neighbors in the five years we've lived here. It's strange. All the husbands walk or drive to and from the train station morning and night, and the wives have their lives doing whatever it is they do, but it certainly doesn't involve us."

I agreed with Lily. "This is all the more reason for you two to join No Longer Desperate Winers."

Katie burst out laughing. "That is a great name. I love it! I'm definitely joining, and you know we'll be spending the night, right?"

I hugged both of them and said, "I'm glad we are back on track. I hate it when we aren't speaking. You guys are my best friends, no matter how many friends I have. You know that."

They nodded. Lily said, "I feel like something is missing in my heart when we are disconnected. You are the bridge between Katie and me." She rushed into the kitchen. I could hear her swearing under her breath. "Hey Cord, you're staying for dinner, assuming I don't totally burn the pasta?"

I laughed. "Absolutely. Just watching your kids eat is enough to make me not want to have kids for years, so I like to do it periodically, not that I'm getting married any time soon."

Katie picked up on my tone. "Hmmm, it sounds like you might be thinking about marriage at some point. That's a definite change for you."

I had to agree. "When I kiss Clint, I can think about forever for the first time in a long time."

Lily heard that from the kitchen. "Ooh, that sounds exciting. Man, sometimes I wish I could be single again. I mean, I love Rory, but I'd love the thrill of the hunt. That first kiss, yum, I can barely remember what that's like." She closed her eyes and wrapped her arms around herself.

Katie and I stared at her. I said, "Does Rory know that you have these urges."

She glared at me. "Of course. He knows he can't be both old and steady plus new and exciting at the same time. As an old married couple, you have to take the good with the bad. And the good far outweighs the bad. But just once, I'd love to be swept off my feet by a hot guy who shoves me in a closet, has his way with me, and I never see him again. But he recites a sonnet and leaves me with a rose." She swoons at the thought.

Katie dismissed her. "You've been reading those romance novels again, haven't you? Somehow, they make sexual assault appear romantic and desirable. I wonder how that works. No wonder it's a dying genre. I'm sure those woke people will have them off the shelves in six months, and the authors banished to French Guiana."

~:~

By dinnertime, the husbands and all the kids were home, so dinner would be a major adventure. Managing to eat any food with four kids, four and under, was a challenge at best. Keeping any of them at the table for more than five minutes at a time proved more trouble than it was worth, so the fathers ended up sitting in front of the TV watching a kid's show on YouTube and eking out whatever food they could scrounge while refereeing wrestling matches and whatever other activities kids this age got into. It all seemed exhausting to me, but the men seemed to take it all in their stride, which impressed me.

I asked Katie and Lily, "So, is this how you survive motherhood? You farm it out to the B Team?"

Katie feigned shock. "Cordelia Corbett, now you take that back. I'll have you know that we spend every second of every day with these children while the men are at work, so spending time with the kids when they come home is only fair."

I nodded. "Yeah, I would get that if I'd ever seen either of you actually spending time with your kids."

They both gasped. Then Lily said, slightly above a whisper, "Cordelia, never say those words. As far as anyone knows, we mothers spend every second with our little darlings. That's the only way to extort our spouses into giving us any peace when they get home. It's the perfect arrangement."

After cleaning up the kitchen, I prepared for my nearly two-hour drive home. I walked slowly toward the door, arm-in-arm with my two sisters. I said, "Let's never let anything like that come between us again. We should always be able to work out our differences."

The three of us did a group hug and agreed, and I felt like everything would be all right.

CHAPTER TWENTY-THREE

Clint had parked in my driveway again, waiting for me to get home, but he didn't look the same as the other night. He wasn't casually lying on his hood. He leaned over the top of his car, smoking a cigarette. I didn't even know he smoked, and I couldn't say I liked it. He gave me a piercing look as I pulled into the driveway, as if I had lied to him, and he found out about it, or something equally as dreadful.

I tried to keep it positive. "Hey, what brings you here so late?" even though it was barely after nine.

He walked toward me, but not directly to me. He dropped his first bombshell. "So, we got the fingerprints back on that revolver from the beach."

I thought that should be interesting. "What did they find?"

He gave me an odd look. "Only your fingerprints were on it."

I thought about it. "Well, I guess whoever buried it either wore gloves or wiped their prints off."

He nodded. "I figured you'd say that. We checked out the borough's security cameras from that end of the beach and saw only you and Martin for a couple of hours except for a couple of joggers. Unfortunately, whatever happened to him appeared to be outside of camera range. But you knew that, didn't you?"

I shook my head. "How would I have any idea about the security camera range?" I smiled, trying to get him to smile, but he remained stern.

I asked, "Did you ever find the Glock that Martin said he buried?"

He shook his head. "No, when he took us to where he said he'd buried it, it was gone. You don't have it. Do you?"

I looked at him like he was crazy. "You're kidding I hope."

He walked across the lawn, sat next to me and said, in an almost begging voice. "Please tell me you haven't lied to me Cordelia. I couldn't take that after everything I've been through."

I started to answer but then figured out it had been a rhetorical question.

He continued but he got louder. "I hate being played. And now it seems we got all of the 'just happeneds' that I have to explain to my co-workers, and I'm starting to feel like maybe I'm the fool. You just happened to be there when your old friend Rachel Lynne Gaston got murdered at the Food Shack; then you just happened to take an interest in her murder, to the point where you drove a hundred miles to interrogate a suspect. Then, with no prior police experience, you somehow convince us to allow you to interrogate our prime suspect, who we release, and just happens to end up dead that same day, and the murder weapon just happens to have your prints all over it."

I could feel my white face turning red against my auburn hair and tried to explain the unexplainable," Listen, Clint, I didn't ask for any of this to happen—"

He interrupted me. "You know what, Cordelia? I didn't either. I didn't ask for my wife to die. I didn't ask to be raising my son by myself. I didn't ask God to make me stop trusting everything and everyone I came into contact with. I really didn't."

I wondered where this all went wrong. I asked, "What happened? Everything seemed fine—"

He interrupted me again. "Don't start with your logical double-talk. You'll only get me confused. Every professional muscle in my body tells me that you are guilty in this case. I wish to God I didn't feel that way, but every time I ignore my feelings, I get burned, and someone guilty walks."

I could barely think. I saw my future going down the drain quickly.

He continued. "But, then to involve me personally, now that's more than clever. Pretending to dump your boyfriend, precious, I've never seen that one. I'll bet you and he laughed about that for hours. You're still working with him, right? He kind of seems to be everywhere around this case even though, when we questioned him, his answers did not jibe with yours."

He counted on his fingers. "Both of you were performing CPR on Rachel Lynne Gaston, then, according to you, you two miraculously ended up together, then you allegedly break up because you need me on your side, then he's on the beach when the squad car leaves the beach with you in it after Martin William Raven is killed. It's all on the surveillance cameras. More just happeneds." He looked me in the eye. "You were already dating Sean when you discovered Rachel in the showers. Weren't you?"

I gasped. "No. I had never seen him before in my life. Sally can testify to that."

He laughed. "Before that day, you hadn't seen Sally since you were sixteen. How would she know?" He continued. "So, you killed Rachel because she was after Sean? I guess it was a replay of what happened between you two when you were sixteen, but this time it went a little too far. So what happened, Cord? Did something in you snap? Did all those years come rushing back? It wouldn't be the first time something like that has happened. You just lost it. Maybe the judge will go easy on you if you confess."

I glared at him. "This is insane."

He continued with his explanation. "What a great scheme, to pretend to try to save her life. Was that Sean's idea or yours?"

I sat down with my head in my hands. "Do you realize how crazy this sounds?"

He kicked the dirt. "I should have known. Smart, pretty girls like you never go for guys like me. I get the C- girl drinking beer down by the creek. The one the football guys already rejected." A tear ran down his cheek. "Well, somehow, a miracle happened when I met Sandy. She was everything, smart, pretty, funny. She had it all. She went to Catholic school, so none of the guys knew her. They never had a chance to meet her and snatch her away from me, so I married her as quickly as I could. The smartest thing I ever did."

He seemed lost in his own world now. "She didn't want kids right away, so we could enjoy each other, and did we ever. We traveled, dated, went to shows, cooked, and just did nothing. Finally, after five years, we figured we'd finally have kids. And almost as soon as he was conceived, she contracted breast cancer. She fought it like a rabid dog but lost the fight two years ago."

I wanted to ask him a question, but I didn't want to interrupt his reunion with his past.

He sat down on my front step. He looked exhausted. "I stayed up all night last night trying to figure out if I'm the fool because the evidence is mounting against you. Frankly, you're the only one supporting your case, and that's not a good thing. Normally, if a case is in the least bit controversial, there might be two or three guys who don't agree with my assessment. But this is the whole force. Until Martin got killed, things were a little more even, but that turned things ugly. And now that you were released under my recognizance, I'm under more and more pressure to bring you in."

I argued. "If I supposedly killed Rachel, which is preposterous, why would I kill Martin? That makes even less sense."

He thought for a second. "Maybe you had him do it. He thought it was a guy who put him up to it, but admitted it was hard to hear the voice over the ocean. Maybe that was you trying to sound like a guy. So, you had to dispose of him too, thinking that he might identify you."

I sat next to him. "What do you need me to do? If I need to turn myself in, I'll do that for you, even though I didn't do it."

He looked at me like I had lost my mind. "This isn't about me, Cord; it's about the case. I need the person or persons who committed these murders to turn themselves in. If that is not you, then it would only complicate things for you to turn yourself in."

I breathed a heavy sigh of relief. "Oh, thank God. I would be willing to do that for you, Clint. I think that means a lot. Doesn't it?" I put my head on his shoulder. He didn't move away from me, which I thought might be a good sign.

He buried his head in his hands. "What am I going to do? I came here so ready to arrest you and bring you in tonight until I saw you, until I heard your voice, until you touched me." He put his arm around me, and we sat in silence for a while. He seemed to want to say something he couldn't say. He stood up again so that we were no longer touching. He couldn't look me directly in the eye. "They're going to take me off the case if I don't bring you in. I'm going to have to recuse myself for conflict of interest anyway. I can't be objective or rational. I thought I could be, but I can't. I recognize that now."

I sat with my arms around my knees, feeling my whole world caving in around me.

He sounded frustrated. "If we had a shred of evidence leading us in another direction, I'd take it in a minute."

I grasped at straws. "How about Sean? You said yourself that he appeared everywhere there was a murder."

He shook his head. "All our guys have gotten on him so far is an obsession with you, but that doesn't help. We know he's obsessed with you." He thought of something else. "Oh, he's also being sued for malpractice. That doesn't surprise me."

I insisted. "Have you investigated him yourself, Clint?"

He shook his head. "Let's say, given our relationship and his relationship with you, I was encouraged not to perform the investigation myself."

I kicked my foot in the sandy soil. "So, this is really how this is going down. Up and down the beach, it's going to be, 'Did you hear the pretty redhead that works at Kohr's got arrested for the two murders on the beach?' 'Oh, she always seemed so nice when she served my orange twist cone.' 'It takes all kinds. Thank God, they arrested her before she got someone else.'"

He pushed back. "I'm sorry, Cord, I don't write the laws. I just enforce them. After you interrogated Martin, what possessed you to go out on the beach, searching, I'll never know, and I don't think you will either.

And that's the problem. The real world doesn't operate the way you do. For you, it's perfectly natural. You felt restless. What does that even mean? When I feel restless, I go to the gym, I don't walk down the beach specifically where a gun is buried, and a man you recently interrogated is murdered. Things that sound completely normal and natural to you sound incriminating and suspicious to the rest of the world."

I sat with my elbows on my knees. "I am who I am, naturally inquisitive. That doesn't make me a criminal. Granted, since I moved to this house, I've been a touch more intuitive than I used to be, but no one would understand that. I can guarantee it."

He glared at me. "So, your deceased grandmother is helping you with this case? Please tell me that's not true."

I couldn't lie. "It's not only that, Clint. She's helped me make new friends and changed my whole attitude about things that I'd never given a second thought about before I moved here. I truly am a different person, more self-confident, more outspoken, and far more intuitive, like my Gram was. I can't explain it, and certainly, a judge would laugh in my face. But there's not a doubt in my mind that my Gram led me to the gun and Martin. Of course, I couldn't say that to the officer when he brought me in. He would have had me put away."

He half-smiled. "Well, you never do anything without conviction, Cordelia Corbett. I have to hand it to you. And despite how crazy this sounds, I believe you."

I felt better having told him everything.

But there wasn't much of a reward when he said, "But, I'm going to have to bring you in any way."

I stuck my arms out so he could zip-tie my wrists together. I was getting used to the drill. I wasn't sure what to say. I tried to understand. "I know you are under a lot of pressure to get this case solved, and I'm the best suspect. So, I get all that. And I certainly don't want you to lose your job because of me. I wouldn't be a very good girlfriend if I allowed that to happen."

I saw a glint of hope in his eyes when I referred to myself as his girlfriend, so I knew this next part would hurt.

I tried to word it as kindly as I could. "Still, I can't help but feel that there had to be an alternative to arresting me. If you truly believe that I'm innocent, how can you book me on a crime you know I didn't commit? So, does that mean there's a little gnawing doubt somewhere deep down in your brain that wonders if, perhaps, I really am guilty? And, if that's the case, I can't be your girlfriend, now, can I? You have to trust me completely, and I have to trust you. If we don't have that, we have nothing." A tear streamed down my cheek. I asked, "Did you tell Shelby that you'd be taking me? She'll be worried."

He shook his head. "I didn't see her. Besides, I couldn't very well have filled her in that I would be arresting you so that she could text you in advance. This is exactly why you don't arrest your girlfriend." He looked more exasperated by the moment, with sweat dripping down his face. I'm guessing he didn't take the break-up well.

He put me in the back seat of his car, and we didn't speak on the one-minute drive to the station.

CHAPTER TWENTY-FOUR

This had all become too routine, and I started to lose my sense of humor. Clint passed me off to another officer that I hadn't met before to book me for the murders of Rachel Lynne Gaston and Martin William Raven. I tried to hold it together, but I felt an odd combination of surrealism and humiliation. While I knew that I hadn't done anything, the fact that everyone else seemed to think I had, including my boyfriend, or I guess I should say, ex-boyfriend, was almost too much to take.

A lieutenant that I hadn't met before, Thomas Stone, took the lead in booking me. He, at least, wasn't unpleasant in the process. He made conversation as he took my fingerprints and mugshot like an everyday occurrence, which I figured it had to be for him. It was the first time for me, so I hoped he hadn't noticed me on the verge of tears as I tried to keep my end of the conversation going.

At the end of the process, he asked if I needed to call anyone. He said they'd prefer if I could keep the number of calls to three or less despite what they say on TV.

I immediately called Katie because she had the widest network and the biggest mouth. "Katie, you're not going to believe this, but I'm in jail."

She chuckled. "Yeah, right, and I'm the *Cat in the Freakin' Hat*."

I cautioned her. "Watch out. Dr. Seuss isn't politically correct anymore. But seriously, I've been booked for two counts of first-degree murder."

She fumed. "Oh my God. What is wrong with this country? We have cities defunding the police and setting life-long criminals free and Point Pleasant Beach arresting my sister for murder. That'll teach you for settling in a Republican stronghold."

This wasn't the time or the place for a political rant. "Seriously, Kate, can you make a few calls? Call Mom, let Lily know, and hey, do you know a decent attorney who practices in New Jersey? I'm going to need one pronto."

She got immediately serious. "Of course, sweetheart. Whatever you need. I'm here for you. I'm so sorry. This is completely ludicrous."

I couldn't stay on the phone long. "Thanks. I love you. I'll talk to you soon, I hope." I hung up and dialed Shelby.

She sounded like she might be crying when she answered. "Cord, are you okay?"

I tried to sound strong. "I've been better. I've been arrested, but I'll be okay. I should be out after the arraignment. Depending on the court calendar, that it'll be tomorrow or the next day."

She sniffled. "I watched out the window when Clint took you away. My heart broke, Cord. What is wrong with him?"

I tried to put a good face on it. "Well, he had to do what he had to do. There are many political pressures, and I'm the logical suspect, so I get it. I just wished he had more faith in me, so I had to break it off with him."

She sounded devastated. "I'm so sorry, Cord. I know how much you loved him."

I wiped a tear from my eye, trying to hold it together. "It'll be all right. You and I will be back together laughing about crazy stuff in no time. You'll see." I thought about it. "Do you want to go back home until I get out? I'd certainly understand."

She immediately responded. "No way. I'm not giving Mom the satisfaction. Besides, between work and school, I'm barely here anyway. The nighttime is a little freaky, but I'll survive. You said it'll only be a day or two, right?"

I hoped I wasn't wrong. "Exactly. You'll hardly know I'm gone." I just remembered. "Hey, can you call Sally? I think I'm wearing out my phone time here. Just let her know what happened and that I might miss a day or two of work. Thanks."

She responded, "No problem. I'll help to fill in where I can."

I needed to go. "Thanks, Shel. You're the best. I'll see you soon."

The lieutenant seemed ready to take me to the holding cell when I hung up. He handed me an orange jumpsuit and pointed to the ladies' room. He apologized, "I'm sorry. We don't have the best facilities. We rarely use our holding cell."

I almost felt bad for the guy. "That's fine, Lieutenant. You are just doing your job. I understand."

He asked, "Do you know if you have an attorney coming for the arraignment?"

I wasn't sure. "My sister is working on it. I gave her your number. Can she coordinate with you on that?"

He nodded. "Yes, that'll be fine. If not, we can use a Public Defender for the arraignment. There's usually not too much to them. We will have to travel to Trenton to Federal Court due to the circumstances of the case. Because of the small number of murders in this area, that might be a good thing. The last time we had a local murder trial, it turned into quite a circus."

I smiled. "Okay, well, it almost makes going all the way to Trenton sound worthwhile."

He started to say something, then stopped.

I asked, "What? Something on your mind?"

He nodded. "Yes, it's probably none of my business, but I'll say it anyway." He seemed to be preparing the right words. "Don't be too hard on Clint about all this. He's just doing his job, and I have to tell you, this is killing him."

I wasn't sure how much to share. "Well, I'll tell you what I told him. If he has doubts about my innocence or guilt, he should clearly bring me in and have me arrested and booked for these murders, but there is no way we could continue to be a couple because that requires absolute trust. So, if he couldn't trust me not to be a murderer, how could he trust me to be his girlfriend? I had to break it off."

He argued, "But in a relationship, you don't have a mayor and a police chief pressuring you every day to arrest a suspect to get the press off their backs. You aren't being threatened to lose your badge because you've fallen in love for the first time since your wife died, something you thought could never happen. You don't have co-workers questioning your instincts because you believe far from customary explanations from your girlfriend for actions she has taken over the past several weeks relating to activities in and around the murders. I'm just saying it's not as black and white as you make it out to be."

I thought about his arguments. "Okay, Lieutenant. I'll consider that."

He nodded. "Thank you. He's a good friend of mine, and I've seen amazing changes in him since he met you. I'd hate to see that come to an end."

I slipped into the ladies' room. I took my time changing into my jumpsuit, realizing that it would be the last alone time I would likely have over the next twenty-four to forty-eight hours. Well, I would probably be alone in my holding cell in a town like this with such a low crime rate but under surveillance at all times. I looked in the mirror and imagined myself to be Nicky Nichols on Orange is the New Black, even though she was far more outspoken and potty-mouthed than I am. Maybe she could be my jail persona. I felt pretty sure that the sweet and innocent Cordelia Corbett one wouldn't cut it. With a slight North Jersey accent, I said, "Hey, you lookin' at me? You betta not be lookin' at me." I laughed to myself. "Now, I have to stop washing and combing my hair, and I've got it." I walked out with a whole new attitude.

I spent the next eight hours trying to sleep and re-designed my life several times. Between fitful naps, I started out deciding that I wouldn't listen to any of the voices, hunches, or feelings brought about by living in my Gram's house. Then, I modified that, believing that I should only listen to the ones that wouldn't put me in danger or get me arrested. A few hours later, I realized I had no way of identifying those potential dangers until it might be too late, so the only choice I had would be to continue doing everything I had been doing. It had worked for the most part, except that I'd been arrested for two first-degree murders.

By morning, I started working on my Nicky Nichols character. She not only seemed to survive prison, but she also seemed to enjoy it. I could do the same if I were convicted. I knew that my fellow convicts could smell fear a mile away, and they would exploit that, so I could never show my fear. I would use the energy my fear generated to create something far more useful: Nicky Nichols 2.0. I reminded myself to binge-watch *Orange is the new Black* if I ever got out of the slammer. It worried me that I had already gotten used to using prison terms. Did that mean I was destined to stay?

Just when I thought I might flip out, a female officer came to my rescue. Her name was Danielle Haggarty. She let me know, "Your attorney is here. I'm going to take you to meet him."

I smiled. "Oh, bless you. If I had one more minute to think in here, I might have gone crazy." I tried out my Nicky Nicole voice, "Even after all the fun we've had."

She laughed, "Wow, great Nicky Nichols impression. You should take that on the road."

I kept it going. "I hope there's still a road to go on when I get out of this hole."

She chuckled. "You've been practicing. Good for you. It's good to have a backup plan in case you never get out."

She waited for my reaction. I said, staying in character, "You're kidding, right?"

CHAPTER TWENTY-FIVE

We just got to the conference room, and she whispered, "You'd probably better shift back to Cordelia for your attorney. Just a suggestion."

I nodded. "Thanks." I wasn't sure I could do it. She had become a part of me. I headed into the room to find a thirty-something attorney in a suit with a briefcase. I wondered if they'd left me with the public defender.

He stuck his hand out and shook mine. "Hi, I'm Paul Thompson, of Thompson, Thompson, and Springer. Your parents use our firm for most of their legal work. My dad founded the firm and has been running it for years. I happen to do most of the criminal work, and I'm the only one in the firm licensed in Jersey, so you've got me." He had a notebook in front of him. He suggested, "Why don't you give me a general background, and then we'll get into the case?"

I smiled. "Well, I'm the middle child, valedictorian of my senior class, voted most likely to succeed, and Queen of the Senior Prom at New Rochelle High. We had nearly a thousand kids in our graduating class, so not a small accomplishment. Since then, I've kind of been the disappointment of the family. I took a job with Goldman Sachs and everyone had me pegged as a millionaire in five years. The only problem:

I absolutely hated it. I hated the job, hated the hours, hated my co-workers. It wasn't for me. The good news: because they terminated me, I got a severance package, so I wasn't destitute when my grandmother, who lived here in Point Pleasant Beach, died and left me her house."

He furiously took notes. "That sounds pretty positive. So, you moved here. Where were you living before that?"

It seemed like a lifetime ago. "I had a rental flat in Greenwich Village."

He wrote that down for whatever reason. "So, you moved here. Then what happened."

I tried to recount things in order. "I decided to contact Kohr's Frozen Custard, where I worked when I stayed with my Gram the summer I turned sixteen. I figured that would cover my property taxes and my other expenses while I figured out what I wanted to do with my life. So, my first morning here, I headed to Kohr's. As luck would have it, my manager from fourteen years ago still worked there; in fact, she owns the place now, and she immediately hired me as Assistant Manager."

He nodded as he wrote. "Impressive. So, you had a management job on your first full day of residency. I would say that's a step in the right direction."

I agreed. "I know. Right?" He seemed like a nice enough guy so far. I hoped he had a clue when it came to lawyering. "Anyway, to celebrate, the Manager, Sally Kohr McIntosh, and I decided to go to breakfast down the beach at the Food Shack, an unusual place that combines a restaurant with a gift shop and a bathhouse, right on the beach."

He smiled. "Believe it or not, as many times as I've gone to the Jersey shore, I've never been to Point Pleasant Beach. I've tended to go further south, usually to Sea Isle City or Cape May. So, I'd never heard of the Food Shack until today. I'll have to stop down on the way out of town and have a look around."

I agreed. "You should have lunch there. The food is awesome." I figured I'd better finish my story, or they'd call me back to my cell before we had completed our business. "So, we were paying our check when we heard a scream from the direction of the bathhouse. A lady said that she'd found a dead woman in the showers. Sally and I went to find out what had happened. Basically, everyone had left the scene, so they left it up to me to start CPR and for her to call 911. Eventually a guy passing by assisted with the CPR also, by the name of Sean, who turned out to be a local therapist. So. While I'm performing CPR, I noticed that this woman looked familiar, but not like from now, but from my past."

He said, "Hold that thought. Performing CPR, you and this Sean weren't able to save her? Did you see anyone suspicious nearby?"

I shook my head. "No, but a couple of women reported seeing a guy running toward a red mustang and driving away at a high rate of speed. We have already checked out that angle and don't believe he is responsible for the woman's death. Her name, as you probably guessed by now, was Rachel Lynne Gaston; by the way, a pretty famous social media influencer. Although, I figured out I knew her when I was sixteen. At that time, her name was Rachel Lynne Redmond."

He seemed curious. "So, this is important and seems to be a key part of the prosecution's case. How do you know so much about the victim in this case, though you've had no contact in fourteen years.?"

I tried to answer most believably and credibly. "Well, once Rachel and I were thrown together again by fate, I couldn't let it go. I felt like I had crossed her path for a reason and that I'd been placed in that restaurant at that time with a purpose. For whatever reason, I've been feeling that way a lot since moving into my Gram's house. I can't explain it. Maybe, I'm supposed to somehow right the wrong of all those years ago. We had been friends and ended up enemies over some stupid boy. Maybe this is my chance to make it right."

He looked worried. "Okay, let's talk about Martin William Raven. What has your involvement been with him?"

I smiled. "You'll be happy to know, far less than Rachel. Until a couple of days ago, I didn't even know his name. I had gotten quite close to the detective on the case and convinced him to let me talk to Mr. Raven. I had a feeling that I'd be able to get a lot more out of him than the police had been able to before they released him, and he proved me right. He told me about a man who gave him a Glock 17, 9 mm handgun that he had never revealed to the police. We had a very good rapport. Before he died, he claimed that he buried it somewhere on the beach, but it hasn't been located yet."

He took more notes. "So, why are you a suspect in his murder?"

I rolled my eyes. "Okay, so this isn't so good. The day they released him, earlier in the week, I felt restless and took a walk down the beach. First, I found a Colt revolver buried, although this wasn't the gun he had described to me that the man had given him. I then found him shot dead in the ocean not far from there. But I swear, I had nothing to do with it.

"I think I might have been a minor suspect in Rachel's murder, but when I called 911 when I found Martin's body and produced a potential murder weapon, they worked harder to find a motive for me to have killed Rachel. It's all bogus as far as I'm concerned. They're saying I murdered Rachel out of jealousy. I hadn't even seen her in fourteen years, so that makes no sense. They are saying I was already seeing this guy Sean before the murder even though I only met him that day."

He scratched his head with the end of his pen. "We're going to need some people to corroborate your story. You didn't do it. Right?"

I said adamantly, "Of course not. No."

We both sat quietly for a few minutes. Finally, he broke the silence. "Okay, here's the plan. We need to get the ballistics reports from the police on both of the bullets from the victims and the weapon you unearthed. So, they still haven't found the Glock 9 mm that Mr. Raven spoke of?"

I thought about it. "Not as far as I know, but we should ask. That should have a huge bearing on the case. For instance, if the gun given to Martin turns out to be the murder weapon used on Rachel, could the killer have been trying to implicate Martin to exonerate himself?"

He took more notes. "You're right. That could be the linchpin in this case. And, as far as I'm concerned, while you happened to be in the vicinity of both murders around the time of the murders, this is a small town, so were a few other people, I would imagine."

He got out his calendar. "Okay, I'll take care of that. The only other thing we need to worry about right now is the arraignment, which is scheduled for tomorrow in Trenton, 402 East State Street, Room 2020. You were lucky to draw Judge Torianne Bongiovanni. She's been a fixture in that court for nearly twenty years. She'd become a legend before I graduated law school, and I will read you a quote from the American Conference website that always cracks me up. It's literally from her kindergarten report card: 'Torianne is a born leader, but she sometimes has a little difficulty in working & playing with others because of a reluctance to relinquish the spotlight (at times) to other children. She is much more mature than most kindergarten-age children, which probably makes it hard for her not to direct & dominate her classmates at play.'"

I laughed. "I like a judge with a good sense of humor, especially one who can laugh at herself."

He nodded. "She definitely can, but she's also very fair. You drew a very good judge. You can't put a price on that."

~:~

By the time I got back to my cell, I felt confident in my attorney. I knew my parents wouldn't send me someone they didn't believe in when my life might be in the balance. He seemed confident and relaxed, not fretful and panicked. I liked that too. I hadn't even noticed if he had a wedding ring on. Maybe I had learned from my last two ventures into the relationship world to take it a little slower.

I started to wonder about something that had been in the back of my mind from the beginning. Had Rachel come to Point Pleasant Beach to meet someone? As John Michael Owens had told me, Rachel had told him to meet her here. She tried to fit him into her schedule, which meant, to me, that she had something else scheduled. Or someone.

She had booked a motel, which meant they weren't staying together. To me, that meant that they had probably never met and that he lived here. I guessed it could also have meant that neither of them lived here, and they were meeting at the motel, but I hadn't gotten that impression from the front desk clerk.

I thought about other alternatives. Maybe they had known each other in the past and were meeting on a chance encounter. But why would she stay in a motel? It seemed like she wanted to meet him in public. Maybe she didn't trust him. Maybe she feared him. Maybe she felt afraid that what would happen did happen. He could have been far bolder or more stupid than she anticipated. I guessed the answer to that would lie in who ended up getting convicted for her murder. So far, he looked pretty smart.

CHAPTER TWENTY-SIX

The forty-five-minute ride to Trenton seemed to take no time at all. A female police officer named Andrea Davis escorted me, and we had a blast, discussing everything from make-up to sunscreen to the best fitting sports bras. I could never find one comfortable enough to run in, and she promised me SheFit would be the way to go. I told her, "Okay, Andrea, I'm coming after you if I can't run five miles with no pain."

She agreed. "I've run marathons in these. I've got your back, girl. We larger chested women have to stick together. We can have fun too."

We had arrived. "Okay, but I am definitely holding you to it. And I know where you work. It's within walking distance of my house."

The Clarkson S. Fisher Federal Building and Courthouse stood proudly on the corner of State Street and South Stockton Street. It was a stately building with murals, statues, and various artwork throughout the building.

It amazed me how remarkable the time, dollars, and energy put into buildings were when this one had been constructed back in 1932; when history insists nothing had been going on but the Great Depression. Clearly, far more went on than that.

The courtroom had been decorated with murals and other impressive artwork. It gave one the feeling that very important work was performed here. I felt honored to be attending court, even as a defendant. It stood as part of what had been great about this country, which hadn't been torn down or destroyed by those trying to rewrite our history.

I understood that there would be multiple arraignments today, so we would be called in order of our docket number. I sat in the second row of the gallery with Paul. He explained to me, "Pretty soon, the bailiff will introduce the judge, and we will all stand. She will either seat us or make opening remarks and then have us sit down. That's all a matter of style."

All of this stuff seemed pretty basic and came along with any Law & Order episode, but if he felt better mansplaining it to me, I would pretend to listen. I replied politely, "So, what do I have to know when she asks me to plead?" I pretty much knew the answer to that, too, but I wanted to make sure I didn't mess it up in any way.

He impressed upon me. "Yes, make sure that you do not plead guilty under any circumstances. That cannot be reversed. I've had clients do it by mistake. And, of course, the judge asked them if that was what they meant, and they said 'yes.' Then it was too late. You need to make sure you plead not guilty."

I nodded. "Got it. Not guilty." Okay, I was playing with him a little bit.

Just then, the judge entered with a flurry of activity. The bailiff announced for everyone to rise, then announced the Honorable Torianne J. Bongiovanni, Presiding. She motioned for us to sit but remained standing. She looked over the relatively sparse crowd in her court. She spoke clearly to all of us.

"Today, we will have multiple arraignments, so we need to act efficiently and expeditiously. If I have a question, please answer it. If I ask for more information, please provide it. If I do something unusual, that's okay; it's my court and has been for nearly twenty years. No one is going to tell me how to run my court. Any of you who have seen my kindergarten report card know that." She smiled and sat down.

She shuffled through papers. I call docket number HI35989, The United States Government versus Cordelia Candace Corbett.

My knees suddenly got weak. I never expected to be first. I figured

I'd watch at least ten other cases first, so I'd have it down before she got to me. But finally, my legs pulled me up. Paul stood with me, and we came forward to the defense table. The prosecution came up to their table to our right. I hadn't even thought about them being here. That made me nervous, having someone fighting against me.

Once we were all seated, she addressed us directly. "First, let's deal with the plea. Cordelia Candace Corbett, you are charged with the first-degree murders of Rachel Lynne Gaston and Martin William Raven. How do you plead?"

I knew that my one and only job was to say the words, 'not guilty.' But I suddenly felt so outraged even to be considered a suspect in the murder of these two people; I couldn't control myself. I took a chance. "Judge, can I ask you a question?"

She looked surprised but answered, "I'm feeling benevolent today, so why not?"

I pondered my question. "What if I'm so outraged by these charges and so confused that I have even been arrested for them that 'not guilty' doesn't seem sufficient?"

She sat for a second with her mouth open.

Before she could respond, I continued. "Don't get me wrong. I love this country, and I believe in the sanctity of the judicial system, as I do all aspects of the U.S. Government. But it didn't seem like 'not guilty' would express it for me today."

A brief torrent of applause came from the gallery.

The judge finally appeared to have found her voice and her gavel, which she pounded mightily. She sternly said, "Order," as she glared at the gallery. "Any more outbursts like that, and you will be escorted out. Is that understood?" The few people responsible nodded. Then she turned to me. "Now, Miss Corbett, I appreciate the respect with which you posed your question. You'd be surprised at the language I have to contend with these days as a judge. I feel like I have to remind my contestants that this is not reality TV. This is reality, a whole different animal. That being said, the nice people from the police department don't generally take people into custody willy-nilly without evidence, such as weapons, forensics, autopsies, witnesses statements, DNA and other evidence gathered at the crime scene. Would you agree with that?"

I nodded. "Yes, your honor."

She continued down that road. "And for the evidence that was provided to and reviewed by your attorney, did they use generally accepted police procedures to gather the evidence that brought them to the conclusion that you were their prime suspect?"

I looked at my attorney who nodded, so I did also. "Yes, your honor."

She put the final nail in my coffin. "So, they didn't fabricate evidence, falsify yours or others' statements, or otherwise illegally obtain evidence in this case?"

I shook my head. "Not to the best of my knowledge, your honor."

She reached her own conclusion. "So, it sounds like you reached the top of the suspect list all on your own without any help from the police, is that right?"

I replied, "Yes, but—"

She'd completed our volleyball match. "So, please give me your plea."

I acquiesced, "Not guilty, Your Honor."

She smiled. "You seem like a very nice girl, Cordelia, and I hope to God that you are innocent too." Then she addressed the youngish female Federal Attorney at the prosecution table, "Ms. Novasdebien, please address bail."

She referred to notes in front of her. "Your honor, we have severe concerns about the defendant. She has not demonstrated significant stability in her life and has only recently, after losing her Wall Street job, secured a job on the boardwalk in Point Pleasant Beach as an ice cream scooper."

Paul raised his hand. "Objection. She is an Assistant Manager, your honor."

The Federal Attorney smiled sarcastically. "Okay then, she went from Goldman Sachs to Kohr's Frozen Custard. I think that speaks for itself. She's also harboring a high school student at her residence for no known reason, which has created a serious rift with the student's mother next door. And while the student is eighteen, there is not technically a legal issue; it speaks to judgment and character. So, based on those issues, I offer bail at one million dollars."

I whispered to Paul, "Where would I get that kind of money?"

He assured me, "That translates into about sixty-thousand in cash."

I felt sick. "I don't have that kind of money either."

He asked, "Just so I know, how much money could you get easy access to, lines of credit, savings, family, that kind of thing?"

I thought about it. "I'd hate to tap into family if I didn't have to. I could probably do up to twenty-five thousand if I absolutely had to." That would drain my savings.

He whispered, "I'll aim low, and hopefully, we can end up in the middle somewhere. A hundred thousand would cost six thousand, and two-hundred and fifty thousand would cost slightly over fifteen."

The judge had been awaiting Paul's reply. "Mr. Thompson, your response, please."

He seemed to be collecting his thoughts. "Your honor, Cordelia Corbett is one of the most responsible young ladies I have ever met. After she inherited her grandmother's house in Point Pleasant Beach, she could have rested on her laurels for a while, but the first thing she did was find a job. That same day, she went to breakfast with her Manager from Kohr's when Rachel Lynne Gaston was found dead, and while I know this isn't a trial or even a preliminary hearing, it's beyond me how you get charged with a crime that you couldn't physically have committed. And she is being charged with the murder of a woman she hadn't seen in fourteen years. There is clearly something wrong here. And, of course, we'll get into more of the details during the preliminary hearing, but in the meantime, bail should be set at a minimum due to the extraordinary circumstances of this case. I would suggest a hundred thousand dollars."

The judge considered the amount. "Thank you, Mr. Thompson. I'm going with my gut on this one. Miss Corbett has a residence in Point Pleasant Beach and is gainfully employed unless we make her bail so high that she can't afford to live. I'm going to grant bail at a hundred thousand dollars. I don't see her as a flight risk." Then she addressed me. "Cordelia, don't make me regret this."

I nodded. "Yes, Your Honor."

The bailiff called the next case.

CHAPTER TWENTY-SEVEN

I hadn't realized that my parents and sisters had shown up for the arraignment until it ended, and we were outside, and I was getting ready to drive with Paul back to Point Pleasant Beach. They all came out of the Federal Building together. I felt so excited to see them after my forty-eight hours in hell. I ran to my mom and gave her a huge hug. "Thank God you're here. You can't imagine what this ordeal has been like." It could have been much worse, but I craved the whole family's attention right now.

She smiled through her happy tears. "You made me so proud in court, Cordelia, and how you stood up to the judge. You have grown into such an amazing woman." She hugged Paul and said, "Thank you so much for everything. The fact that she set bail at a hundred thousand dollars was a tribute to the job that both of you did in there. It couldn't have gone better."

Katie asked, "Hey, since we all rode together, why don't we take Cord back to Point, so we can catch up and map out next steps. I think Paul said it best in court. How could they arrest you for a murder that you couldn't possibly have committed? And why would she have committed the murder? None of it makes any sense. We need to just forget about this case for a while."

Luckily my dad had driven the seven-passenger Tahoe, which he rarely needed on Long Island, but it sure came in handy today.

We played all sorts of juvenile car games on the way back to Point Pleasant Beach, trying to savor a moment from the past before we delved into the future. We played I Spy with My Little Eye, the License Plate Game, the Alphabet Game, and Name the Artist on the Radio. We ran out of miles before we ran out of games.

Lily complained. "I almost won. Can't we stay in the car until I win?"

Mom laughed. "You're just like you were when you were eight. You used to ask the same thing. And the answer is still the same. No."

When we got into the house, Dad brought up something they evidently had been discussing as a family while I was in jail. He cleared his throat. "As a general contractor, there have been times when I've needed a Private Investigator. Tom Handy from up in Dutchess County is among the best. He's also become a good friend over the years. I wonder if I should give him a call."

I felt immediate resistance. After all, I had taken it upon myself to investigate both murders with no support from anyone. Of course, that landed me in jail, so perhaps he had a point. I pushed my feelings down. "That sounds great, Dad. I'd love to get someone down here with a new perspective. Maybe I'm too close to things. Besides, I've pretty much exhausted any ideas I had on who might be responsible for Rachel's murder, and they didn't pan out. I'd be happy to meet with him."

He seemed thrilled. "That's great, Honey. I'll give him a call as soon as I can and see about getting you two together. I have a feeling he could be helpful."

Lily teased me. "I've met him before. He's kind of cute. And single."

I groaned. "Don't even go there. I'm not in the market for a man right now. I've already had two failed trial runs since I got down here, and I've proven to myself that I'm far too out of practice to be jumping back into the dating game any time soon."

Mom looked in the fridge. "Cordelia, you have no food. I thought maybe we could all have a meal together."

Lily chimed in. "Katie and I will run over to Stop and Shop. Just tell me what we need."

She looked in the cabinets. "Everything, just about everything. Cordelia, do you ever eat here?"

I explained. "Well, with my work schedule, pretty much only breakfast and lunch every other day. So, I don't really get a chance to cook much."

She looked at me. "No wonder you're wasting away to nothing."

I complained. "Mom, I'd hardly say a hundred and thirty is wasting away at five foot five. I think a hundred and twenty-five is average."

She sized me up. "But you are hardly average figured, Cordelia. They have to account for at least five pounds."

I laughed. "It's okay, Mom, we can call them breasts now. It's not the fifties."

Mom protested, "I wasn't even alive in the fifties. I'm not that old." She proceeded to make a list. "Okay, girls, here you go. And don't come back until you have all of it." She thought before they reached the door. "Do you need money?"

Katie laughed. "I think we can handle it, Mom."

I added as they were about to go, "Hey guys, since I might have a little time to myself this weekend, can you stop at the Little Point Book Shop and pick me up a book, maybe a mystery."

Lily agreed. "Sure, I love that place. It may take us an hour longer once we get in there and start browsing."

My mom rolled her eyes. "You better not take that long."

Lily laughed, "Just kidding," on her way out the door.

My parents sat on the couch, and I sat on the love seat after my sisters left for the store.

My mom asked, "So, other than this mess, how has life been since you moved down here?"

I tried to think of the best face to put on it. "Well, I love my job. I can't believe that Sally is still at Kohr's. It's made my transition down here so much easier, already knowing someone. And the fact that she was willing to trust me enough to make me Assistant Manager on day one made me feel really good. We have a great rapport and a wonderful staff.

Of course, most of them are high school kids, so you have to keep your eye on them, but they mean well for the most part." I also remembered something else. "I'm not sure if you heard that Shelby next door moved in with me."

My mom cringed. "I'll bet her mother wasn't thrilled about that."

I chuckled. "You can say that again. She spoke downright nasty to me. But I didn't care. Shelby is eighteen, so it was between her and her mother. Shelby's been a Godsend. I never really liked living alone in the city, so this fit right in with my plans. And she's so mature for her age. Sometimes I wonder if it's more for me than it is for her."

My mom tried to catch up. "So, you've seen a couple of guys since you been down here already? Tell me about them."

I tried to relax and not react like she was interrogating me. "Well, the same day I got my job at Kohr's, the day I went to breakfast at the Food Shack with Sally, and Rachel Lynne Gaston got shot, I met Sean McPherson. He assisted me in trying to revive Rachel, and we hit it off immediately. Of course, the fact that he was of Irish descent didn't hurt since I rarely meet anyone Irish, much less with the perfect Irish name."

She seemed excited. "So, how did that end so quickly?"

I tried to reconstruct the series of events that led to our demise. "I guess in the final analysis, a series of events happened. He came to the stand and got ice cream, and we ended up in a fight because he thought I concentrated more on the murders than I did on him. Considering we'd been dating for a day, it seemed kind of early to have our first fight."

Mom nodded. "Not much of a honeymoon period."

I continued with the saga. "Then, I met Clint Daniels, a detective with the local police force. At first, he completely rubbed me the wrong way. Then, he started to grow on me, especially when I met his adorable five-year-old son Josh and found out that his wife had died. But, when he arrested me, that whole thing pretty much fell apart too. So, maybe I'm meant to be alone right now."

My dad seemed happy with that outcome. "Well, sweetheart, you won't find me complaining about that any time. You can always come home and spend as much time with us as you'd like. Your bedroom is always available."

I smiled. "Thanks, Dad. I think it's kind of bizarre that we are now twenty-eight, thirty, and thirty-two, and you haven't redecorated any of our bedrooms yet, but whatever works for you guys."

He laughed. "Oh, we'll get to it one of these days."

I gave him a look. "Oh really? I'm thinking with two out of the three of us married with kids, and you haven't done it yet, it's not happening."

He grinned. "Oh, you never know. It's unpredictable."

Before long, the girls were back with food, and everyone helped with the cooking. It seemed like old times.

While they entertained one another, I slipped away to call Sally. She answered on the first ring. "Hey, girl, how are you?"

I smiled at her concern. "I'm ready to get back to work. Tomorrow's Saturday. Which shift do you need me on?"

She sounded excited. "Why don't you work the late shift. That'll give you a few hours to recover. I can't even imagine what you've been through. You'll have to tell me all about it. I can't wait to see you." She sounded ready to go, but then she remembered, "Hey, that Sean guy came looking for you. I didn't tell him you were in jail."

I smiled. "Thanks. I appreciate that. I wonder what he wanted. He can't seem to take 'no' for an answer. I wonder if he heard that Clint and I broke up. These small towns are murder."

She laughed. "Yeah, these days, in more ways than one. I'll see you tomorrow." She hung up.

CHAPTER TWENTY-EIGHT

By the time Shelby came home from school, the family had left, and the kitchen had been restocked. I sat vegging in the living room on my phone. She immediately yelled, "You must be home because there's food in here! This is so great—bread, crackers, peanut butter. I could live for weeks on what's in the cabinets alone."

I came out to greet her. She threw her arms around me and asked, "How's my favorite criminal?"

She had decided to keep it light, which I appreciated. "I'm doing all right. My whole family came here after my arraignment, and my dad offered up the services of a private investigator. At first, I resisted a little because I've kind of taken on that role, but since I'm stuck here, I figured, hey, I'll accept helping if they are offering."

She smiled and nodded. "Wow, very mature. I guess I'm rubbing off on you."

I punched her on the arm. It felt good to be home. I thought of something else that had been bugging me. "Hey, since you are so mature, maybe you can help me with something. Do you think I'd been justified in breaking it off with Sean? Or had I been making excuses so I could be with Clint?"

She winced. "Truth?"

I nodded. "Truth."

She smiled. "I'd have to go with what's behind door number two, so let's tell our contestant what she's won."

I had a feeling. "Darn, I knew you were going to say that. Well, not exactly that, but, well, you know what I mean."

She explained. "It seemed like once you met Clint, you were far more critical of Sean. He could do no right. He was competing with a ghost. I'm pretty sure he felt it too. It had to be frustrating for him. Almost the harder he tried, the more you backed off."

I lit up. "Well, maybe he'll get his chance once again. According to Sally, he showed up at Kohr's to see me the other day, so he must still be interested. And Clint really blew it when he arrested me. He had so many other options. He could have recused himself completely from the case and disclosed his conflict of interest. But he chose to arrest me. He obviously didn't love me like he said he did or like he thought he did. I mean, the guy is still grieving over his dead wife. He's probably incapable of loving the way I need a man to love me right now, so I respect that. I'm staying out of his way and out of his life."

Shelby agreed. "You should give Sean another chance. You two make a cute couple. And, God, the Irish kids you two could make. It's mind-blowing."

I laughed. "I know, freckles from here to eternity. Poor kids. They'd have to learn how to fight on the playground, young, like I did."

Shelby laughed. "Look at us. Moments ago, Sean could barely hang on as a distant part of your past; now you're having children together. Isn't love a strange and wonderful thing?"

I gave her a look. "Okay, it's a huge leap from here to having babies with the guy, but I'll try to be open-minded. It's been a crazy couple of weeks." I looked down at my phone, trying to decide what to do. "Maybe I'll call him. What's the worst thing that can happen?"

She smiled. "Exactly."

I dialed his number on my cell phone. He answered on the second ring. "Cordelia, I didn't expect to hear from you."

I wondered if he'd heard I'd been in jail or if he actually missed me. I smiled. "Oh? So, is this a good or a bad surprise?"

He didn't hesitate. "They brought me in for questioning on the Gaston and Raven murders. I was afraid you'd still be in jail."

I confessed. "I just got out on bail. They seem to think I killed Rachel out of jealousy, and that she had something going with you."

He laughed. "That's ridiculous."

I asked, "And you told them that and would testify to it?"

He sounded sincere. "Of course. That's preposterous. Who makes this stuff up?"

I said weakly, "Apparently Clint."

He chuckled. "Oh, the jealous boyfriend."

I tried to keep my positive tone. "Speaking of that, I wanted to apologize again. I'm sure I've done more than my share to contribute to our issues, and for that, I really feel dreadful. I wondered if, perhaps, we could start with a clean slate."

He sounded joyous. "That would be tremendous, more than I could have asked for, Cord. God, I hope I'm not dreaming."

I smiled. "Nope, you are not dreaming. This is a real call. I really like you, Sean. That may even be the source of our issues. I may have been overly sensitive because I care so much."

He suddenly sounded suspicious. "Hey, what about the detective?"

I stayed in the moment. "That's over, Sean. Honestly, there wasn't that much in the first place. We went to lunch and shared one kiss. I realized after that happened, I'd made a mistake." I waited for a response. When I didn't get one, I asked, "So, do you think we can start over?"

He answered immediately, "Of course. The detective knows that it's over with him. Right?"

I laughed. "Yes, when he arrested me, I made it crystal clear." I figured if we were going to be open and honest, it needed to start here and now.

He sounded serious. "I'd heard you were in jail, but I didn't want to pry. What did they bring you in for?"

I confessed. "The murders of both Rachel Lynne Gaston and Martin William Raven. I spent two days in jail. I got out this morning after the arraignment."

He sounded surprised. "Oh my God, I'm so sorry. I hope you know that I would have been there for you had I known."

I smiled. "Thanks, but I would have had no reason to expect or deserve that after how I treated you."

His voice took on a tender quality. "Cordelia, it's not about whether you deserve to be treated a certain way or not. I love you, and that's forever, that's whether you like me, love me, or hate me. That never changes. I hope you never forget that now."

I couldn't remember, for the life of me, why I had broken up with him. But I felt, now, like we deserved another chance. I asked him sweetly, "Can you come over now?"

He whispered, "Is the kid home?"

I laughed, "Yes, Shelby is home, but it won't matter. You're not getting into my pants that easily, Mr. McPherson. You're going to have to court me. I want it done right. I want wine and roses. I want action behind those words. My grandparents dated a hundred times before she allowed him a single kiss."

He gasped. "Wow, I hope you don't want to go that slow."

I smiled. "I want you to know who I pattern my life after. Don't expect a wham, bam, thank you ma'am kind of courtship. If that's what you are looking for, there's a bowling alley in Lakewood."

He made a point. "I'm fine with slow, Cord. I don't want to be broken up with every other week. I have a heart too, you know."

I agreed. "You're right, Sean; I've been wild, crazy, and impetuous. I won't let that happen again. If you had a class ring, I would wear it proudly around my neck."

He chuckled. "You're the craziest thirty-year-old woman I've ever known, but you are a breath of fresh air."

I smiled sweetly. "So, will I see you a little bit later."

He agreed. "Yes, I'll be there after I wrap up a couple of things here."

I said, "Okay, I'll see you then," and hung up.

I found Shelby in the kitchen, eating a peanut butter and jelly sandwich with a vengeance. She said between bites, "I forgot how good these things are."

I reminded her. "Thank my sisters. They bought everything."

I noticed John Grisham's *A Time to Kill* sitting on the countertop and grabbed it. I wouldn't exactly call that a mystery, but I hadn't read it, so it would have to do. I made a mental note to stop into the Little Point Bookshop over the weekend. I'd gone by it at least fifty times since I'd moved here and never stopped. It looked like a welcoming place with the blue bench and red table and chairs out front, a place you could buy a book and spend the day reading if you so desired—my kind of place.

Shelby finally asked as I perused the Grisham best-seller, "So, how'd your conversation go with Sean. It sounded pretty friendly from out here."

I chuckled, "I guess I don't have to fill you in much, then, do I?"

She pouted. "I still want details. I could only pick up some general stuff."

I smiled. "He seemed amenable to giving me one more chance but did note that he doesn't want his heart broken every five minutes, so I'd better make up my mind once and for all. He didn't actually say those words, but it seemed pretty clear that I'd hurt him very badly, and I don't want to do that again. He's a very nice guy, and he's putting his heart on the line for me. He's not making any secret about the fact that he loves me whether I love him or not. That's pretty special."

He must not have had much to wrap up because his car pulled into the driveway moments later.

CHAPTER TWENTY-NINE

He looked good when he came in through the kitchen door. I ran over to him and kissed him. He kissed me back, and we shared the most romantic moment of our relationship to date despite Shelby watching everything from the sidelines.

I felt breathless when we finally came up for air. I finally said, "Shelby, you remember Sean. Sean, Shelby."

They both acknowledged the other but with minimal interest.

Shelby said, "Hey, I've got paperwork to fill out for graduation, so there's no time like the present. I'll be upstairs if you need me." She nearly flew up the stairs.

We sat on the couch. I hadn't expected quite this level of physical attraction. I guess I had been holding back because everything now said 'go, go, go.' And even though I had no intention of acting on my feelings, it felt nice to know that I had them. From the look in his eyes, I could tell he felt the same way. So, we needed a distraction badly.

I asked, "Do you want to watch TV, play a game, do a puzzle, sit on the front steps?"

He looked at me and laughed. "Why are we so darned nervous?"

I admitted, "I didn't realize how hot you were."

He smiled. "Thanks. That's got to be the nicest thing you ever said to me."

I smiled back. "I guess I should talk more." I stood up and started pacing. I said, "I'm sorry. I wasn't prepared for this."

He had an idea. "Let's go for a walk on the beach. I think it's easy to take for granted how close we live. Sure, I run there, but that's so different from walking. Besides, what's more romantic than walking hand in hand on the shore?"

That sounded good to me, anything than being stuck in here like caged animals. "Great. I'd love to." We took off up the road toward the ocean and hit the sand in less than two minutes.

We took a right and headed south. I hadn't walked north past Kohr's since moving here. After we walked in silence for a while, I asked, "So, why haven't you given up on me? I've been pretty dreadful to you. Did something in you know I'd be back?"

He seemed to think about my question for a while, which made me feel good that he didn't blurt out the first thing that came into his head. "I can't say I ever knew that you'd come back. Like I said on the phone, Cord, there's a part of me that will always love you no matter what. And that part of me will never give up on you. Does that make any sense to you?"

I thought about it. "You are talking unconditional love here, right? It reminds me of the Alanis Morissette song, 'You Owe Me Nothing in Return.' It talks about that kind of love. Katie used to have that CD, and I listened to that song repeatedly, trying to figure it out."

I looked over at him, being careful not to trip over anything.

He stayed quiet, so I continued.

"I have to be honest, Sean; I'm not sure I'm capable of that kind of love. When I love, I want to get love back. I wouldn't be okay with you telling me you loved someone else or that you wanted to take time off from me. I want my love to be all about you and your love to be all about me. That's the kind of love that I want. So, the fact that you were able to keep loving me even when I broke your heart makes me uneasy."

He looked at me like I'd gone crazy. "Okay, I followed you right up to the end. But, where the fact that I kept loving you even though you broke my heart made you uneasy, I couldn't follow. I'm sure it had something to do with that crazy Alanis song. But don't put me in her category. I said that my feelings for you were strong enough that they were able to withstand two brutal breakups, and they still kept ticking. I think that's pretty darn good."

I smiled. "Okay, I'll put Alanis aside for now. What matters is that we are trying a third time. Most people don't even get a second chance, so the fact that we have a third is beyond a miracle. I'm willing to accept that."

We walked for a while, holding hands and feeling very much like a couple. It felt right. We passed a few other lonely singles but no other couples. I felt exclusive and lucky, like no one else in the world was as lucky as we were.

We walked nearly an hour and a half to Mantoloking and figured we had better turn around. I looked at the huge beachfront properties and said, "Wow, looking at these houses makes me almost feel poor."

He laughed. "Yeah, well, a couple of these houses are worth ten times what our houses are worth, so it makes sense."

We stood, Sean standing behind me with his arms around me, pulling me close, staring out at the ocean. It felt right. I turned around to face him, and we kissed again, deeply. I could hardly breathe, staring up into his eyes, reflecting the full moon. I finally said, "I'm glad that we didn't miss this because of my impetuous stupidity."

He smiled. "Don't be so hard on yourself, Cord. You're as new to this relationship stuff as I am."

I chuckled. "Oh really. When's the last time you were in a successful relationship?"

We started our walk up the beach. "Well, what do you mean by 'successful?' We didn't kill each other, or actually mutually satisfying?"

I wasn't sure. "Does anyone ever have the second one? You're the therapist. I guess you would know better than I do."

He didn't have to think. "Sure, they do. People graduate from my services every day and come back years later to tell me how successful and satisfying their relationships have been."

I wondered, "So why have yours been such an abysmal failure?"

He gave me the best answer he could think of. "Because I hadn't met the right woman yet."

I looked at him for any indication that he might be lying. I let it go. "Okay, whatever you say, Mister Therapist, but we'll have to let time determine if that one's true."

We stayed outside for a while after we got back to the house. Finally, we hugged and kissed, and he headed toward his car. He asked, "Will I see you tomorrow?"

I had no idea. "I'm working the four to midnight shift, so that's going to depend on your schedule. Call me."

He opened his car door. "I will. I'll talk to you one way or the other." Then he started his car, pulled away, and left.

I thought to myself how lucky I was that I'd had third thoughts. I wrapped my arms around myself against what had suddenly become a cool evening.

Shelby sat at the kitchen table, working on her graduation paperwork. She smiled, "So, how'd that go?"

I got a dreamy look on my face. "I don't think it could have gone better. We walked for miles down the beach, talking and laughing, holding hands, kissing. You know, that sort of thing."

She smiled. "I knew you two were a good pair. I'm glad you didn't give up. Sometimes a relationship needs a few false starts. I'm glad he didn't give up either. That means a lot. So, where do you go from here?"

I scratched my head as I sat next to her. "We're open to taking it one day at a time. But I'm pretty sure we are exclusive for now. I have no desire to see anyone else, so I can see where this goes."

She changed the subject. "Hey, I almost forgot. You left your cell phone here, and it rang, so I answered it. He identified himself as that private investigator who knew your parents. He said he'd be coming down here to see friends tomorrow and wanted to drop in. Bottom line, I told him that ten a.m. tomorrow would work for you."

I thought about it. "Well, as it turns out, that's just fine. He's going to be assisting with the case. I don't think I ever mentioned him to Sean, but I probably should. We may be spending a bit of time together. I get the impression he may be the jealous type." I bit my lip. "And Lily said he's cute."

She laughed. "That's all you need. You'd better keep your eye on the case."

I nodded solemnly. "Yes, Ma'am."

I set the alarm to nine, so I'd be all set when Tom Handy arrived at ten. He came right on time, and Lily wasn't off-base; aged mid-thirties, and definitely a high school football player. His persona said 'clean-living' all the way, and he impressed me immediately. I stuck my hand out to shake his. He grasped mine firmly and looked me straight in the eye. "You must be Cordelia. Your dad said your were a looker, but I had no idea." He winked and smiled.

I blushed a bright tint of red. "I'm sure you say that to all the girls." This should be interesting.

CHAPTER THIRTY

We settled at the kitchen table. I noticed he sat a little closer to me than he needed to. He smelled really good. I needed to focus. Thankfully, then, he started right into business. "Okay, so your parents filled me in on most of the details. I won't waste your time making you repeat a bunch of stuff you've probably had to tell people over and over again."

I liked his style already. If I had to tell the story one more time, I thought I would scream. I had thought of something, though. "Hey Tom, before I forget, there's one piece of the puzzle that I thought of lying awake last night. I couldn't understand how the police could have constructed a story where I killed Rachel Lynne Gaston while I ate in the restaurant, while she was in the bathhouse. But I remembered something that might be important."

He seemed interested. "Oh?"

I thought back. "Well, if they talked to any witnesses in the restaurant, right before we paid the check, and all hell broke loose, I went to the ladies room. If I recall correctly, the way the place is laid out, the restaurant, and the bathhouse share the restrooms. So, technically, it would have been possible for me to go into the bathroom through the restaurant, go out the back door into the bathhouse, shoot Rachel, and return to the restaurant undetected."

He thought about it. "Well, you didn't, did you?"

I laughed. "Of course not, but I hadn't even been able to come up with a scenario that the prosecution could use in court, but now I have one. It at least helps to prepare my defense."

He seemed unimpressed. "I don't even like to think that way. If this gets to trial, I haven't done my job, which is for it to never get past the preliminary hearing."

That amazed me. "Wow, you could do that? My boyfriend would be forever indebted."

He muttered under his breath. "Damn it. Why do the pretty ones always have boyfriends?"

I winked at him. "You know you said that out loud, right?"

He tried to maneuver a fake volume button and rolled his eyes. "I hate it when this thing gets stuck. How embarrassing. Your parents are going to shoot me. Your dad has a gun, you know?"

I chuckled. "They're fine. They don't even know him yet."

He rubbed his hands together like Snidely Whiplash. "Oh, so there's still a chance then?"

As much fun as we were having, I decided I'd better keep it to business. I reminded him, "Okay, Tommy, I admit I could have a lot of fun with you, but I think that could be detrimental to my case, so I think we'd better set up a few ground rules. The first rule is if we're doing or saying anything that we wouldn't with my boyfriend in the room, then it's off-limits. Rule two is," I thought for a minute. "I'm pretty sure with rule number one in place, we won't need a rule two."

He looked like he might say something but held his tongue. "Okay, Cordelia, if that's how it's going to be, boring and by the book, then that's how we'll play it. Tell me exactly what your connection is to Rachel Lynn Gaston."

I winked. "You're going to torture me now purposely, aren't you?"

He threw a napkin. "Flag on the play. You broke rule number one. No way you would have winked at me if your boyfriend had been sitting here."

I rolled my eyes. "Okay, I get it. Maybe a little harmless flirting would be more fun and make the time go more quickly, but how, then, do we know where the line is between flirting and something more?"

He picked up the napkin. "Fifteen yards. My ball. I did my part in good faith, so now I don't know if I feel like playing by the rules."

I complained, "Oh, come on now. One little broken rule and you're calling the game?"

He tapped the table impatiently with a half-smile. "Okay, answer the question."

I thought back, bored that I had to go through this again. "I knew Rachel fourteen years ago when she was Rachel Lynne Redmond. She was the granddaughter of my Gram's best friend. She and I hit it off immediately and we were inseparable the summer we were sixteen until she stole my boyfriend. I haven't spoken to her since."

He repeated the next most popular question. "What happened the morning she died?"

I said, "I had lunch with my boss, and we were about to pay the check, and we heard a woman screaming that someone had been shot in the bathhouse. My boss and I went back there and found a woman in the shower. She had been shot and was bleeding. I tried to revive her. I yelled for help and a man, who now happens to be my boyfriend, came to my assistance. We both tried CPR on her. We were eventually spelled by EMTs who soon pronounced her dead. It wasn't until I had been performing CPR on her for a while that I noticed she looked familiar from some time in my past."

He chewed on the end of his pen. "Oh, so this is where the boyfriend comes in. Interesting. So, when and why did he arrive?"

I thought about it. "I guess he'd been running by. That's on his running route, where he runs every day. But I honestly didn't think about it all that much in the excitement." I thought again. "Wait a minute. He had jeans and a tee-shirt on, so that couldn't have been it. I'm not sure." I had another thought. "But, now the police think I knew him before this and that I killed Rachel because of some love triangle with Sean, some replay of my sixteen year old jealous rage."

He moved on. "Okay, we'll worry about that later. The point is, he was there." He looked through some notes. "So, it's my understanding that you did your own detective work with the waitresses in the restaurant.

So, what did that yield?"

I laughed, "Well, so far, a couple of good friendships, but not much else."

He rolled his eyes.

I added, "Okay, that's not completely true. I got a little clearer picture of Rachel's visit here. She stayed alone at a motel near the Food Shack, where all this took place. She'd planned on meeting a guy, who drove a red Mustang convertible, right around the time she got killed, almost to the minute. His name is John Michael Owens. He lives in Nazareth, Pennsylvania. I thought he might be the killer initially, but he convinced me otherwise."

He nodded. "I'd like to talk to him."

I agreed. "I think you should."

He cracked a smile. "I'm happy you approve." He then asked, "Was there anything else that came out of the employees answers to your questions at the Food Shack?"

I thought about Martin. "Yes, one of the waitresses saw Martin William Raven, the homeless man who later got murdered on the beach, accept a handgun from a man about a hundred feet down the beach from the restaurant."

He raised his eyebrows. "Would she recognize the man?"

I shook my head. "No, he wore a hood."

He swore. "They should outlaw hoodies. It's ridiculous." He held that thought. "But what else do you have on victim number two? I'm assuming you are done with the first one."

I smiled. "He turned out to be such a nice guy. I met him briefly, actually helping the police interrogate him. He had lost a friend and co-worker in a fire and struggled to work through it. Later the same day, I felt restless and went down the beach. I found myself unearthing a Colt revolver; not the type of gun he had been given, which was a Glock 17, as he had told me during the interrogation."

I buried it again, and kept walking down the beach. I saw something in the water, and it was Martin. He was dead from a gunshot wound." I thought of something else. "I never found the Glock. I wonder if the police have gone back there with a metal detector."

He scanned his notes. "Good question. Can you write down the names, numbers if you have them, or where I can find them, of anyone and everyone you spoke to? I need to talk to everyone again. Sometimes a second opinion is worth a thousand words."

I nodded. "Sure, no problem." I hesitated. "Does that include Sean?"

He missed the inference; then he got it. "Oh, I see—the boyfriend. I don't see why not unless you think it will cause a rift between you two. I certainly don't want that."

I thought about it. "No, it's not so much that. I don't know that it would be an effective use of your time."

He seemed to want to say something but held back. "Okay, you may be offended by this, but it's my job. You may think this guy is all that because you've been dating him for five minutes. I don't know if it would be the smartest thing to exclude him from the process, just because you're playing kissy-kissy with him right now; when two weeks from now, you could as easily be testifying against him in court. I've seen it a thousand times."

I had to agree that I'd been pretty fickle lately. "Okay, Tom, I'll give you that one. Talk to Sean like everyone else."

He warned me. "You do know he'll be expecting a pass. I've also seen that a thousand times from boyfriends and husbands, and you'd be shocked how often they are involved. It kind of makes me sick."

He seemed ready to go as soon as I had completed writing the list of people he should speak to and where he could find them or their contact information. I handed him the list.

He took it with a smile. He shook my hand and said, "I'm not surprised I took to you as quickly as I did. Your folks are nice people. You come from good stock, Cordelia Corbett. And, hey, if you're ever between boyfriends and you'd like someone to hang out with, give me a call or text me." He handed me his business card. Then he noted, "And I don't mean 'Hang out' the way the kids do today. I mean, hang out."

I pretended to be disappointed. "Oh, I'm sorry to hear that." I batted my eyelashes.

He shook his head, turned, and walked out the kitchen door with a smile.

CHAPTER THIRTY-ONE

A few hours later, Shelby and I were headed to work. She asked, "So, how'd it go with that Tom guy?"

I searched for the right words. "Interesting. He asked a few pointed questions and plans to talk to everyone I did. I think it's a good approach. I'm sure that he'll come up with others as a result of the people he talks to. He's a professional; I've only been doing it as a hobby for a couple of weeks."

She wanted more. "I kind of meant more personally. What did you think of him?"

I got it now. "Oh, tremendously dangerous. We had to establish ground rules, which I broke at least twice." I wondered if I would have to come to terms with the fact that I wasn't a very good girlfriend. I wasn't ready to admit it yet, but it seemed possible. I tried to imagine Tom and Sean in the same space discussing this case. It didn't even register. At least I wouldn't be there.

Work on Saturday night felt like heaven. My biggest worry: giving someone the wrong change or forgetting to put nuts on someone's sundae. I love the mindlessness of the work, and the time went by so quickly that I could hardly believe it when midnight came.

Walking home with Shelby, while I felt tired but relaxed, she seemed agitated. Finally, she nearly exploded. "Cord, did you see the new girl, what's-her-name. Natalie, flirting with Billy all night. 'Oh, Billy, can you help me with this ice cream machine. It seems to be stuck.' 'Oh, Billy, which one is the waffle cone?'" Shelby did the international gag sign, sticking her fingers down her throat. "Seriously, she didn't know which one the waffle cone was? Had she been raised by wolves?"

I felt confused. "I thought that you had decided not to date Billy because he didn't fit your long-term plan."

She agreed. "Well, you're right. I'm not saying I want to be with Billy. I just don't want to work with someone who is blatantly flirting with him right in front of my nose. Does she have no dignity?"

I argued. "Well, maybe she doesn't know that you had interest in Billy at one time."

She shook her head and fumed. "Oh, she knew I had in the past, and I believe she still thought I fancied him. You should have seen the looks she gave me the whole time. She did it on purpose to get my goat."

I smiled. "Well, the best thing you can do is to let it roll right off your back. Then, she won't get any satisfaction out of it."

She nodded. "I suppose. It's so annoying."

I thought about it. "You know what I would do? Kill her with kindness. Treat her like your best friend. She won't know what to make of you."

She groaned, "Man, school is going to be out in a couple of weeks. I thought I'd be through with these people."

I laughed. "You know the problem with working in our business. I can't take you out for ice cream to make everything okay. After working with it for eight hours, you'd probably throw it in my face."

We walked arm in arm the rest of the way home, both pondering how to get out of the fine messes we'd gotten ourselves into.

I had to get through a nine-to-five Sunday workday, and I'd be home-free for my Monday and Tuesday weekend. Granted, I hadn't worked a full week last week due to circumstances out of my control, but that couldn't be helped now. It wasn't like I hadn't had my share of stress. I'd spent my first two nights in jail ever. That had to count for something.

About halfway through the day, Sean appeared at my window, which I initially thought would be great, until I saw the sour look on his face. It suddenly hit me that Tom had contacted him, and I hadn't even warned him that would be happening. But to be honest, he looked even madder than that. I felt tempted to tell him I couldn't take a break right now, but Shelby dutifully stepped up, leaving me no choice but to face the music.

I exited through the employee door, working on a credible story, but I knew I'd never make it in time. Even admitting I wasn't a good girlfriend might not be enough to survive this one. He looked hot.

When I got outside, I tried to kiss him, and he turned his head and backed away, never a good sign. He started talking immediately. "Why is your family sic'ing a private investigator on me? Did they find out that I'm seeing you, and they want to get dirt on me so that they can eliminate me from the relationship? Are they trying to slander me around the community, so I lose all my patients and have to relocate to Scottsdale, Arizona?"

I wasn't sure where to start. I tried to keep it light. "Um, none of the above?"

He fumed. "Oh, come on, Cordelia, don't get all cute and sweet with me when you very well knew that he would contact me. He told me that you did."

I nodded. "Well, yes I did, but he's a friend of the family. He's trying to gather as much information as possible to assist in the defense. I know it's a pain, but I promised him you'd meet with him, so can you be a sweetie and do it."

His face reddened. "So, when did this come up? Why didn't you mention it the other night?"

I took his hand. "I had other things on my mind."

He wasn't buying it. "This is really bad timing. I've got stuff going on with the practice. I've got a woman suing me for malpractice. I've got lawyers all over the place. This is the last thing I need."

I tried to be a good girlfriend, but this started to get annoying. "Okay, I get it, Sean, but put yourself in my shoes for a minute. I know I don't act like it because I choose not to, but I'm scared to death. I'm out on bail for first degree murder. I think that trumps your malpractice. Now, if you could buck it up and take care of this, I'd really appreciate it."

He hesitated, then said, "Fine," and walked away

I whispered to myself as I walked back to the Ice Cream stand. "I've dated this guy less than two weeks, and we've already had three major fights. We won't need to fight for a year once we finally get together."

I held my breath that I didn't hear anything from either Tom or Sean for the rest of the workday, so I felt encouraged when I saw no new texts on my phone as Shelby and I walked home.

She seemed a little lost in her thoughts as we walked.

I asked, "Is everything okay? You've been spending a lot of time on your Garnet Gulls graduation documents lately. Is there anything I can help with?"

She said, "Well, to save on cost this year they are holding the graduation in the gym. So, what that means is that every graduate is limited to only two immediate family members."

I suddenly saw her dilemma. She felt disloyal to me and didn't know how to exclude me without feeling bad. I smiled. "I understand that there's no room for me at your graduation, Shel. I'm really flattered that you want me there."

She shook her head. "Well, Cord, it's not that exactly. I don't want my parents there. They haven't been a part of my life for months. They are being totally unsupportive of me right now. I don't feel like it would be honest of me even to have them there. It would be fake."

I considered the ramifications of that. "I understand how you feel today, but how about twenty years from now when I'm a faded memory, and you have a lifetime of regret that you didn't have your parents at your graduation?"

She thought about that. "I'll give it some thought, Cord." She hugged me. "I knew you would help me think about it differently. I felt so stuck in my anger. Maybe you're right. I should at least talk to them about it."

I smiled. "There's my girl."

She changed the subject. "So I saw you and Sean talking out there. It didn't look good."

I nodded. "Yeah, Tom went to talk to him. Sean thought he should have caught a break since we were dating. Evidently, he's got some legal stuff going on with the practice, and this is the last thing he needs right now."

She shook her head. "I'm sorry, but that's pretty lame compared to what you're going through. Did you come to an agreement?"

I thought about it. "Well, sort of. I guess the next time I see him, we'll see what 'Fine' meant."

She chuckled. "You two are a piece of work. I wonder if you just have so much spark, you're always going to ignite into flames, or if you're so hot that you're going to burn out like a candle that burns so fast, it's gone in one evening."

I looked at her. "Do you think those are the only two alternatives?"

She nodded. "Well, it's certainly not going to be a casual relationship under any circumstances. That's clear."

I laughed. "It reminds me of a song from years ago; my sister had the CD. I think it might have been from a band called Semisonic, a song called 'Chemistry.' This verse kind of reminds me of us: 'So for a while, we conducted experiments in an apartment by the River Road. And we found that the two things we put together had a bad tendency to explode.'"

She smiled. "Hey, at least it's not boring. That was Sally's concern about Sean. Maybe there's something to be said for that. Hopefully, this is just another bump in the road. I get why Sean, as your boyfriend, would have wanted to be trusted instead of being treated like some random person on the street. It's a tough call for sure."

As we got near the house, I suggested, "Hey, why don't you stop by your parents' house and talk about the graduation. It's probably about time you had a face-to-face chat anyway, and it's been long enough for tempers to have cooled."

She nodded. "Okay, wish me luck."

"Good luck," I yelled behind her as I continued home. I hoped the timing was good because I valued Shelby's company, and I would miss her a lot if she ended up going back to her parents' house. I crossed my fingers.

CHAPTER THIRTY-TWO

From the time I got home without Shelby, the clock seemed to slow nearly to a stop while she discussed her graduation with her parents. I clearly hadn't admitted to myself how important our relationship had become to me. I paced the kitchen, checking my watch every five minutes, wondering if she would ever return.

Finally, after I'd been home nearly an hour, which felt like about four, she breezed through the kitchen door and immediately sat at the table, grinning.

I stared at her and asked, "So? How'd it go?"

She seemed excited. "It went great. We didn't argue. They were both understanding. They spoke to me like an adult. They weren't demanding. It felt like the perfect visit."

I went immediately into suspicious mode but kept my mouth shut. I forced myself to be positive. "That's so good. I'm happy to hear it. So, what's the final result? Are they coming to the graduation?"

She nodded. "Yes, they wanted to go. Are you still okay with that?"

I should have no problem with that. "Yes, they are your parents. I hope I can get graduation pictures here, though, before you go?" I could feel my heart tug a little bit, even with the short time she had lived with me. I asked, "How did the rest of the visit go? Are they still okay with you living here?"

She smiled. "Well, we mostly talked around that. I could tell my mom wasn't thrilled about it, but didn't want to get into an argument that might put the graduation ceremony in jeopardy, so she let it go for now. I'm not under any illusion that she actually supports it. Once I graduate, I expect a full-court press to get me home, including the continued threat of tuition withholding. But, what she doesn't know is that I've already applied and been approved for enough financial aid to get through at least my first two years of Community College. I've already been accepted to Brookdale at Wall, which is my closest option, and I have the financial aid to cover it, so that's what I'm doing. After two years, I'll decide what University I want to attend and figure it out."

I stood up and ran around the table. I gave her a huge hug. "So, you're going to stay here at least another two years? That is the best news I've had in like forever. I thought your parents would entice you back to their house with money and gifts."

She got an odd look on her face. "Well, I do have a kind of favor to ask. I am saving every paycheck, but I don't know if I'll be able to afford a car by the time school starts. Do you think I can borrow yours if I need to?"

I smiled. "Absolutely. I barely use my Jeep. Someone might as well use it. She's sad sitting there day after day. I know you're going to want your own car at some point, but saving for a good one makes sense rather than blowing all your cash on a crappy one and then having to spend all your money on repair bills all the time. I should know. I've been there."

My cell phone rang. My caller ID said: *Tom.* I said, "Tommy, are you still in town? I wasn't sure of your plan?"

He laughed. "First of all, you're the first person I've let get away with calling me 'Tommy' since my mom right before I graduated second grade, but it feels right with you for some reason. Second, I wanted to stop by and give you a wrap-up before I left town. Are you around?"

I pointed to the phone and mouthed, "Tom," to Shelby.

She nodded and gave me the thumbs up.

I responded happily, "Sure, I'll be here. Give me a few minutes to get cleaned up. I worked at the ice cream parlor all day. Let's say 6?"

He agreed. "Okay. Can I bring a pizza?"

I felt starving. "Perfect. Thanks." I smiled as I hung up.

Shelby started at me. "Wow, I see what you meant about dangerous. That guy lit you up like a Christmas tree. And seriously? Tommy? And now he's bringing pizza for the wrap-up? I guess I'd be a bit concerned, too, if I were Sean. You'd better watch your step."

I blushed. "This is a simple debriefing. Nothing more, nothing less."

She smiled. "Then you won't mind if I stay down here and share a little pizza?"

I nodded nervously. "Of course not. The more, the merrier." I tried to convince myself that it would be fine. He would give me much-needed information to help the defense team during the preliminary hearing before returning to Upstate New York. Then, what were these butterflies about? I headed upstairs to shower, do my hair, change, and remind myself this wasn't a date.

As I dried and curled my hair, I threw on my favorite off-the-shoulder one-piece beach romper. It showed enough but not too much. It might be a little much for a business meeting, but it felt like summer, and what was the point of living on the beach if I couldn't dress as if I did.

He arrived five minutes later. When he came in with the pizza, he said, "Wow," then shifted his glance to Shelby and said, "Hi, I don't believe we've met. I'm Tom."

She shook his hand. "Smooth transition. Nice to meet you. Cord said that I could stay and hear your presentation."

He nodded. "Perfect. I'm putting my thoughts together, so that'll give me a chance to summarize them for an audience." He seemed disappointed not to meet with me alone, so it was probably a good strategy to have Shelby there. I had enough boyfriend issues right now.

I smiled and repeated, "Perfect."

He opened the pizza box. "Everyone, please grab pizza while I go through what I learned while I visited for the weekend."

Shelby and I grabbed a piece and started eating while Tom settled into his presentation.

He opened up a laptop where he had presumably taken notes. "Okay, I visited the local police department first. I always find that to be an interesting starting point. It gives me a grounding point and a chance to see the police's attitude toward my client, in this case, you."

I smiled, "So, what do they think of me?"

He responded enthusiastically. "For the most part, you got positive marks, which I can say is highly unusual in my experience for a defendant, especially for a defendant in a double-first-degree murder case. They thought you were a polite and model prisoner during the short period you were incarcerated in the local holding cell."

I nodded. "I also felt respected and well-treated there."

He continued. "That's good to hear too. You have no idea how your behavior as a prisoner can impact your outcome in court later on. There have been multiple studies done on this. After all, we are only dealing with people here, and you can never separate that from the case. People have very long memories.

"Here's an example. Let's say that you are a cop, and you arrest a suspect, and the suspect knees you in the groin when he's being loaded into the squad car during the arrest. You can see that you started the relationship with this suspect on the wrong foot. Now, you might 'accidentally' hit his head on the vehicle when getting him out of the vehicle. Now, you two might trade verbal barbs while he is in custody several times before the arraignment. What is your attitude going to be toward this suspect by the arraignment?"

Shelby responded. "Not good, and that's going to stick with both of them."

He nodded. "Right, and that could have an impact on the outcome of the trial, even though all of this happened well after whatever alleged crime was committed."

That impressed me. "I never even thought about this kind of stuff. Good thing I'm a naturally respectful person."

I asked, "Were you able to get access to the ballistics reports?"

He rolled his eyes, smiling. "You are dying to take the wind out of my sails, aren't you?"

I smiled. "Well, honestly, someone has to."

He gave me a look that probably meant to stop flirting in front of Shelby. "Yes, I did. We were able to confirm that the Colt revolver is the murder weapon in the death of Martin William Raven, but not Rachel Lynne Gaston."

I asked, "Do they know what killed her?"

He nodded. "It's a bullet consistent with a Glock 9 mm, the kind that Martin William Raven referred to during his interrogation. So, even though we don't have the weapon, we know that it's possible that a similar Glock was used."

I nodded. "Interesting." I thought of a question. "Do they know who registered the Colt revolver?"

He checked his notes. "Let me check exactly what they said." He scrolled through a few more pages. "Okay, it's officially a stolen weapon registered to Steven Mark Stevens from right here in Point Pleasant Beach."

I scratched my head. "Who's he?"

He shrugged. "No idea. I tried to call him but had to leave a voicemail."

I asked, "Well, obviously, the police have to have spoken to him. What did they have on him?"

He gave me a blank look. "They haven't been able to speak with him either."

I felt frustrated. "Don't you think that's odd? This guy couldn't be bothered to come into the local police station to confirm the identity of his stolen weapon?"

He agreed. "Of course, I think it's odd, and I intend to follow up with the guy, but there was only so much I could do while at the police station. I think I did pretty well."

I patted him on the back. "Oh, I'm sorry, didn't I give you enough kudos for pretty much getting what I could have done by walking a couple of blocks and spending a half-hour."

He seemed ready to move on. "Okay, smart girl, let's move on to the Food Shack. Since I know everything you got and who you spoke to, I'll concentrate only on what you didn't get."

I agreed. "That sounds very efficient."

He looked proud to have unearthed something I'd evidently missed.

"There is a very important employee who cleans the restrooms daily, the showers twice daily in the bathhouse, and deep cleans the kitchen bi-weekly in the restaurant. The kitchen closing and opening staff does the daily cleaning of the kitchen. Her name is Yvette, and she pretty much works seven days a week. And sometimes she sees things, and sometimes she hears things, and she's often invisible."

That excited me. "That's great. I thought I'd gotten everyone. Great job." I completely meant it.

He savored the moment. "She told me she saw the man who shot Rachel Lynne Gaston."

I wanted to be sure I heard him correctly. "The *man* who shot her? Then that couldn't be me, then, could it?" I could have kissed him. I asked, "Can she identify him?"

He shook his head. "Other than his gender, probably not. She only saw him from behind."

I smiled. "But it's still good for me. Right?"

He searched for the words. "Well, maybe."

I got a sinking feeling. "Why maybe?"

He continued. "She's not exactly legal."

I got it. "She's an illegal alien?" I thought I remembered something. "Wait, that shouldn't matter. Right? Wasn't there a court ruling that they couldn't deport you for testifying for a defendant in court'"

He nodded. "Yes, it's illegal in Federal Court for an alien to be harassed or otherwise deported from this country simply because they have been identified as an illegal alien in a court proceeding." He considered this. "But most illegals either don't know this or don't believe it."

I wondered, "Even though she didn't see him from the front, did she have any impressions: height, weight, hair color, body type, clothing, anything?"

He smiled. "I know how you feel. I tried to get everything I could from her. I even tried some of my high school Spanish, but I got nothing. I'll keep working on her. I also figure if she saw someone, maybe someone else did." He almost redeemed himself. "I did record the conversation so I could get it translated, so maybe there's hope."

CHAPTER THIRTY-THREE

He outlined the rest of his day, not turning up anything monumental other than Yvette, who, it appeared, would probably leave town if compelled to testify. Then he seemed ready to talk about Sean. He rolled his eyes. "Okay, last but not least is your boyfriend. Boy, he is a piece of work."

I already felt offended. "Why's that, because he's not you." I tried to keep my emotions in check. I took a deep breath and let it out slowly.

He looked me in the eye. "He didn't like me or anything about me. He made that clear from the first second we made contact. He proceeded to tell me why I wasted his time, why he didn't appreciate it. He spent probably a half-hour with me describing where he'd been when the murders took place. It seemed all well and good. I didn't believe a word he said."

I stood up, put my hands on my hips. "Now hold on right there. Are you being completely objective, or are you being super hard on him?"

He looked at me like I'd gone crazy. "He was the unreasonable one. I asked the questions I ask everyone. He took them all personally like he'd been hand-selected as the loser of the year." He thought about it. "If you asked me, he acted extremely sensitively, as if he had something to hide."

I decided to stop pacing. I sat down at the table. "Are you sure you both didn't have a little too much testosterone going on? Maybe you should call it a 'draw.'"

He thought for a second. "I don't know, Cordelia. Maybe you're right. I did feel awfully jealous every time he referred to you as his girlfriend. I think he did it on purpose, and it did get to me. And, I know I have no right to feel that way, but I do,"

Shelby stood up and headed for the stairs. "I'm out. I'll see you in the morning, Cord. Nice meeting you, Tom."

Tom smiled in her direction. "Nice meeting you too."

I closed my eyes for a second, then opened them, staring into Tom's. "Tom, I like you. I really do, and I sense that you know it. Damn you. But I'm not in a place where I can act on that right now. There are many reasons that we would both regret that. So, let's try to get through this and stay friends. Okay?"

He nodded. "Okay. Whatever it takes." He continued. "Anyway, all I can report on my interview with Sean is that it ended up being inconclusive,"

I smiled. "Thanks for trying. I appreciate it anyway. I'm sure my parents do, too."

He looked uncomfortable. "I can't honestly say that I would rule him out for foul play. He seems a little squirrelly to me. But maybe you're messing up my radar. I know that outfit isn't helping."

I looked down. "Oh, this old thing."

He stood up. "Well, I'm going to use this opportunity to head back upstate. I'm sure we'll be in touch over the next couple of weeks. Do you have a preliminary hearing date yet?"

I checked the calendar. "Yes, it's the 15th, three days before Shelby's graduation. That should be quite a week. I would love to find out it's not going to trial."

He headed toward the door. "Well, that's pretty rare. Most prosecutors will stop at nothing to prove that there should be a trial even if they have no case. But stranger things have happened. See you in a couple of weeks."

I waved. "Fingers crossed." I watched his car back out, wondering how things would have been if we'd met under different circumstances.

The Monday night wine group had begun to gather in the living room the next evening. Mo and Jackie had each come with a new friend as a result of our social experiment. It seemed remarkable what happened when you rejoined the world and got off your phone. The results were shocking. We might need to slow down, or we could run out of space.

Mo introduced me. "Cordelia, these are our new friends, Natasha and Olivia. They live right down the street from me. Jackie and I took a walk in the neighborhood and met them."

Natasha spoke with an Eastern European accent. "It was miracle. We live here for year, and no one speak to us. Mo and Jackie were so friendly and nice. And now they bring us to you. This is best time since we move here from Czech Republic. Thank you."

I smiled. "I think you will like anyone you meet here. It's our goal to expand our horizon of friends. We started the idea in this house, and we won't be happy until the house is full of happy wine-drinking women." I handed them each a glass. "My sisters will be here soon. I challenged them to bring a new friend, too. We'll see if they succeeded." I hoped they would be on their best behavior.

Just then, my cell phone rang: Sean. I answered on the first ring. "Hey, there, what are you up to?"

He sounded okay, which surprised me after the whole Tom episode. "I knew you were off for your 'weekend,' I hoped we could get together since you work on normal people's weekends."

In the rush to get everything ready for tonight, I wasn't sure if I'd ever even filled him in about the No Longer Desperate Winers. I guessed I hadn't. I went into the kitchen. "I'm sorry. I think I forgot to mention a Monday evening tradition I have going here with a few of my friends. We're about trying to meet new friends and drink wine. But unfortunately, it's women only."

He sounded a little annoyed. "So, you're not available at all?"

I smiled, trying to make it sound fun. "Nope, in fact, it's a sleepover. All innocent fun. Believe me; I could use some about now."

His voice softened. "Okay, I get it. Can I reserve a little time with you tomorrow anyway? I've got a couple of sessions in the morning, but it's a light afternoon."

I had no idea therapists didn't have to work all day, every day. What a racket.

I agreed. "Yes, sweetheart. I'll be available all day, just for you. Whatever you want to do. Come up with something fun. Let's make an afternoon of it. Maybe we can go down to Cape May or something."

He sounded excited. "That's my girl; I'm happy to hear the excitement in your voice. I know things have been tough for you, and I haven't always been helping. Yes, I'll plan an afternoon in Cape May. I'll pick you up at Noon."

I agreed. "Okay, see you then," happy to have dodged a relationship bullet.

I went back to the front room as Katie and Lily arrived, friendless. I commented. "Hey guys, the goal was to see how many new friends you could bring to tonight's party."

Katie said, "Yeah, about that. I don't think Westchester County is as friendly as down here. We didn't have much luck. In fact, people looked at us like we were trying to abduct them to another planet."

Knowing how aggressive Katie could be, I suggested, "Maybe, I can help with your approach. How many times did you try?"

Lily said, "We tried the approach that Jackie and Mo used, walking around the neighborhood. It worked for them."

I saw their problem. "I'm not sure that's duplicatable everywhere with everyone. You might want to try striking up a conversation in line at the store, at the hairdressers, or while waiting to get your car serviced. Just do something non-phone related. You might be surprised."

They both nodded. Lily said, "Okay. Maybe we were hoping for too much, too soon."

I agreed. "Yes, sometimes a short conversation can grow into a longer one the next time you see the person, and it can grow into a friendship over time. This isn't a sprint; it's a marathon. Just remember to lose the phone."

I brought them over to where the other four were congregated, talking and laughing. "Hey, these are my sisters, Lily and Katie. This is

Natasha and Olivia. They are our newest members. Olivia, can you tell us something about yourself?"

She smiled. "Yes, I just learn English after I move here, so I sometimes struggle with word. But I happy to be with you today. Natasha and me are best friend, and we save all our money to move here. We are so happy to be here now and not Eastern Europe, where we come from. We enjoy the freedom of this country and how friendly people are here. Thank you for welcoming us."

Katie was on her best behavior. "We welcome you with open arms and are happy to have you here. You should be happy you came to New Jersey and not New York, where we live. I think you'll be far happier here."

Lily gave her a look and took over. "We may not always agree in this country, but we always agree that it's better to be free than not to be free. I, for one, would love to hear more about your country and the lessons you learned living there and moving here."

I sighed, "Or we could keep the discussion completely casual, non-political, and enjoy the wine." I dug out board games, which I thought would be a lot more fun than a lot of heavy conversation. My Gram had a huge collection of board games. "We have Monopoly, Scrabble, Trivial Pursuit, Sorry, Trouble, Jenga, Yahtzee, Pictionary, Uno, Clue, Life, and several decks of playing cards. We even have chess and checkers for those of you who are really old school." And we were off to game land for the rest of the night.

CHAPTER THIRTY-FOUR

Waking up at 6 a.m. on Tuesday morning, I found the floor of my room covered with blankets, sleeping bags, pillows, and bodies, as well as my bed. My sisters decided that my bed was a far more comfortable place to sleep than the floor, so we were all on it. It wasn't an unfamiliar place, as we often ended up together during a severe thunderstorm, on Christmas eve, or other times when we felt lonely.

From the middle, I needed to crawl down and off the end, since Lily and Katie were on either side of me, so I could go downstairs and make coffee. I peered over the end, ensuring I wasn't stepping on anyone as I crawled out. Luckily, I found a clear path through the ocean of blankets and sleeping bags to the door.

When I got down to the kitchen, it surprised me to find Shelby at the table. I put my arms on her shoulders and peered at her laptop screen. "Hey, girly, what's up with you?"

She yawned. "I'm trying to figure out what courses to take once I start college."

I laughed. "You haven't even graduated yet. Why are you up at 6 a.m., working on this now?"

She sounded frustrated. "I feel like my life is on hold. I want to make sure I don't miss any deadlines. I got a reminder in my email to get my schedule set up because classes fill up soon. I started to panic that I'd get closed out of the classes that I wanted."

I wasn't sure. "Where do you stand on the timing of your financial aid?"

She hesitated. "Well, it's supposed to come any time."

I nodded. "So, you don't have it yet? I'll bet that's not helping you sleep." I went to my purse, which sat on the counter, and dug out my wallet. I pulled out my credit card and said, "Here, use this. We'll settle up later."

She looked at me with disbelief. "You can't do that. What if the financial aid falls through?"

I chuckled. "Then I guess I'm out three thousand dollars. I've wasted money on less important things than you in the past. I'd consider it an investment."

She looked panic-stricken. "What if I fail or drop out or—"

I put my hand on her shoulder. "Don't worry. You'll be fine."

She stood up and hugged me. "Thank you so much for your confidence, Cord. You make me feel so much more of an adult than my parents ever do."

I smiled. "And, that's exactly how we become adults." I let her go. "Now, get that done before I change my mind." I went to make coffee, feeling like a proud mother. My phone sat plugged in on the kitchen counter to make my point of leaving the phones out of the mix last evening. A text came through, which I thought odd at this time of day.

It came from Tom. It read, "Hey, Cordelia, could you text me when you get this. I think this is your day off. Can you maybe do me a favor and interview the guy who had the gun stolen, Steven Mark Stevens. He's retired and available all day and doesn't appear to live too far from you. Just find out anything you can about the theft, when it happened, if he has any suspects, that kind of thing. Thanks."

I responded. "No problem. I'll get in touch with him this morning."

He replied. "Thanks. It's good to have someone on the team who's willing to help. That's a rarity in my business."

I responded. "I'll let you know what I find out."

Shelby noticed me texting. "Hmm, isn't this a 'put down your phone' event?"

I smiled. "Yeah, last night was. That ship has sailed. Besides, Tom needs help with an interview. A guy who had the murder weapon that killed Martin stolen from him."

She made fun of me. "Ooh, Tom's texting you at 6 a.m. That's interesting."

I brushed it off as nothing. "He wanted to get a jump on it before I got my day started, I'm sure."

She didn't comment. "Okay, I'm all set." She handed me back the credit card.

I took it and put it back in my purse, saying, "Thanks." I sat at my laptop, looking up Steven Mark Stevens, the gun owner. Sure enough, he had a Linked-in Account that listed his full name and his home address on his resume. He lived at 280 Laurel Court. Just down from Sean. I wondered if they knew one another. His phone number was listed, so I wrote it down. I figured that calling at 6:30 might not be good form, although you never knew with a retiree.

I figured I'd try him at 7. In the meantime, I wanted to formulate a few questions. I said to Shelby, "Hey, can you type these on Word and print them out? That would save me a ton of work. And if you don't pay me back, I could take like twenty-five dollars off your tab."

She rolled her eyes. "We aren't going to be doing that with everything from now on until you get paid back, right?"

I put my finger on my chin. "I thought it might be fun."

She shook her head. "No, that would not be fun." She winced.

I relented. "Okay, I'll be good. Anyway, I'm brainstorming, but write down what I say, and then we can edit if we have to. Number one, how long has your gun been missing? Number two, is this the only gun you had that has gone missing? Three, but this is only applicable if he answered 'no' to number two. What other gun or guns have gone missing, and did they go missing simultaneously? Four, have you talked to anyone about your guns, either before or after the gun or guns went missing? Five, are you a gun user, collector, or both? Six, where do you store your gun or guns? Seven, did you report your lost or stolen gun or guns to the police? If so, when?"

She looked at the screen. "Okay, anything you want me to edit, or did you get it on the first take?"

I pulled my chair closer to hers and reviewed her screen. "It looks great. You can print it as it is. You saved me a ton of work."

She teased me. "More than Twenty-five dollars' worth?"

I chuckled. "I'll tell you what. I'll make you breakfast. Pancakes, bacon, and eggs okay?"

She jumped up and hugged me. "Oh, yes! I'm starving but too lazy to bother."

By the time my cooking got fully underway, people had started wandering in as the aroma of bacon made its way upstairs. Just like it happened when we were kids, Lily came downstairs first. It would take Katie at least another half-hour to join us.

Lily yawned as she hung off my shoulder. She looked for the plate. "Where is the bacon?"

I smiled. "It's still in the pan. But you can't eat it all before everyone comes down."

She grinned. "I know. But I can have one piece, right?"

I nodded. "Yes, one piece."

Within an hour, everyone had come downstairs, and were having coffee and eating breakfast. Something could be said for having a sleepover that accelerated friendship building. We had no more of the shyness and politeness that dominated the first hour or so. The gloves were off, and we all were now more like sisters than strangers. It did my heart good to see how quickly we had progressed. The kitchen rang with laughter. As we finished breakfast, people started heading home.

I hugged everyone on their way out the door. I yelled to everyone remaining. "Hey, don't forget we will be here again next week, and our goal is for everyone to bring a new friend until we run out of space."

After eight, I called Steven Mark Stevens. He answered on the first ring. "Stevens here"

I tried to sound friendly. "Mr. Stevens, I'm working with Handy Investigation to get information regarding your stolen firearm related to the death of Martin William Raven. Would you have any availability this morning?"

He hesitated. "Yes, can you meet at ten? I have an appointment at eleven."

I nearly jumped up and down. "That sounds great. I can come to you if that would help. Are you still at 280 Laurel Court?"

He agreed. "Yes, I guess there are no secrets on the Internet."

I smiled. "I'll see you at ten."

CHAPTER THIRTY-FIVE

Mr. Stevens had a youthful look for a retiree. I would have pegged him in his fifties, but you can never tell age these days. He welcomed me into his two-story traditional Jersey Beach home, which also appeared to have a built-in pool in the back yard with a pool house.

He led me toward the rear of the home, to the kitchen, in a similar location to the one in my house. He gave me a broad smile. "I have to admit that I expected a tough, chewed-up and spit-out ex-cop, riding out her last few years before her pension kicked in. So, excuse me while I put my eyes back in my head."

I blushed nine shades of red. I said, "Thank you, Sir, I think."

He apologized. "I'm sorry. I didn't mean to embarrass you. My messed-up expectation of you surprised me more than anything you actually did. You just looked young and pretty." He smiled and decided to change the subject. "Anyway, so you're here to talk about weapons. I have to give you credit. The police have yet to visit me, and they literally are located less than a hundred footsteps from here"

I pulled out my questions. "Thanks for seeing me so soon. My name is Cordelia Corbett. We are actually neighbors. I live up on Trenton

Avenue."

He looked at me wide-eyed. "You're Catherine's granddaughter. I should have seen the family resemblance. I am so sorry about your loss."

I nodded. "Thank you. She was a wonderful woman, and she's still with us."

He smiled. "Well, now I certainly will provide you anything I have that you need. Your grandmother led a big part of this community. She will be greatly missed." He thought for a minute. "Wait, did I hear that you were arrested for the murders? That didn't make sense to me when I heard it. Now that I've met you, it makes even less sense."

I decided to get into my questions and referred to the sheet in front of me. I asked, "Is it okay if I ask you a few specific questions?"

He nodded. "Absolutely," apparently forgiving me for ignoring his question about the murder.

I started my questioning, reading from my list. "How long has your gun or guns been missing?"

He stood and went to a wall calendar. "About two months ago, I noticed them missing. I store them in the pool house, and I don't go in there all the time, so all I can say is that it was two months ago when I noticed they were gone. They could have been missing longer."

Number two was easy. I asked, "You said 'them,' so you didn't lose just one gun. How many guns do, or did, you have, and how many were stolen?"

He looked embarrassed. "I have collected many guns over the years and felt that they were safe, locked in gun cabinets in the pool house. My record-keeping has not been all that great since I never expected any of them to be stolen. I have done my best to cross-reference my weapons, but there may be one or two that I can't match. As of right now, I have fifty-five handguns. I believe that at least five of them were stolen."

The number came as a surprise. "Wow, have any others shown up in crimes until now?"

He shook his head. "No. Not that I've been told anyway."

I just thought of something. "Did you have a Glock 17, 9 mm?"

He brightened. "Yes, one of my favorites ever. It broke my heart. Did you find it?"

I shook my head. "No, but it's likely that it had been used in the other beach murder where we have no weapon."

He wondered, "I'm curious. How do you know that gun had been used for that murder?"

I wasn't sure how much to tell him. "Martin William Raven told me the day he got killed that a man had given him that gun. I think in an attempt to frame him for the murder. And even though the gun hasn't been found, the bullet in Rachel Lynne Gaston's body was consistent with a bullet of that caliber."

I asked, "Could you show me where you store the guns?" On the way out past the pool, I asked, "So, are you just a collector, or do you use them too."

He laughed. "Oh, I used to do a bit of target practicing in my day, but now I just look at them."

I referred to my list. "Do many people know these guns are back here?"

He thought for a minute, "No, a few family members I told since they look after the place sometimes when I travel. But no one else would have a reason to." He joked, "Well, I told my therapist once before my ex-wife moved out just in case." He thought about it and chuckled. "I guess it wasn't that funny."

I smiled. "Certainly not if you were her." I checked my notes to make sure I'd asked everything. "So, sir, I only have one more question, did you report everything that you told me to the police?"

He thought about it. "Well, not everything because they didn't ask. But I did report the ones stolen that I could identify. It's caused me to improve my storage and identification system, so if I ever do lose another weapon in the future, I'll at least know what I lost, and since I check them regularly, I'll have a better idea of when."

I wondered, "Can I ask you one thing that's been bothering me. If you're living in the house, why do you store them out there?"

He laughed. "I actually did that as a safety measure. At one time, I drank heavily and used to fight with my wife the more I drank. I became increasingly afraid that I might shoot her in a fit of rage. Physical distance from the weapons seemed like the smartest thing." He looked at his watch. "Hey, speaking of anger issues, I've got to see my therapist. Did you have anything else?"

I smiled. "No, I think I have everything I need." I headed toward my car.

He headed up the street toward Sean's house.

I got home before 11, with plenty of time to prepare for our afternoon in Cape May. I wondered if Sean had planned the day or if that would be my job. I jumped on Trip Advisor, looking for the most fun things to do. Of course, they had the beach, but we had one of those here, so next came the lighthouse, which would be a must. I couldn't wait to visit Jersey Shore Alpacas. I wasn't sure that would be Sean's thing, though. I thought he might enjoy the Wildwood Aviation Museum, but I wasn't sure I would.

Similarly, I thought I'd love the Washington Street Mall but thought he might be bored to tears. Finally, I found the answer we had both been looking for, Willow Creek Winery. They had something we both could probably appreciate, alcohol.

He was trained as a psychologist. Did that mean he'd appreciate museums? We could visit the Emlen Physick Estate, a Victorian House and Museum combination. Most men would run in the other direction screaming for a football game or an oil-changing pan, but I had no idea about Sean. Would he enjoy the Historic Cold Spring Village, the Nature Center of Cape May, or the World War II Lookout Tower? It suddenly scared me that I had no idea. I didn't know the first thing about this man's likes or dislikes. And what did he really know about me?

I decided to go upstairs and change again. I'd already changed three times because I had no idea how we would spend our day. My outfit would be completely different for Alpaca petting than for Museum browsing. My turmoil reached a fever pitch when he pulled his Volkswagen into the driveway. What did the fact that he drove a Volkswagen say about him? I didn't have time to look it up on the Internet.

I ran downstairs in white capris, a pink floral blouse, and white sandals. It was my most middle of the road outfit. I could wear it anywhere, and I would fit indoors, outdoors, informal, semi-formal. Well, okay, not semi-formal in the high school dance sense, but sort of business casual.

I nearly forgot to answer the door as I evaluated myself in the full-length mirror in the living room. Finally, I threw caution to the wind and threw the front door open to find Sean standing there, looking confused.

We stared at one another for a second, and finally, he said, "Hi. You were expecting me. Right?"

I tried to look casual. "Of course, silly." I took his hand and led him inside. "How'd your half-day of work go?"

He shrugged. "Oh, you know. Everyone's got problems."

I realized I had no idea. "Actually, I don't. Do you really think *everyone's* got problems? I like to think that most people are pretty happy." From the expression on his face, I knew this wasn't the correct way to negotiate Sean McPherson. I needed to change paths. "Oh, wait, I'm sure you didn't mean that everyone had problems; I took it literally." I needed to change the subject fast. "So, do you know what you want to do in Cape May?"

He looked at me without focusing. "How about we get out of here, and then we can focus on that?"

I glared at him. I didn't like his tone one bit, but if this is how our day would go, I'd be much happier to stay here. I asked him directly, "Bad day at the office?" I tried my best Lucy Ricardo accent.

He didn't get it. "Why are you talking like that?"

I rolled my eyes. "I thought I'd lighten it up, oh never mind." I tried to stop myself, but I couldn't. "Hey, you know what? I don't think this Cape May trip is such a great idea. Maybe we should do it another time. I'm not really in the mood."

He looked me in the eye. "Come on, Cordelia. Not everything can be storybook every hour of every day."

I didn't need to look at him. I headed toward the bedroom stairs. "In my world, they do. So, why don't you go back to your world without me? I think that's what you need right now. Maybe that'll knock a little sense into you."

I didn't look back but heard the door slam and the car door close when I got upstairs. By the time I lay crying on the bed, he had left.

CHAPTER THIRTY-SIX

I wore an orange jumpsuit, and my auburn hair was tangled and unmanageable. I banged my silver cup against the bars of the jail cell. I yelled in my best Nicky Nichols voice. "I need water. Better yet, make it whiskey, a double. I'm gonna be in here for a while."

A prison guard with an all too familiar voice came a long way down a dark hallway. He yelled and carried a nightstick, "Keep it quiet down here, or there's going to be trouble. Serious trouble." I stopped banging my cup, suddenly feeling afraid; I went to hide in my cell, but of course there was no place to hide.

When he arrived at my cell, he smiled a wicked smile through broken teeth, but I still recognized him as Sean, and my blood ran cold.

I sat up straight in bed, sweating. I didn't even realize I'd fallen asleep, but that was a better alternative to being Nicky Nichols in real life. As I struggled to get my bearings, I realized I had but another meaningless fight with Sean in the infancy of our relationship. I couldn't understand the weird chemistry that we had. I still wasn't sure if it was good or bad. I'd withhold judgment until we'd been together for a few more weeks.

I checked the clock: just after two, so I got out of bed, looking for

Shelby. She rarely had full days of school these days. I checked the back bedroom. She lay on her stomach on the bed, doing something on her laptop.

I said, "Hey, girl, what's up?"

She nearly jumped a mile. "Oh, my God, I thought you were in Cape May with Sean."

I smiled. "Yeah, about that, we had another one of our famous fights and didn't go. Do you want to go? We could be down there by three-thirty. I have stuff all mapped out. It involves Alpacas."

She jumped off the bed. "I'm in. I've never met an Alpaca I didn't like. Besides, that cute downtown mall is there. That'll be perfect. Men were never meant for Cape May anyway."

I laughed. "It's funny you should say that. The more I looked at what we could do down there, the more perplexed I became. I settled on a winery. And that would have been fine, but there are wineries everywhere these days."

She hugged me. "It goes to show that you and I make a better couple than you and Sean. I could have told you that."

I agreed. "We certainly don't fight as much."

She nodded. "I know. Watching you two makes me never want to be in a relationship. It seems way too complicated."

I thought about it. "Yeah, maybe it's not supposed to be. I guess we'll see. Anyway, let's talk in the Jeep; we've got an hour and a half to solve the world's issues."

As soon as we merged onto the Garden State Parkway, Shelby got quiet, and I knew she must be thinking about something.

"Hey, Cord, I've been thinking about something. Ever since I set up my parents to attend my graduation, it hasn't felt right. You are the person in my life right now, taking care of things, taking care of me. You handed me your credit card for tuition, no questions asked. You don't know if that student aid will ever come, and you don't care. That's who you are to me. I want you at my graduation. And if my parents can't go as a result, so be it."

I thought of something. "Hey, do you have any friends who are only using one ticket?"

She bit her lip. "I thought of that, but people are scalping them for other family members. It's ridiculous. I've asked around but haven't found anything. And I know I get two tickets, and there's only one of you, but I can't imagine only one of my parents going." She looked like she might cry. "I don't know what to do, Cord."

I didn't want to make it worse. "Let's keep it the way it is, and if you find another ticket, I'll go. If I can't actually go to the ceremony, I'll be right outside waiting to take pictures. How does that sound?"

She nodded. "Okay, and then we can go somewhere for lunch or something, okay?"

I agreed. "Perfect." I changed the subject. "Hey, check out Trip Advisor. That's where I got ideas for the Cape May day trip. See if there's anything else you'd like to do. I'm pretty sure the lighthouse is the centerpiece. We should definitely go there."

She got out her phone and agreed. "Yeah, I've heard that." She looked at me. "So, you've never been to Cape May, either? What kind of Jersey girls are we?"

I laughed. "North Jersey girls, I guess."

She checked the list of things to do. "I would vote for everything in the top ten except for the Naval Air Station and, of course, the winery. Well, I wouldn't mind going to the winery, but I don't want to get you in trouble."

I tsked her. "Oh, tell me you aren't drinking. That's all I need to hear. I'll be sending you back to your parents' house quicker than the police can say 'you're under arrest for contributing to the delinquency of a minor.'"

She protested. "But, I'm not a minor."

I agreed with the hypocrisy of it. "Well, true, except for the drinking part. I'm not a big fan of having different ages for different things, to be honest. I mean, you can vote and join the army at eighteen, but you can't drink alcohol until twenty-one? Who thought that would be a good idea?"

She nodded. "Not me. Not that I like to drink all that much, but a glass of wine here or there wouldn't kill me."

I looked at her. "Don't even tell me you don't 'drink all that much.' I'm counting on you to be an adult, well actually I'm counting on you to stay a kid a few more years."

She smiled. "Okay, Cord. Don't worry. I'll be fine."

I made a hand-to-eye-to-eye motion and mock-glared at her. "I've got my eye on you, girl." I felt like a terrible parent.

We rode in silence for a while. Finally, I asked, "So, where are we going first?"

She looked at her phone. "I think we have to start with the lighthouse. That'll give us our bearings and a start at the most popular visitor's destination other than the beach. And, let's face it, we get enough of the beach in our daily lives."

I agreed. "That sounds like a plan."

Within a few minutes, we were at the Cape May Point State Park, poised to climb the 199 steps to the top of the lighthouse. I asked, "How are you with heights?"

She looked straight up, nervously. "Well, it looks a lot taller this close than it did from a distance. Are you sure about this?"

I smiled. "Absolutely. We can do this." When we stepped inside, my knees suddenly weakened. The white metal circular stairs ran up the middle of the 162-year-old structure. You could see right through them all the way to the top, which meant, from the top, you'd be able to see all the way to the bottom.

She looked over at me. "Are you okay?"

I closed my eyes for a second and forced them open. "Um, I'm okay. I'm not great, though. I wasn't expecting to feel this queasy."

She smiled at me and took my hand. "I have an idea. Let's hold hands, and don't look up or down. Just look straight ahead. It's only 199 steps. Take it one step at a time."

I nodded. "Okay. Let's do it." It sounded much easier, taking it one step at a time. Once again, she seemed wise beyond her years. I took her hand. We started up the stairs. They had a railing in the middle of the narrow sets of stairs. I let go of her hand and held both railings, which worked fine until we came upon a couple descending about halfway up between periodic landings. I briefly panicked as I almost walked head-on into them since I refused to look up.

Shelby took control of the situation, encouraging me to turn sideways toward the center handrail as they passed by. Finally, within a few minutes, we were at the top. I hugged Shelby for helping me and spoke. "Thank you so much for getting me to the top. The view is beautiful. It would have been a shame to have missed it."

After walking around the three hundred and sixty-degree outdoor balcony and taking pictures of the stunning views of the New Jersey and Delaware Shores, I knew we'd have to head down eventually, but I didn't want to think about that yet.

We hung around for about fifteen minutes, mostly because I wasn't ready to face the idea of going down. Finally, I took a deep breath. I asked her, "Ready to go down?"

She smiled. "You'll be fine, Cord," she said, filled with confidence.

I stared at the exit as if it might be my life's final challenge. "Okay, let's go."

We started down, using the same concept we used on the way up, but it proved far more difficult on the way down, finding the steps, trying not to look at my feet. Because every time I looked down at my feet to get a foothold, I could see through the stairs, all the way to the bottom, and went into an immediate panic.

Eventually, she suggested, "I'll walk in front of you, obscuring most of your view. Maybe that will help."

And while, admittedly, it worked a little better, it wasn't great, and it took us nearly ten minutes to descend the 199 steps.

When we got to the bottom, Shelby asked, "So, what do you want to do now?"

I chuckled. "How about the Alpacas. They are far closer to the ground."

She smiled. "I can't wait. Let me look at their hours." She hesitated. "Oh, it looks like we are out of luck. They only schedule private tours due to employment issues, and the last one has already been scheduled for today."

I hit the steering wheel. "This economy has ruined everything. Okay, how about the Washington Street Mall?"

She looked it up. "Yes, we are in luck. It's open from ten to ten."

We were back on track. I said excitedly, "Okay, put that in your navigation, so we can do something that's not quite as mind-blowingly frightening while we're here."

She laughed. "I, for one, loved the lighthouse. You seem to have a minor fear of heights."

I rolled my eyes. "That's so weird because heights have never bothered me in the past. I've been on a ton of rides at Six Flags, and I was always fine."

She asked, "Was that before or after you moved to your Gram's house?"

I thought about it. "Well, definitely before."

She put a finger on her chin. "Interesting."

CHAPTER THIRTY-SEVEN

Time flew by until my parents, my sisters, Katie and Lily, my wine-drinking friends Mo, Jackie, Natasha, Olivia, my live-in 'daughter,' Shelby, and my boss-friend, Sally, were all in the Federal Court Building in Trenton for my Preliminary Hearing. Sean had come too but wasn't sitting with the group. We'd had a tough few weeks. We'd dated a few times, but I felt a real tension between us that I hoped getting this hearing out of the way would help resolve.

In a way, the pressure would be on the prosecution today, because they had to prove to the judge that there was sufficient evidence to move forward with a trial. It wasn't that my attorney was a spectator as such, but it was his job to question the credibility of the prosecution's witnesses and the viability of their case.

Paul Thompson was the attorney I wanted for this job. He was smart, credible, and good-looking, and I could tell at our brief appearance at the arraignment that Judge Bongiovanni liked him. She didn't seem all that impressed with the Federal Attorney, but hey, maybe she preferred men. It wasn't for me to say.

There shouldn't be anything that would come as a surprise to Paul today, as the Prosecution had specific requirements to provide all evidence to the defense well in advance of the hearing. He seemed confident as he briefed me at the defense table while awaiting the judge.

I asked, "Will I have to take the stand today?"

He shook his head. "No. Today is for the Prosecution to prove their case. They need solid evidence and facts. The last thing they want is you on the stand. They know as well as we do that you didn't do it. They are trying to get this to trial, so they can possibly get a plea deal."

My mouth hung open. I felt totally out of my element. "If we know I'm innocent and they know I'm innocent, then what is wrong with this picture? Why aren't I just out on the street living my life?"

He looked me in the eye. "Oh, they could never admit that they know you are innocent. They would deny it to the death. The problem they have, though, is because they don't have the real killer; they're going to try that much harder to prove that you are. If they had the real killer, they wouldn't have to try that hard; it would all come together. Understand?"

I looked at him like he'd gone crazy and said, "Honestly, no. None of it makes any sense to me. I always thought the guilty went to prison and the innocent went free. That's what we were taught in school."

He chuckled, "Well, you clearly didn't go to law school."

I almost choked. "No, that wasn't in the cards."

Just then, the judge arrived. The bailiff announced. "Ladies and Gentlemen, please stand for her the Honorable Justice Torianne J. Bongiovanni, United States Magistrate Judge for the District of New Jersey."

We all stood. She motioned for us to be seated, then she sat.

She addressed everyone. "We are here today in the case of the United States Government versus Cordelia C. Corbett to determine if there is sufficient evidence to bring this case to trial. As most of you know, this is a critical case for the law-abiding citizens of the quiet community of Point Pleasant Beach, New Jersey. Point Pleasant Beach certainly doesn't have the notoriety of Wildwood or Atlantic City. That's because it's a small bedroom community of retirees, commuters, and immigrants who came across the ocean a generation or two ago and chose to make New Jersey their home."

She looked around the courtroom to be sure that she had the attention of each and everyone in the room. When she seemed satisfied that she did, she continued. "Cordelia Corbett's family was no different. Her grandmother, Catherine Carrie McDougal Corbett, was an Irish immigrant who came to the United States during the great potato famine. She and her husband worked hard and made good in this country. She only recently died, leaving her home to her favorite granddaughter, Cordelia."

I heard minor stirring in the gallery as my sisters had to be quieted by my mom, even though they knew it was true. I was Gram's favorite.

The judge pondered her kingdom before she spoke again. "Ladies and gentlemen, we are here today to determine if there is enough evidence to move forward with a trial. That can be a daunting task and one that Ms. Novasdebien will not take lightly; I assure you."

She hesitated a full thirty seconds before she spoke again. "This is perhaps the most difficult part of my job. Determining innocence or guilt once a trial has begun is one thing, but we all know that there will be one outcome or the other. But today, I literally have life's continuum in my hands. Does the young lady go to trial, or does she go free? That's a far more mind-blowing choice for me to have to make, and I do not take my responsibility lightly. So, if I seem highly contemplative, or if it seems like I'm asking the same question over and over again, it's because I don't want to get this wrong. Her life depends on it."

She straightened her robe and shifted her attention to the Prosecution table. Ms. Novasdebien, the ball is in your court.

She stood and referred to notes in her hand. After a few seconds, she said, "I would like to call Frank Stoddard from Precision Testing Lab in Toms River, New Jersey."

A studious-looking man with glasses and a bow tie, probably mid-fifties, approached the witness stand, was sworn in, and took his seat.

The Federal Attorney approached the witness stand with a dramatic flourish, surprising all of us, evidently including him. She immediately started questioning him. "Mr. Stoddard, your firm has been tasked with DNA testing in this case, is that correct?"

He nodded. "Yes, ma'am."

She continued. "You ran several tests for inclusivity of the suspect labeled 29-291838. Is that correct?" She noted to the court. "Please note that this label number is consistent with the DNA collected from the defendant at the Point Pleasant Police Department when she was incarcerated there from May 20th and 21st."

I said under my breath to Paul, "I hate this."

He nodded. "I know. Is this necessary?"

She looked at us as if to say there would be more where this came from. "So, what did your tests determine?"

He checked the results in front of him. "The DNA from the samples we took from both victims, and the murder weapon that had been taken from the scene, were all consistent with the sample taken from the defendant."

I whispered to Paul. "That proves what we already know. I touched both victims and the weapon. This is asinine."

He nodded. "I'll address it in cross-examination. Nothing here but yesterday's news."

She asked, "And the weapon had been confirmed to have murdered which victim?"

He responded. "Martin William Raven."

I assumed they had nothing more because I hadn't touched any other weapons, but they surprised me. The Federal Attorney started with a new line of questioning. "There was another weapon discovered on the beach this week not far from the first weapon, is that correct?"

Mr. Stoddard nodded. "That is my understanding."

I poked Paul and whispered, "What is this about? I haven't heard about this?"

He started looking through his notes. His face turned red, whispering back, "They buried this in with the other evidence. We didn't see it."

I glared at him. "But they reported it to you, so there's nothing you can do, right?"

He nodded.

I watched as we heard about it for the first time together.

He continued. "A Glock 17, 9 mm has also been unearthed on the beach, and it is confirmed to be the murder weapon of Rachel Lynne

Gaston."

There was a singular gasp from the gallery. The judge glared at them, daring them to make more noise. They fell silent.

Jacqueline Novasdebien was on a roll and enjoying her show. She continued her questioning of Mr. Stoddard. "And did you test for DNA on this new weapon?"

He nodded. "I did."

She asked, "And who did it belong to?"

I didn't even have to listen to know what his response would be, but I did anyway.

"The Defendant's"

The gallery erupted.

The Judge pounded her gavel, but it was all over.

CHAPTER THIRTY-EIGHT

We were all in shock as we rode back to Point Pleasant Beach in my dad's SUV. This felt in stark contrast to the mood on the way to the Preliminary Hearing. Even my dad's well-meaning bad jokes were falling flat.

Finally, Katie broke the silence. "We need reinforcements. Tom did a good job when he went down there. But he's up in Dutchess County. Maybe, he could take this on full time until the trial, so stuff doesn't slip through the cracks like what happened today. How did Paul miss that DNA test? Not that he could have defended against it, but maybe he could have if he'd been prepared, but how could Cord's DNA have been found on a gun she never touched or even saw in her life?"

Dad responded. "I don't know, Katie, maybe we can research DNA planting. There is no guarantee putting Tom on this full time that the outcome would have been any different."

Lily smiled. "Well, at least she probably wouldn't be dating that guy Sean if Tom had been on the case full time. He gives me the creeps."

I rolled my eyes. "Sean's more intense than most guys. He's a therapist. What do you expect? Besides, I don't think Tom and me dating is such a good idea."

Katie teased me, "Why, because you'd never get to work on time? Oooh. Maybe he's a little too hot to handle. Is that it, Cord?"

I confessed. "I need to concentrate on this case. We both do. I admit there might be a spark or two between us, and that's the last thing either of us need when preparing for a murder trial."

Lily nodded and said sarcastically, "Yeah, stay with Sean; you won't have any distractions at all. That's for certain." She wondered. "Whatever happened to that cute detective you were seeing?"

I shook my head. "I could never quite get over the fact that he arrested me for these murders. He saw no other choice, and I saw plenty of other options. So, I guess we agree to disagree."

Mom slipped in, "Well, it couldn't hurt to talk to Tom. He's very competent, a friend of the family, and adores you, Cordelia. He can't stop talking about you whenever he's around. What's the worst case?"

I turned red. "The worst case is that we fall in love, get married, have kids, and I end up spending the rest of my life in prison. That's the worst case."

Katie poked me. "You're so dramatic. I thought the middle child was supposed to get lost in the shuffle."

I protested. "I do. That's the problem. You all do what you think is best for me and forget that my opinion is the most important one. So, yes, I like Tom, but I think the best thing I can do for my case and for me right now is to concentrate on it, not on him."

Dad agreed. "Okay, Cordelia makes a point. She's the one on the hook here. It's not time to play with her life."

I smiled. "Thanks, Dad."

I had one caveat. "Now, if there comes a time when I think having Tom in the picture would be helpful, I will call him directly."

Because she lives with me, Shelby had come with us but had been relegated to the rear seat of the SUV. I yelled back, "You doing okay back there, Shel?"

She yelled, "It's fun watching a fully functional family operate. No one jumped out of the car or stabbed anyone in the eye, so I'd call that discussion a success. Just the opposite of how my family would have done it."

Katie kept her in the conversation. "Hey Shelby, how can you stand living with someone as moody and dramatic as Cordelia?"

Shelby chuckled. "You must have the wrong, Cordelia. Mine is delightful and wonderful. I love her."

Lily whined, "Oh, you're no fun, Shelby, we never tell Cord how we really feel. We don't want her to get a swelled head."

She nodded. "Oh, so it's you guys' fault why Cord never felt like she was good enough. Way to go."

Katie couldn't respond directly, "Wow, you're a feisty one for your age. I'll bet you give the boys a run for their money."

She nodded. "You have no idea. Why do you think I'm living with Cord?" She winked.

I laughed. "Don't listen to her. She's a sweetheart. She's nicer than me most of the time."

When we finally got home, I felt exhausted and thrilled to get out of the constant banter.

I said to Shelby after they were gone, "I love my sisters, but they wear me out."

She nodded. "I get that. They kind of wore me out, too."

I suggested, "Let's lie on the couch and watch Hallmark movies. I love them because the plots are always the same, so if you fall asleep in the middle, you don't miss anything."

She agreed. "I'm in."

I headed to the kitchen to make a big bowl of popcorn.

During the movie sometime, my phone rang: Sean. I debated letting it go to voicemail but finally answered it. He started talking immediately, "Well, that didn't go so well. So, what's your plan, Cordelia? Obviously, this combination of attorney and private investigator that your parents have provided isn't working. Will you consider using my attorney now? This could be a matter of life and death." We'd had this argument a thousand times. It appeared around to be a thousand and one.

I yawned, on the verge of a nap. "I don't know, Sean. I'm comfortable with my team. I know your heart's in the right place, but I have to go with my heart. Sorry."

He sounded frustrated. "Tell me you'll think about it."

I smiled. "Okay. I know I drive you crazy, so thank you for being patient with me." We hung up. I often wondered what he saw in me. He rarely seemed truly happy and often just seemed to tolerate me. Our relationship had gotten far more parent-child than I would have preferred; he had become the parent, but he was good to me.

He said flatly, "Okay, I'll see you later. Love you." He hung up.

Shelby asked, "Mr. Wonderful?"

I nodded. "He's not so bad, Shelby. You'll see when you get a little older."

She smiled. "Yeah, he's fine if you want to date your dad."

I leaned back on the couch. "Maybe I'm not in the market for the romance of my life right now. I needed to ease back into the guy market, and I'm happy. He gives me my freedom. I get lots of time to spend with you and Sally and the wine crew. It's kind of a perfect arrangement."

Shelby thought about it. "Now that you mention it, I'd miss you if you were with someone who wanted to dominate your time."

I nodded. "See, it all makes sense, for now, so don't question it." I thought of something else. "Hey, Shel, can you believe you're graduating in three days? Oh my God! It's come so fast." I teased her, "Wow, I'd better come up with a graduation gift pronto."

She looked at me in panic. "You'd better have my gift! I'm counting on you, Cord."

I laughed. "Oh, yeah, I have it already. I almost forgot, it's so small." I'd been dropping inaccurate hints for weeks. I actually bought her a used car from a little of my severance. I figured if I didn't, she'd be using my Jeep constantly, so it wasn't completely an altruistic gift. It was kind of for both of us.

She hit my arm. "You are so bad."

My phone rang again. I felt very popular suddenly. It was Sally. She sounded concerned, "Hey, Girl, I wanted to see how you are doing after that surprise attack in court today."

I tried to sound positive. "Well, once they started down that road, it was nearly predictable that I would be implicated. So, when they got to the punchline that they had found my DNA on that Glock, I wasn't all that surprised. It felt like a setup. My team is going to focus there and figure out how my DNA could show up on a gun I've never seen or touched."

She suggested, "Hey, any time to take a walk later? I feel like it's been forever since you and I had one-on-one time. I mean, we see each other nearly every day, but we rarely connect on anything but a superficial or work level."

I smiled. "I'd love to. Do you want to meet here or at Kohr's?"

She thought. "Let's meet at Kohr's. I have to check out a couple of things. I like to surprise the staff on my day off sometimes just to make sure they're not smoking joints in the back."

I agreed. "Good point. I'll meet you there in a half-hour."

She agreed. "Okay. I'll see you then." She hung up.

Shelby commented. "Oh, I see, so I'm your back-up when you've got no one else to hang out with."

I looked at her to make sure she wasn't serious. Thankfully, she burst out laughing. I laughed too, relieved that I hadn't hurt her feelings.

CHAPTER THIRTY-NINE

Sally cracked the whip at Kohr's when I showed up. Evidently, the staff had become far too used to no management showing up on Mondays and Tuesdays and had become far too lackadaisical.

Finally, after doling out assignments that would no doubt keep the staff busy well into the night, she joined me out front.

She laughed. "I had a feeling they were getting too comfortable with neither of us working on Mondays and Tuesdays. Too many staff have requested those days, so I figured those were becoming their party days. So, if either you or I drop in randomly, that'll keep them on their toes enough to keep them working."

I agreed. "That's fine with me. It's only five minutes from the house." We started down the beach.

She asked with a hint of seriousness in her voice. "So, Cord, how are you really doing?"

I dug deep. "I'm really okay, Sally. I know that I didn't commit these murders. I have to hold on to the fact that the truth will eventually come out. What is crystal clear is that someone is making a lot of effort to frame me. And it's clear that he has stepped up his game. So, to me, that's the bad news and the good news. It's bad news because now there is hard evidence against me on both murders.

"But the good news is that whoever is trying to frame me, likely the real murderer, is taking more risk to create false evidence. That means to me that he is getting more desperate and more nervous about the outcome of the trial. Somewhere in his mind, he thinks this evidence ties up the final loose end, but I think it's the opposite. I think it opened a door for me. I'm not sure what it is yet, but I'm pretty sure that it did."

She looked at me. "You're something else, Cordelia Corbett. I'd be shaking in my boots if I were you right now, but you seem more confident with this new evidence rather than less."

I thought about it. "I am more confident, because this confirmed that I'm being framed. I only had a feeling that I had been before this. I guess that's the difference. To be honest, I hadn't put a name to it until now, but you helped me do that. So, thank you, Sally. My defense team thanks you too. I'm sure they saw this as a real setback. I know that Paul felt terrible that they had missed this piece of evidence, because the Prosecution very cleverly slipped it in. Well, that only works in the short run. We'll all be on an even playing field during the trial."

Sally asked, "So, how's it going with Sean? He seems like a nice enough guy."

I nodded. "I know. No one thinks he's good enough for me. But he's good to me."

She looked me in the eye. "I don't know. I feel like he talks down to you all the time like he's got all the answers, and he needs to tell you what they are. He's got mansplaining down to an art form."

I made up excuses for him like I normally do. "Well, he does have a Ph.D., and he's very smart. Besides, he's nearly ten years older than I am, so he probably does know more than I do."

She walked for a while in silence, then said, "You've got your reasons for being with him. I'm not going to second guess you. I'm with Jim, and for some pretty crazy reasons, and you never give me a hard time about that."

I smiled. "Thanks for noticing. Yea, you two aren't the traditional couple for sure."

She seemed to be thinking deeply and finally changed the subject, "So, Cord, what is the plan at this point? How are you going to get off from these murder charges?"

I thought about it. "My team, Paul and Tom, will get back together and start from the beginning. I guess we'll revisit the research that I did early on regarding Rachel Lynne Gaston and who might want her dead."

She had a thought. "How about someone who didn't want her dead?"

I was confused. "Why would someone who didn't want her dead kill her?"

She smiled. "Well, I read a lot of mysteries and watch a lot of movies. Most murders aren't planned, and most people are killed by someone they love or someone who loves or loved them. So, when searching her website, you might look for the friendliest person, someone who might have been in a budding relationship with her. Maybe it was a new love that went bad."

She dreamed up a scenario. "So how about this. She strikes up a friendship on her website with a guy; at first, it's a flirt here or there, so it would be easy for you to follow on her site. Then eventually, they go private, so this guy seems to disappear from the site. But, in fact, they're talking privately. So, let's say they decide to meet up in his hometown of Point Pleasant Beach."

I followed her so far. "Okay, so, they meet up here. Why does he kill her?"

She put a finger to her lip. "Well, that's both the easy and the hard part. I'm not sure it matters."

I looked at her incredulously. "Well, of course, it matters."

She laughed. "Well, I don't mean that literally. I just mean he had it bad for this woman. He had it built up in his head big time. So, the result could have been for any number of reasons; she didn't react to him as he'd hoped; she wasn't as smart or pretty as he'd hoped, maybe they go into a fight, or maybe he thought they'd have sex, but she didn't want any part of it. There are any number of reasons, but the specific one doesn't matter all that much."

I thought about it. "Yes, so he's sure that he's in love, that she's the one, she gives him the cold shoulder or treats him like the stranger that he is, and he goes berserk. He can't handle it because, in his mind, she's his, she's committed, they will be spending a lifetime together. But for her, he's just another guy, sure a nice guy that she has some things in common with, but in the end, just another guy."

She agreed. "That's what I think."

I tried to fit it in with what I already knew. "Okay, so I know that right around the time she got killed, she was scheduled to meet with John Michael Owens with the red Mustang who Mo and Jackie saw fleeing from the Food Shack. Do you think the killer knew about their appointment, and he planned to pin it on him?"

She nodded, "I'd bet on it. I'll bet that he met her the night before, and that night didn't go as planned. I'll bet he planned on staying with her in the motel or enticing her back to his house, neither of which he could pull off."

I asked, "So, why not kill her in the motel and call it a night?"

She thought about it. "Not his style. This guy is too calculating for that. He was afraid someone at the front desk spotted him coming to the room, or maybe that he had to ask for her room number. Something made it too risky to do it at the motel after she broke his heart. So, he knew about this meeting with John and decided to pin it on him, but something didn't work out in the timing, he showed up early or late, but something didn't mesh, so he shot her in the shower, and then had to improvise."

I froze with that thought. "Oh my God, Sally, I know who it is."

She looked at me like I'd gone crazy. "How can you know who it is?"

A tear ran down my cheek. "He said he *loved* me. He said he'd *do anything* for me." Now I was getting angry. "He said he'd *always* protect me. How stupid could I be?"

She looked confused as she watched me process. Then a light went off for her. "Sean? You think Sean did this? How? Why?"

The more I thought about it, the more sense it made. "Think about it, Sally, his temper, the fact that he's never satisfied with anything or anyone, how distant he is."

She had her doubts. "That could be anyone. So, he's got attachment issues. That doesn't make him a killer."

I felt so stupid. "Sally, think about the day Rachel died. We were paying the check, and a woman screamed, finding Rachel shot moments ago in a shower in the bathhouse. I ran in, started CPR and yelled for assistance. Who came in? Sean. Because he was right there. He never explained how he got there. He was there because he had just shot her, probably stashed the gun somewhere, and came back."

She picked up the story. "Then, he gave the Glock to Martin William Raven, so he could get him to take the fall, and he killed him with the other Colt. But, through some sort of luck, you unearthed the Colt and got your fingerprints all over it. But how did your DNA get on the Glock?"

I thought back. "And who was on the beach to watch me being taken away by the police? Sean was." Then I thought of another connection. "The guns. The guns. He stole the guns. When I visited the guy whose guns were stolen, he said in passing that he had told his therapist where he stored his guns. I didn't put two and two together at the time, but he was going to a therapy appointment after I met with him. He lived down the street from Sean and was headed in the direction of his house for his appointment."

She stared at me with her mouth wide open, then responded, "Oh my God, the killer is Sean. It has to be."

I thought about something and asked, "There's one more thing I have a hunch about, but I'll have to research. Maybe you know. Can DNA be transferred to an item, like a gun?"

She thought for a second. "I have no idea, but I'm sure an Internet search will either tell us the answer or tell us where we need to go to find it. Or maybe Precision Testing Lab in Toms River might be a good place to start. That guy Frank Stoddard seemed pretty knowledgeable."

CHAPTER FORTY

I agreed and said, "Hey, maybe we should go see him. Do you think he'd take fifteen minutes with us?"

She grabbed her cell phone, put it on speaker, and called their general phone number from their website.

The operator answered. "Hello, how can I direct your call?"

She sounded like she knew what she was doing. "Frank Stoddard, please."

The operator responded. "May I tell him who is calling?"

She thought for a second. "Yes, this is Sally Kohr McIntosh from the Cordelia Corbett defense team. I had a question regarding the DNA testing on the case."

She replied. "Please hold. I'll put you through."

We high-fived. I whispered, "Good job."

He came on the line. "Stoddard."

She sounded very business-like. "Mr. Stoddard, I wanted to follow up on the results you reported in court at the Cordelia Corbett preliminary hearing this morning in Trenton. Do you have a few minutes?"

He seemed friendly enough. "Sure, what have you got?"

She chose her words carefully, "As you can imagine, as part of the defense team, we were taken aback when we found out that our client's DNA showed up on a weapon that she had never been anywhere near. Off the record, is there any way for DNA to be transferred from one object to another or from one source to an object such as a gun?"

He hesitated. "Well, Miss, it's a controversial subject that we are treading very carefully around, and I think you can understand why. If every criminal could suddenly accuse someone of transferring their DNA anywhere, they didn't want to admit being, it could set crime-fighting back twenty years. On the other hand, we can't ignore technology and what DNA transfer makes possible either."

She encouraged him. "So, it is possible then."

He reluctantly agreed. "Unofficially, and off the record, yes, it is possible, but I can't tell you that officially yet."

She smiled. "Well, thank you for being open and honest with me. Good-bye now." She hung up.

I grinned. "This is great." Then I tempered my excitement. "Except, we'll never get him to testify to that in court. Well, at least Paul can do something in cross-examination with it, I'm sure." My emotions were all over the place. "I am so hurt and angry right now. I could kill Sean. He played me like a fiddle. How could I have been so blind? At least I didn't give my heart completely to him."

She took my hand. "There was something in you that didn't allow you to give yourself completely, so that's a good thing. You also took that time to bring lots of new friends into your life. Think about how things were for you when you moved here, Cord. You were a mess. Now, you've got me, Shelby, Mo, Jackie, Natasha, and Olivia. I get jealous sometimes, sharing you with so many people. When you first got down here, I had you all to myself."

I hugged her. "That's sweet, Sally. To be honest, if it weren't for you giving me the job, none of the rest of the good things would have happened to me. You gave me a huge boost in confidence. New York kind of chewed me up and spit me out, and you had the grace to help pick me up and dust me off. So, thank you."

She held me at arm's length. "Okay, so now what do we do?"

I thought about it. "Well, we could give all of this to Paul and Tom and let them do what they do."

She pouted. "That doesn't seem very satisfying."

I looked her in the eye. "You're not thinking what I'm thinking, are you?"

She smiled. "Well, if you're thinking that we should make this girly-man face the music, then I'm thinking what you're thinking."

I laughed, "You said that so much nicer than I would have." I had an idea. "Let's stop by the house and inform Shelby what's going on, so she can be our backup if something unpredictable happens."

She laughed along with me. "What could happen?"

We were flying on air when we arrived at my house through the kitchen door. I yelled upstairs, "Shel, are you home?"

She called from the couch in the living room, where I'd left her watching Hallmark movies. "I'm still down here."

I felt like I was talking a hundred miles an hour. "Sally and I have to go to Sean's house."

She yawned, "Why? And why are you talking so fast? Did you have three cups of coffee again?"

I laughed. "No, it's better than that. Are you ready for this?"

She stretched. "I guess. I don't know. It depends on what it is."

Sally couldn't wait. "Sean's the killer."

Shelby looked at both of us like we were crazy. "Our Sean. The Sean who doesn't step on insects because they could be descended from a relative."

We nodded.

I said, "Yes, that Sean. We have proof."

She didn't sound convinced. "You have proof, proof that the police and the Federal Prosecutors don't have?"

I started getting annoyed. "Yes, Shel, they are people like the rest of us. They can make mistakes. Obviously, I didn't kill anyone, so they've made a lot of mistakes."

She nodded. "Well, that's true."

I had to tell her like it was. "Okay, Shel, you're going to have to suspend your disbelief for a while, because we don't have enough time to explain how we concluded that Sean is the killer. Just take our word that it is well thought out and makes sense."

She wasn't happy with that but agreed. "Okay, so you're going to do the 'mom' thing? I get it."

I tried to draw her in. "Okay, but you are going to play a super important role, should you decide to accept it."

She agreed. "Okay, I'm in. What do I need to do?"

I spoke to her directly. "No, Shel, this literally could be a matter of life or death. Sally and I are going to confront Sean, and you'll be our outside person. If things go bad, you will call the police. We must come up with a signal, or a time frame that will be too long, or both. We have no idea how he will react or how prepared he might be to be found out. If he's super paranoid, he will have a backup plan all devised. We have to be ready for that. Since he's already killed twice, he probably won't hesitate to kill again."

Sally chewed on her lip. "And why are we going to confront him?"

I thought about it. "Oh, I don't know, Sal. We could pass this off to Paul and Tom, and Tom could do his best to research Rachel's site to find something on Sean, and maybe he could find what he needs, and maybe not. Maybe, he could get a witness to remember Sean at the motel Rachel stayed at this long after the fact, or maybe not. And maybe Paul could get him to admit all this on the stand, and maybe not. Maybe the jury will buy Sean's story, and they won't buy mine. Am I okay with putting my future in their hands? I don't think so. That hasn't worked out so far. What's worked out so far has been taking my future into my hands. And that's what I'm going to do here."

Sally considered my speech. "You've got a point, Cord. I think we need to develop a very simple coding system for Shelby, because we may not have much time to spare when we're in trouble, like one word texts. But it shouldn't be so obvious that he knows what we are up to if he confiscates our phones."

I thought for a second. "Okay, Shel, type this in the notes section of your iPhone. We'll use M as the decoy letter. So, mops means call the cops. Mood means we are good. Mad means bad."

She studied her screen. "How do I know mad doesn't mean sad or glad?"

I went through it again. "Because it means bad. Just check your notes, and I'll check mine, so they match."

She asked, "What's the code for 'He's beating the hell out of us?'"

I checked my phone. "Mops."

She looked at the codes again. "Okay, I got it. But what if I don't hear anything?"

Sally and I looked at one another.

I shrugged. "That's the tough one. I guess we all must agree on what a reasonable time is before you call the police if you don't hear anything." I considered that carefully. "How about fifteen minutes?"

Sally looked at me seriously. "That could be the shortest or longest fifteen minutes of our lives."

CHAPTER FORTY-ONE

We tried to psych each other up on the ten-minute walk to Sean's house. We didn't let him know we were coming. We figured it was better to surprise him than to give him time to prepare. If I were visiting him alone, I would just walk in. But since we were coming as a pair, and it wasn't really a social visit, we rang the front doorbell. I immediately texted Shelby, so she'd know we had arrived.

He'd probably been working out because he had gym shorts and a tee-shirt on when he came to the door. He looked a little annoyed with me. I could see his expression through the window in the storm door as he opened it. "Cordelia and Sally, to what do I owe this pleasure?"

I thought I could hear a touch of sarcasm in his voice. I said with a pleasant lilt, "Oh, we were in the neighborhood, so we thought we'd drop in."

He led us inside, then said, "Seriously, I'm sure you're here for a reason. I'm in the middle of a workout that I'd like to get back to."

Sally stepped in, which was good because I was about to give him a piece of my mind. "Actually, we did have a couple of questions about Cord's case that we thought you might be able to clear up."

I looked at my watch. It had been two minutes since I texted Shelby. We had thirteen left before she called the police. I suddenly worried that we hadn't coached her on what to say to the police, but I guess we'd have to worry about that later.

Sally was on a mission. "We were talking earlier, and it seemed an odd coincidence that your neighbor whose guns were stolen uses you as a therapist."

He didn't look at either of us; he stared at the wall. I didn't think he would respond, but then he said, "Yes, that's an odd coincidence. An odd coincidence."

I spoke a little bit louder than she had. "Yes, and an even odder coincidence that a gun I had never seen or touched in my life showed up on the beach with my DNA on it."

He nodded. "Equally as odd."

I started getting angry. "And my DNA is all over this place, on coffee cups, toothbrush, shower, soap, you name it. If someone had to collect a sample of my DNA, other than at my house, this would probably be the place to come, wouldn't it?" I glanced at my watch. Five minutes in. So far, so good.

He looked confused, obviously an act he'd been working on. "And why would someone collect your DNA?"

I wanted to cover so much more material before the police came, if they came. I finally snapped. "Okay, let me spell it out for you, little man. We can start with the stolen guns if you want to, but that's not where this saga starts. So, let's start at the beginning. Let's start when you fell in love with Rachel Lynne Gaston."

I watched for a reaction and waited for a denial. I got neither. Seeing both as a good sign, I continued. "You and Rachel had the perfect relationship as long as she never had to meet you. Mister Perfect online. Picture perfect. But you don't have the kind of personality that translates well in person, do you, Sean? Something's missing there. I don't know what it is. A soul? You tell me. You're the only one who really knows, Mister Therapist."

He sat silently for a few minutes. I looked at my watch. We were eight minutes in. I wrote 'Mops' on my text line to Shelby should I need it without any notice, but I didn't hit the send button. Yet.

Finally, it looked like he would speak. His face started to redden with an angry glow. "I never liked you, Cordelia. I never even planned on framing you for the murders. Still, you made it all too easy, your prurient interest in Rachel's death, your sudden desire to be an amateur sleuth like you thought you lived in Nineteenth-Century Ireland or something.

"I figured I'd frame the homeless guy, but you made it too hard for that to be believable. You couldn't keep your nose out of things. So, the only answer was for you to take the fall, and it all went so beautifully. Today in court was magnificent. The judge bought it hook, line and sinker. I could almost hear the prison doors slamming behind you."

He shook his head. "But, even with this, you couldn't leave well enough alone. You had to go snooping around, and now you have to die, you and your ice cream scooping friend." He pulled a semi-automatic pistol out of a rarely used drawer in his kitchen.

I hit send on my phone and said to Sean, "What good is that going to do?"

He chuckled, "What does it matter now? What're a couple more murders among friends, right Cordelia?" He asked, "So what gave me away?"

I wanted to waste as much time as possible until the police arrived. I was a bit afraid that police wouldn't have the desired impact in his present state of mind, but I wasn't sure of a good alternative. I tried to reconstruct when it became obvious to us that Sean was the murderer.

"Well, when we thought about the logistics of Rachel's murder, I realized it had to be someone nearby. When I thought back and remembered that you were immediately available to assist with her attempted revival, it hit me that time was so tight, and no one saw anyone else; it almost had to be you. Then when you add the stolen guns from your neighbor, who also happened to be a client who had told his therapist where he stored his guns, it pretty much fell together from there."

He pointed his pistol at me. "Very good reasoning. I always knew that someone might figure it out, which is why I had to provide the prosecution with better alternatives. And, had it not been for you thinking too much, as usual, I believe today's positive DNA test would have been the nail in your coffin.

"This is a shame. It's going to be far messier this way. Of course, I'll never be implicated. It'll be the poor retired man with dementia and alleged stolen guns. It will turn out that none of his guns were ever stolen. Once he's dead, I'll be able to break doctor-patient confidentiality and tell the whole story."

Just then, a loud knock came on the door. "Police Department." Shelby must have sent them early. There would have been no way they could have gotten here by now.

With his gun trained on us, he ordered, "Downstairs."

I glared at him. "You're kidding! This is over."

He mumbled, "This is far from over." He pushed both of us. "Downstairs. Now." He had a finished basement that I'd been in a few times, but it had a locked room at the end I'd never been in. He quickly unlocked it.

I was shocked. It looked like a Medieval torture chamber with hand locks on the walls, and he quickly zip-tied our hands and taped our mouths as we heard the police knock again. He said, "I'll be back to do you up right after I get rid of them. You'll be sorry that you messed with me." He closed and locked the door.

I realized that we had to act fast while the police were still in the house. I also remembered, perhaps too late, that we hadn't discussed with Shelby what story she would use with the police to get them to come. 'My friend, who's the suspect in a double murder, thinks her boyfriend did it, please go to his house,' probably wouldn't cut it. She must have thought of something. I'd have to ask her later, assuming we came out of this alive.

I realized, in his haste, he'd made mistakes because one boring day, I'd watched a video on how to get zip ties off if you were ever a captive. I never thought I'd need it, but here I was. The first thing I needed was my mouth, so I immediately tried to figure out how to get the tape off. Not to mention, Sally and I needed to communicate with one another.

I listened and could hear muffled voices upstairs. They were still here. Suddenly I realized if we could hear muffled voices, they'd be able to hear us yelling for help if we got our mouths free.

We tried to work cooperatively. Sally rubbed her upper arm against the edge of the tape covering my mouth, hoping to get the edge started so it would begin to peel off. This was really strong tape. I wondered where criminals bought the tape for these purposes. You thought of the funniest things at times like these.

Within a few minutes, it started to give, and she got it off. I immediately started yelling, "Help, help, help, help, help."

Within a few seconds, we heard the key in the door and expected to see a very embarrassed Sean with a couple of cops. Unfortunately, we only saw a very angry Sean, his face bright red. "You are so lucky they left before you started yelling." He pushed me roughly away from the door and re-taped my mouth. He directed us toward the wall with hand and foot locks, cut the zip ties, and locked us to the wall.

He leaned on a table and started talking to himself as if we weren't there. "Okay, they're taken care of for now. That'll give me time to think. I can't kill them here. I have to take them somewhere they can't be found. Wait, now the police knew they were here. What do I do with Shelby? I have to dispense with her."

Suddenly, we could hear voices upstairs yelling. They were yelling our names. It was multiple female voices, but I couldn't recognize them from all the way down here. I couldn't believe our mouths were taped, and we couldn't respond.

Sean seemed to freeze. I thought he might close the door and hope they didn't discover us in here, but then he thought better of it. I figured he decided to get out and lock the door behind him. Then, we'd probably never be discovered since we couldn't make a sound. My heart sank.

But, as the door closed, I heard Jackie's voice yell, "He's down here, girls, hurry."

I heard a struggle, and then he said in a disgusted voice, "Get off me."

Mo laughed, "Not on your life, sissy boy."

Then I heard Jackie on the phone giving the police the address. "Yes, I know you were just here, but you're gonna want to see this, multiple women in custody against their will. I see a lawsuit against your force coming very soon based on the shoddy job you did while you were here, but we can talk about that later. We will see you in a couple of minutes, I trust."

Mo yelled, "Stop squirming, or I will put your lights out. You have no idea how much pleasure that would give me." I wish I could see what was going on out there, but with the door mostly closed, I could only imagine what they were doing to him. I was relieved that the worst seemed to be over thanks to my new band of wine-drinking friends.

CHAPTER FORTY-TWO

A couple of uniformed officers arrived within ten minutes, along with Detective Clint Daniels. While the uniformed officers prepared to take Sean away, Clint tried to sort out what had happened. He'd been carefully avoiding me, even though our eyes had met several times since he arrived.

Finally, I asked politely after he carefully removed the tape from my mouth, "Do you think someone could find the keys to these things before they take him away? They kind of hurt."

He half-smiled, "I kind of liked having you captive for a while."

Sally rolled her eyes. "Then, how about me?"

He acquiesced. "Okay, for you, Sally." He left the room briefly and came back with a set of keys. In a couple of minutes of trying various keys, we were free."

We both shook our arms and legs, trying to get feeling back into them.

Clint said to both of us, "I'm going to take statements from everyone else, then you two. Can you stick around for a while."

Sally looked at her watch. "Well, I've got to get back to the store, so

I'd like to go first if I could." She winked at me. I knew she planned to leave me alone with Clint.

I nodded. "That's fine. I have nothing planned."

He smiled and said, "Okay, I'll be back in a few. Just relax. The worst is over."

There were a couple of chairs in the corner of the room, so we sat down to talk. I started. "I guess this didn't turn out to be our brightest moment. We could have been killed."

She reflected on it. "Well, yes, but we weren't, and we got you off the hook and exposed him for who he really was. In fact, we not only got him to admit he stole the guns but that he planned on killing the gun owner and blaming him for the murders as a backup plan. That's probably something that never would have come out in court."

I thought about it. "How did I not see this all along?"

She smiled. "I don't know. Maybe, in a way, you did. You always kept a certain amount of distance from him. That had to be intuitive in a way."

I shook my head. "I have no idea."

She reminded me of something. "But you know what really saved our lives?"

I wondered, "What?"

She smiled. "It was your idea of making a new friend every week. You heard out there who came to our rescue. Shelby must have alerted the No Longer Desperate Winers. He didn't stand a chance."

I laughed. "No way I would mess with Jackie and Mo, and now with Natasha and Olivia as backup, not a chance."

Just then, Shelby came in. I stood and motioned her over. We hugged for a long time.

She whispered. "I was so scared. I didn't know what to do. When the cops came, I hung around to make sure everything was okay. When I saw them leave, I knew something had to be very wrong, so I called Mo. I had called her earlier to be on standby, but she must have assembled everyone and come over immediately. Thank God. We went right in when they arrived. The house was unlocked."

I held her at arm's length. "You know you saved our lives, right?" I pointed to the wall. "He had us strapped to those things. God only knows what he had planned next, but he is some kind of psycho."

She gasped. "I had no idea. I freaked when I saw the police go in and you did not come out. I knew he had to be hiding you somewhere, so we split up to find you and him as fast as we could."

~:~

Eventually, all the statements were taken, and everyone headed home, and it was just Clint and me. I asked, "Hey, it's been quite a day. Can we go back to my house, and I'll give you my statement there? This place gives me the creeps."

We sat down at my kitchen table, and he got out his iPad. Before he could ask me anything, I touched his hand. "Clint, how have you been?"

He nearly melted in front of me. Tears streamed down his face, and he sobbed for a good ten minutes. And as soon as he started, I immediately joined him, crying uncontrollably. I couldn't help it. There was something about this man that touched my soul deeply. That's why I had been so hurt when he arrested me for the murders. It could have been anyone else, but I lost a part of myself when he lost his faith in me.

After we both gained our composure and I took nearly an hour to describe Sally and my nearly life-ending experience at Sean's house, he broke from the process and asked, "So, why Sean? How could you choose him over me?"

I rolled my eyes. "God, men are so obtuse. I never chose him over you. I chose him because of you. I chose him because he wasn't you. I chose to spend dead, meaningless, but painless time with him so I could try to forget about how much I loved you. How could you not see that?"

He thought about it. "Because that makes absolutely no sense."

I shot back, "It makes as much sense as you arresting me for two murders you knew damn well I didn't commit. Come on, Clint. Picture me committing either of those murders. It's ridiculous. You let your coworkers get to you so bad; it was shameful. Well, what happens now? Now that they all have to go back and eat crow? Will they? I doubt it. They'll move on like they never thought I did it in the first place. That's what people do. And they'll get away with it because you'll let them. After all, you have to work with them every day."

He pulled a ring out of his pocket and got down on one knee. "Cordelia Corbett, will you marry me?"

~:~

The next evening, the No Longer Desperate Winers plus Shelby were called together for an emergency meeting. I welcomed them as they arrived, and they made small talk, and hugged one another, sharing tales with one another of the success of last evening's mission with those who hadn't participated.

Katie mock-scolded me. "Cord, you could have called me. I would have come down."

I hugged her. "I know. It was just one of those 'time is of the essence' things or you would have been the first one we called," I lied. But she seemed satisfied.

Jackie still seemed on a high from last night. She was talking a mile a minute with her new best friend, Mo.

I loved looking around the room, seeing what we had accomplished in such a short time. It made me wonder what more we could accomplish from here. I was excited and optimistic about our future, and thankful to be alive.

Finally, when everyone was assembled with a glass of wine in their hand, except for Shelby who had ginger ale, I took the floor. "I'd like to welcome everyone here tonight, first to celebrate being alive, because there were a couple of times yesterday when I wasn't sure that would be the outcome."

Everyone clanked glasses.

I continued. "But that's only one reason I called all of you here tonight." I paused, not really sure how I was going to present my impending decision. I figured I'd just jump right in. "Okay. Clint proposed last night."

I was met with a combination of smiles, frowns, gasps, chuckles, and what I thought I discerned as a few sarcastic comments.

I didn't relinquish the floor. "Okay, not all at once. I really do want your feedback, because frankly, I could tell you what my initial reaction was, but why spoil the fun. So, I'm going to ask you individually what you think. So, please, be brutally honest. This is my life we are talking about here." I looked around the room. "Sally, I'm calling on you because I know you're leaving Kohr's uncovered right now and I really appreciate that."

Sally smiled. "Yes, and I'm not going to feel like going back there after a glass of wine, but I'll be a trouper." She took a second to gather her thoughts. "I know that marriage is a huge commitment, but I think you and Clint have been dancing around each other for long enough, it's time to go for it. I say you go for it."

I was shocked, knowing how independent Sally is. I wiped a bead of sweat from my forehead and just said, "Wow. Thanks. I think." I moved on to my sisters. "How about you guys, Katie and Lily. What do you think?"

Surprisingly, Lily jumped in first, which was something she rarely did when Katie was around. "Cord, you know first-hand of the trials and tribulations I've faced with the institution of marriage. But, does that mean I don't think anyone should get married? Absolutely not. I still think, overall it serves a purpose in society. Even with the issues I have, do I want to get divorced and be alone raising my kids? No, absolutely not. So, considering everything, if you love him, I'd say 'yes.'"

Katie was ready to jump in. "There isn't one of us here who isn't going to allow ourselves to be influenced by our own situation. So, dear Cord, I'm afraid you're going to have to look within when all is said and done. Some of us have had wonderful experiences with marriages, and some of us, not so much. But you need to listen to your heart. First of all, you need to decide if you are ready to settle down with one man for the rest of your life. This is not something to be taken lightly. And, sure, you can always divorce, but are the scars that will stay with you thereafter really worth it? I'd say probably not." I thought she was done, but then she gave me a penetrating stare. "Cord, if you hear anything from me tonight hear this. What was your initial reaction when he took out that ring? That was your heart speaking. Was it, 'This is so wonderful. I can't believe this is happening?' or was it, 'Oh my God, what do I do now?' That response will guide you to the next step."

Sometimes Katie could be a real pain in my neck. But, she kind of had said it all. And, as I listened to the others, I couldn't help but think about what she had said. The only other person in the group who knew me intimately was Shelby. And, even though she was only eighteen, she often had insights of someone twice her age.

Finally, she took the floor. "Cord, I've probably been the one person to see you in action with Clint more than anyone. I've seen you silly. I've seen you fighting. I've even watched while he arrested you. And that was painful. One thing I do know is that you love each other very much." She gathered her thoughts. "Having lived with you for a while now, I also understand your needs, and your desire to make something of yourself. I know you never want to be dependent on a man, and getting there may take a while, even though you inherited your Gram's house. So, while I think you might eventually end up with Clint, I think the answer has to be 'No' right now."

～:～

Two days later, when I didn't have to work the four to midnight shift, I had arranged for Clint to come over to talk. It was for drinks or dinner. I didn't want to extend things any longer then then had to go if they got uncomfortable.

He knocked on the door, and kissed me immediately when he came in. He seemed very upbeat, like he could positively think me toward the decision he desired. "How's it going Cord? I hope you've been well. You look beautiful tonight." It almost seemed like if he just kept talking, I wouldn't say anything that might break his heart.

I felt my face get hot. What could I say? I loved him, but this didn't feel like the right time. It felt more like an apology. I said, "I'm sorry, Clint, I'm going to have to say no. That doesn't necessarily mean no forever, but at least 'no for now.'"

He stood up, kissed me, walked out to the driveway, started his car, and drove away.

A single tear ran down my cheek, but I knew 'no' was the right answer for me and one I would never have said if it hadn't been for my Gram. And such was the beginning to my new life in Point Pleasant Beach, New Jersey.

ACKNOWLEDGMENTS

To Mary Lou Monahan, who heads up Cortero Publishing a division of Fireship Press. Mary Lou was willing to take the Point Pleasant Beach/ Cordelia Corbett Mystery Series when many publishers passed on the opportunity. And for that I will be eternally grateful. I hope my readers will feel the same way. Thanks, also, to Jacqueline Cook at Cortero Publishing who made the publishing process a smooth and pleasant one.

*If you enjoyed reading **Under the Influence**, please leave a review where you purchased the book.*

ABOUT THE AUTHOR

J. T. Kunkel is a lifetime singer/ songwriter. When he tried his hand at professional songwriting, and his producer instructed him to relocate to Nashville, he opted to keep his day job in Finance. Writing a novel had been a dream of his, and after completing a memoir after a bout with a life threatening illness, he decided to take a chance at fiction. This is one of many results. He lives in the Northeast with his wife, Susan, and their King Charles Cavalier, Gracie.

Other Titles from Fireship Press / Cortero

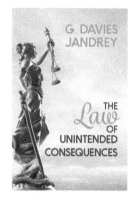

The Law of Unintended Consequences
G. Davies Jandrey

Sturdy, stalwart Detective Marie Stransky is called to Santa Rita Park, a gathering place for the homeless and addicted, Marie studies the strangled body of a young woman. The cigarette burn on her right wrist pegs her as a victim of a stalker that has already killed two homeless women. Then there is the young Mexican woman found shot in a wash. Homicide department head, Lieutenant Carl Lindgrin, a man Marie loves to hate, dismisses the murder as gang related, but the tattoo of a unicorn on the girl's shoulder visible in the autopsy photo gives Marie pause. What self-respecting gangbanger has a tattoo of a unicorn? And the bodies pile up.

Provincial Justice
A Kate Mahoney Mystery, Book 1

Gerry Hernbrode

Set in Tucson, Arizona, Provincial Justice is a tale of greed, lust and, of course, murder.

When Julie Mason, the district Superintendent, is found dead in the first-grade classroom of Elijah Stewart, the teacher becomes the prime suspect. Though Kate imagines there are plenty of people who would like to see Julie Mason dead, or at least out of the business of education, she is certain that Elijah is not one of them and sets out to prove it.

"Provincial Justice is a fascinating read. Moving between dream visits from the Mother Provincial of the convent, giving Kate advice, and the squalid, dangerous lives of her students. Each world is beautifully described."
—Nancy Farmer, author of The House of the Scorpion

Cortero

An Imprint of Fireship Press

Interesting • Informative • Authoritative

All Cortero books are available through
leading bookstores and wholesalers worldwide.

Printed in the USA
CPSIA information can be obtained
at www.ICGtesting.com
CBHW051522200224
4524CB00008B/104